continued . . .

"Readers will find themselves drawn into the investigation of the death. Throw in a little ghostly activity [and] the promise of a pirate's treasure and the reader will be hooked."

—*Fresh Fiction*

A TOUCH OF GOLD

"Paranormal amateur sleuth fans will enjoy observing Dae use cognitive and ESP mental processes to uncover a murderer . . . Readers will enjoy."   —*Midwest Book Review*

"The Lavenes once again take readers into a setting with a remarkable past, filled with legends and history . . . The characters are vivid and fascinating."   —*Lesa's Book Critiques*

A TIMELY VISION

"Grabbed my attention on page one . . . Puzzles are unraveled and secrets spilled in a fast-paced paranormal mystery full of quirky characters you'll want as friends."

—Elizabeth Spann Craig, author of *Death Pays a Visit*

"I could almost smell and feel the salty sea air of Duck as I was reading. The authors definitely did a bang-up job with the setting, and I look forward to more of Dae's adventures and the hint of romance with Kevin."

—*A Cup of Tea and a Cozy for Me*

"This is a mystery with strong characters, a vivid sense of place, and touches of humor and the paranormal. *A Timely Vision* is one of the best traditional mysteries I've read this year."

—*Lesa's Book Critiques*

Praise for the Renaissance Faire Mysteries

TREACHEROUS TOYS

"An engaging whodunit made fresh by changing the season . . . This exciting amateur sleuth is filled with quirky characters as team Lavene provide another engaging murder investigation."
—*Genre Go Round Reviews*

HARROWING HATS

"The reader will have a grand time. This is an entertaining read with a well-crafted plot. Readers of the series will not be disappointed. New readers will want to glom the backlist so they don't miss a single minute." —*Fresh Fiction*

"The Renaissance Faire Mysteries are always an enjoyable read . . . Joyce and Jim Lavene provide a complex, exciting murder mystery that amateur sleuth fans will appreciate."
—*Midwest Book Review*

DEADLY DAGGERS

"Will keep you entertained from the first duel, to the last surprise . . . If you like fun reads that will let you leave this world for a time, this series is for you."
—*The Romance Readers Connection*

"Never a dull moment! Filled with interesting characters, a fast-paced story, and plenty of humor, this series never lets its readers down." —*Fresh Fiction*

continued . . .

GHASTLY GLASS

"A unique look at a Renaissance Faire. This is a colorful, exciting amateur-sleuth mystery filled with quirky characters, who endear themselves to the reader as Joyce and Jim Lavene write a delightful whodunit." —*Midwest Book Review*

WICKED WEAVES

"This jolly series debut . . . serves up medieval murder and mayhem." —*Publishers Weekly*

"[A] new exciting . . . series . . . Part of the fun of this solid whodunit is the vivid description of the Renaissance Village; anyone who has not been to one will want to go . . . Cleverly developed." —*Midwest Book Review*

LOOKING FOR
MR. GOOD WITCH

Joyce and Jim Lavene

BERKLEY PRIME CRIME, NEW YORK

**BERKLEY
PRIME
CRIME**

**An imprint of Penguin Random House LLC
375 Hudson Street, New York, New York 10014**

LOOKING FOR MR. GOOD WITCH

A Berkley Prime Crime Book / published by arrangement with the author

ISBN: 978-0-425-26826-1

PUBLISHING HISTORY
Berkley Prime Crime mass-market edition / October 2015

PRINTED IN THE UNITED STATES OF AMERICA

10 9 8 7 6 5 4 3 2 1

Cover art by Mary Ann Lasher.
Cover design by Lesley Worrell.
Interior text design by Laura K. Corless.

Penguin
Random
House

*For all the lovely witches we've met since writing
our first book. Thanks for all your support
and encouragement. Merry Meet!*

PROLOGUE

"Good night, my little witch."

I held my breath as I waited for possible retribution.

Joe wasn't supposed to know about my witchcraft, hadn't known for the thirty years we'd been married—until the last few days. It had been necessary to tell him. He could never mention it outside of an enchanted space where the information was protected from the Grand Council of Witches.

He'd forgotten as he was falling asleep. There was nothing to do but wait.

Just as I became sure no one had heard us, a bright light filled our bedroom. My heart beat fast as I thought of what could happen to Joe. A rush of water, as though I were standing under a waterfall, filled my senses. I fought for the next breath, even though water is my element.

And then it was gone. The bedroom was dark, and we were alone.

I took a large, cleansing breath and let it out.

Joe patted my side. "Okay over there?"

"Yes." *For now.*

CHAPTER 1

Heat of Fire,
Burn away
All the trace of yesterday.

SIX MONTHS LATER

"Fire is the element of change, will and passion. All forms of magic involve fire." Elsie Langston used her ritual sword to draw a circle around the fire that burned brightly in the cave under our shop, Smuggler's Arcane. The fire followed the circle and made the area brighter.

"I am a fire witch. My direction is south. My color is red. My time is midday. My tool is the sword." Elsie's faded red curls bobbed up and down on her head as she spoke with conviction. She'd been an active witch for sixty years. Her bright green eyes were powerful with all she had seen and done over a lifetime.

"Fire is the realm of sexuality and passion, the spark of divinity which is in all living things." She laughed. "In other words, I'm one *hot* mama!"

Everyone in the cave laughed.

We were attempting to teach our new witch, Dorothy Lane.

It was a slow, painful process. We had been at it for months, but it wasn't getting any easier. Elsie, Olivia and I had learned our magic at our mothers' and grandmothers' feet. Explaining it to someone was more difficult than we'd imagined.

Dorothy had been adopted into a family without magic that had no idea who or what she was. Olivia was actually her mother, but they hadn't been reunited until after Olivia's death.

It was complicated.

Olivia's ghost had clung to a half life to spend time with her daughter. She wasn't a practicing witch anymore, but she still possessed important knowledge of the craft.

"I am Olivia Dunst, and I am an air witch." Her voice wasn't as solid as Elsie's, but it was still strong with purpose. "Dorothy, honey, would you mind drawing the circle in the sand with my rune staff? It's a little hard for me to hold a solid object for so long."

"Oh sure, Mom." Dorothy popped to her feet from one of the carved and weathered chairs around the circle. She wore her straight brown hair in a short pageboy style that swung into her face as she moved. She drew a circle in the sand with Olivia's rune staff.

"Thank you, honey." Olivia's face wasn't as solid as it had been before she was killed either. She was still pretty, and her carefully coiffed hair was still blond. She was elegantly clad in the outfit we'd chosen for her to be buried in even though we'd known by then that she was a ghost. "My direction is east. My color is yellow, and my time is dawn. Obviously my wonderful staff is my tool."

The runes collected on the staff through the years began to glow in Dorothy's hand. The magic with Olivia's staff was only possible because of their blood tie. Elsie or I couldn't have done it.

"Air is the element of the intellect, the most powerful tool for change. It is psychic, and essential to all spells and rituals." Olivia's voice grew stronger as she concentrated on her words. The runes on the staff continued to glow, but there was no actual air magic from her words or actions.

"*Most* powerful?" Elsie joked. "I don't think so. Right now I'd say not too powerful at all."

"Elsie!" I hissed. "I shouldn't have to tell you that this is a solemn ceremony of declaration."

"Sorry, Molly." Elsie put her hand over her mouth. "When did you get to be such a poop?"

Everyone laughed at that too, of course.

"Sorry," I said. "I guess I was wrong about it being a solemn declaration, Dorothy."

"Oh." Dorothy batted her lashes quickly. It was her habit when she was confused or nervous. "Does that mean it's a party or something?"

"No." Elsie heaved a deep sigh. "Molly's right. It's a solemn declaration of ourselves and our magic. I'm sorry. Is anyone else hungry?"

"It's probably the boredom," Brian Fuller said. "We could speed this up some. I'm not sure how solemn it's supposed to be, but it could be faster."

"That's because you're not trained to be a witch," Olivia told him. "You've gone a long time on natural ability—and, of course, your *wonderful* good looks." Her opaque form fluttered. "What was I saying?"

"Let me hold the rune staff." Brian took it from Dorothy.

He wasn't a blood relative of Olivia's, but he was a powerful air witch, more powerful than Olivia had ever been. Brian wasn't a member of our coven. We were hoping he would be at some point, but he hadn't declared himself. He was a virile young witch with a headful of unruly brown hair and seductive blue eyes. My mother would have said he was trouble with a capital T.

"I am an air witch!" he declared loudly toward the ceiling

of the large cave. "I am Brian Fuller, son of Schadt and
Yuriza Fuller, grandson of Esmeralda and Abdon Fuller. My
time is dawn. My direction is east. My magic is powerful."

As his words echoed through the cave, a windstorm grew
and beat at the walls and swelled the air. It rose like a hurricane around us, swirling rocks and sand.

"Cool!" Dorothy yelled from the middle of the storm.
"How'd you do that?"

"You have to suck it up from inside you and let it go,"
Brian told her. "If I were using my wand instead of Olivia's
staff, it would be even better."

Brian was also a little bit of a show-off.

Olivia's ghostly form was blown around by the elemental
forces he had called. She banged back and forth against the
walls like a sock puppet. "Brian, could you turn this off
now, please? I feel a little dizzy."

"This is all well and good," I said to Brian. "But you
aren't in control of the air you've summoned."

Brian shrugged. "Sure, I am. I can stop it anytime."

"Please do so." Olivia's voice sounded as though it were in
a tunnel. "I don't like to think what my hair is going to look
like."

"It looks just like it always does," Elsie shouted above
the wind. "It's not like you need a brush once you're dead."

"Yes, get it under control," I added to Olivia's pleas.

"No problem." Brian tapped the staff on the ground. Nothing happened.

He grinned at Dorothy. "It's because I'm using someone
else's magic tool." He took his wand out of the pocket of his
brown cargo shorts but still held Olivia's staff. "I command
the spirits of the air to cease."

"I think it's worse." Dorothy put her arms protectively
over her head.

"You have the same problem we do." Elsie held tightly
to her chair as the wind buffeted it. "Except you have too

much power and not enough training. We have a lot of training but we're short on the power."

"Oh, right, Elsie," Olivia called out. "Exactly the same but *completely* different."

Brian put down Olivia's staff and addressed the problem with his wand. "I am an air witch, and I demand this to end. Stop!"

The hurricane whistled through the cave. It was beginning to dislodge rocks from the ceiling, and they fell at our feet.

He looked at me. "Molly? Any ideas?"

I considered the problem. "Perhaps if you try your wand *and* the rune stick again. Olivia, I know you have no real magic, but it's your staff. Could you come down and help him?"

Olivia was trying hard to keep her form together. "I'll do my best. It's not easy being a dead witch. I haven't mastered my ghostly powers to replace my magic yet."

She managed to drop from the ceiling, where the storm had whipped her, and alighted at Brian's side to grasp her staff with him.

"Now, concentrate, both of you," Elsie suggested. "My hair is literally blowing off my head."

Olivia and Brian worked together, but the storm only barely subsided. I beckoned to Elsie and Dorothy, and we all put our hands on the staff to add our magic. Though all our magic was not of the air, still the turmoil slowed and finally stopped.

We all stared at one another with our hair standing at odd angles on our heads (except for Olivia) and then started laughing.

"Okay." Brian made a swipe at his hair with one hand. "That's what I'm talking about. I'm not bored or mostly asleep now. Are you, Dorothy?"

"No." She pulled her pretty blue top back on her shoulders and pushed at her short hair. "But maybe there's something to be said for training *and* control."

"Don't let them kid you," he said. "Magic is all about fun and excitement. If you don't have fun with it, you get old and cranky—like my grandfather."

We all knew that Brian's grandfather, Abdon, was more than cranky. He was an obnoxious egomaniac. He was a member of the Grand Council of Witches. Their rules made most witches cringe.

"I guess we're through with fire and air," Elsie said. "Molly, would you declare for water?"

I nodded and grasped my mother's amulet, which hung around my neck. "Water is the feminine element of the subconscious mind. It is wisdom, strength and growth. It is the heart of life." I closed my eyes. "I am Molly Addison Renard. I am a water witch who lives between the river and the sea. My direction is west. My color is blue, and my time is twilight. My tool is the cauldron. Let the water flow from every direction and heal the earth."

There was complete silence around me as I finished my declaration. My feet were wet, but I hadn't noticed until I'd finished.

Opening my eyes was a surprise. The Cape Fear River, which is normally at the mouth of our cave, had begun to flow inside. Not only was I standing in gray-green water to my ankles—so was everyone else.

The cave had been here in the old port city of Wilmington, North Carolina, since the time of smugglers. I wasn't sure if it had come this far over its banks in a hundred years or more. It had never happened in the last twenty years that we'd had held ceremonies here.

"Molly, what in the world is going on?" Olivia was the only one with dry feet. "And where is the cauldron necklace you should be using as your tool? Did you take it off?"

"Let me take care of this problem first." I closed my eyes and held the amulet, seeing in my mind's eye the water flowing back where it belonged.

"That was almost as good as my hurricane." Brian applauded. "Dorothy, what do you have in mind—an earthquake?"

Elsie came to my side with curiosity and confusion in her green eyes. "Molly? I've known you all your life. When did you get the magic to do something like that? Where did you get it? You didn't even have that kind of power when we were young."

I opened my eyes. The water was gone, leaving a few fish and some marks on the sand where it had been. We quickly put the gasping fish into a bucket of river water that we kept in the cave for ceremonial purposes. "I'm sorry. I stopped wearing the cauldron because I didn't need it. There's magic stored in this amulet that relates to my family and other water witches."

Dorothy smiled. "That's a good thing, right? Maybe you won't have to give up being a witch and move to Boca after all. We can all stay here together and look for your missing spell book. I'd like that."

"Me too." Elsie hugged her. "And Olivia has a hundred years as a ghost before she has to leave. It sounds like a party to me. I'll have to look through my mother's old things and see if she left me something powerful to reclaim *my* magic."

"Shall we finish our declarations before Molly gets all out of sorts again?" Olivia asked. "Dorothy, it's your turn."

"Okay." She smiled. "I hope I don't do anything catastrophic."

Dorothy closed her eyes to concentrate. "Earth doesn't represent the physical earth, like you told me. It is the realm of abundance and prosperity. I am Dorothy Lane Dunst, and I am an earth witch. My direction is north. My color is green. My time is midnight. My tool is the stone." She held up the emerald cull she'd found on the riverbank. "Is that it?"

"Sweet." Brian focused on Dorothy. "I want a magic gemstone."

"You have to draw a circle in the sand with your stone," Olivia told her. "Mind the fish."

Dorothy dropped to her knees and drew a circle near the fire in the sand. "What should I say?"

"Your stone represents you and your earth magic," I coached. "You're imbuing your tool with your magic."

"Okay. Part of my earth magic is in my stone now. My strength and magic come from the earth, but not the dirt." She looked up and smiled. "How was that?"

"Did you feel anything?" Olivia asked her.

"No. Not really. What am I supposed to feel?"

"No one can tell you that," Elsie added. "You feel what you feel. But I'm not feeling any magic from it. Try it again with more conviction."

Dorothy pushed her hair away from her face and puffed out her cheeks. She grasped the emerald cull in one hand and began drawing a circle again in the sand with the other. "My earth magic is now in my stone. My strength and magic come from the earth, but not the dirt."

"Not feeling it," Elsie said. "Something wrong?"

"I'm just thinking about all those new books that have to be shelved at the library. New books mean that old books are going to be thrown away. I always hate choosing which ones have to go."

"That's the problem," Olivia said. "You're not concentrating. I told you to give up your old job at the library. I left you plenty of money. There's no reason for you to work at all. I never worked a day in my life."

"But I love my job," Dorothy said with a pleading expression on her face. "I don't want to quit." She glanced at me. "Molly, you were a teacher for many years. You still did magic."

"That's true," I agreed. "So did Elsie. My parents didn't leave me a lot of money and a house. I had to work for a living. You have to learn to compartmentalize. When you're doing magic, that's all you're doing. You can't think about work or anything else."

Dorothy sat on the sand. "I'm sorry. I know that I have to

concentrate on the magic, but it's really hard, since I know all those books are going to be thrown away."

"The best thing for a clear mind is to get rid of the problems," Elsie added. "I have an idea. Don't throw the books away—bring them here and we'll give them away to customers when they come in. I'm sure there are plenty of witches who have children."

"What a great idea." Dorothy grinned. "Could I really do that?"

I agreed with Elsie. "Why not? I'm sure it would be fine."

Dorothy made a loud squealing sound, as she frequently did when she was excited. She got up and hugged Elsie and me before giving Olivia the air hug they'd started doing. She turned to Brian and stopped.

"What? Don't I get the group hug too?" He held out his arms.

She slowly walked into his embrace. The two of them tightly hugged each other. Brian let out a deep, satisfied sigh and pulled her closer, turning his head toward her face.

Dorothy took a sudden step back. "There you go." She awkwardly patted his shoulder.

Elsie and I exchanged knowing glances. The relationship between Brian and Dorothy had been slowly transforming into something more. We couldn't agree if it was a good thing or bad thing. Romance between witches in the same coven could be a distraction to a witch just learning what to do.

"I think we should go upstairs now," Olivia said abruptly. She definitely didn't like the idea of Dorothy and Brian having a relationship. No one was good enough for the daughter she'd only recently found again. Besides, Olivia had dated Brian right before her death. It was a bit awkward.

Just as we were about to ascend our newly rebuilt stairway (young male witches are good for many things) that led from the cave to a trapdoor in Smuggler's Arcane, there was a flash of blinding light and the overpowering scent of roses.

"Cassandra." Elsie shook her head. "I was hoping not to see her again for an eon or so."

"Ladies." Cassandra Black, one of the heralds of the Grand Council of Witches, appeared in the cave. She was tall and thin with long black hair that flowed past her waist. She claimed to be at least a thousand years old. I might not have believed it if I'd never looked into her dark eyes.

"Cassandra." I knew her appearance wouldn't be for anything good. We rarely saw her. When she showed up, it was usually because of a crisis in the council—the governing body of witches. "It's wonderful to see you."

My heart was beating fast. Despite my outward calm, I was still terrified that the council had heard Joe's mumbled remark about me being a witch.

Those without magic who learned of the existence of the witching world were condemned to have their memories wiped away. It was a curse that had destroyed many witch–non-witch marriages. Wiping away memories was a tricky thing. Many times those memories held more than just information about witches. It could leave a person slack-jawed and blank.

"Thank you, Molly." Cassandra smiled graciously. "I'm afraid I have some bad news. The council has asked me to spread the word."

"Why doesn't the council send out an email like everyone else?" Dorothy asked.

Cassandra's midnight eyes dismissed her. "Someone is killing witches, and the problem seems to be headed your way."

CHAPTER 2

It is forever within you.
Blessed are the witches.

"What do you mean someone is killing witches?" Elsie demanded. "I always thought we put up with council interference in our lives because the council *protected* us from such things. Remind me again what you do if you don't protect us."

It was a massive statement for Elsie. She tended to look the other way on most things.

I had to agree that it seemed the council was slack on their job, but I was relieved that Cassandra wasn't here to take Joe away from me.

"We're a little touchy today, aren't we?" Cassandra's black gown swung around her as though a breeze were blowing. "None of you has any idea what the witching world was like before the council was formed. There was complete chaos. We can't control every situation for you. We do our best to keep you safe. Telling you about possible threats is one way we accomplish that."

"Thanks for that." Brian snickered.

Cassandra speared him with her gaze. "What are *you* still doing here? I don't think your grandfather would be happy to learn that you're part of this coven now."

"Excuse me?" Olivia swooped down low. "Are you saying we're not good enough for Brian?"

"Begone, wraith!" Cassandra held up one hand and turned her head away. "I don't speak to the disembodied."

"I think it's about time the disembodied got their own council or guild, like the witches, werewolves and other supernatural creatures," Olivia said. "We deserve respect too, you know. I might just be the ghost to create that organization."

Cassandra turned back to her, eyes blazing. "You exist by the indulgent sufferance of the council. Normally when a witch bizarrely chooses to become a ghost, we dispose of her."

Olivia pushed her form into Cassandra's face. "Just try it. I'm not going gently into that good night."

Dorothy pulled her back—so to speak. She reached for her mother's arm. Her hand went inside Olivia.

"Oh, Dorothy." Olivia shook all over. "You know Mother doesn't like to be touched in her current state, honey. It makes me feel like spiders are walking on me."

"Sorry, Mom." Dorothy nodded at Cassandra, trying to hint at a coming conflict if Olivia didn't back down.

Olivia sighed and moved away from the herald. "I'm not kidding about raising an army of specters to defend our rights. I haven't even been dead a year and I'm already feeling oppressed."

Cassandra took a deep breath and turned to me. "Molly, I know you have your hands full with your new witch and your friends. But this is serious business. Already nine people have died. I'll be speaking to the covens at the full moon celebration tomorrow night. I'm asking for everyone's cooperation. This affects every witch in Wilmington."

"I understand. I'll do what I can to help." I wondered why she'd singled me out. She knew I was retiring soon, like Elsie.

Perhaps it was because Brian's magic bordered on the rogue, and Dorothy's magic was still lacking ability. Elsie was clearly angry about this warning. That left only me.

I assured myself that it had nothing to do with Joe and me.

"That's it," Cassandra declared. "Have a nice day." She disappeared in a puff of rose-scented smoke.

"I'd be tempted to run for council just to learn that trick," Elsie muttered. "I think we were on our way upstairs."

When we were finally upstairs in our shop, Dorothy said, "I'm surprised witches have been around as long as they have. Nine dead witches!"

"It's unusual." Elsie started a pot of tea. She had to do it without magic. While she was strong in her declaration during the ceremony, many of the day-to-day magic that we took for granted had begun to elude us.

It was nothing when we were younger to make tea, wash the dishes and get dressed using our magic. Now, we had to be careful that we didn't break the dishes, shred our clothes and make something poisonous in our teapots.

Olivia had escaped retirement with her passing. Elsie and I were still tasked with finding three witches to replace the three who'd taken over our coven from our mothers and grandmothers. We also had to hand over our spell book before we could retire with the large group of witches who lived in Boca Raton.

We'd located Dorothy, who could replace Olivia. But our spell book had been lost to a thief at the same time as Olivia's death. So now we needed two witches and a good spell to find our book.

Many witches had extended family to give their covens to, but Elsie had only one daughter, Aleese, and she was without magic. I had one son, Mike, who was also without magic.

Olivia had her one daughter, who fortunately had powerful magic though she was unschooled. She would head the coven, but for the first time, two spots would pass to witches outside our three families.

Dorothy got the tea. She did it standing on a step stool. I sighed. She couldn't remember to use her magic for these small things yet.

"Whatever are you doing, honey?" Olivia asked her.

"Getting the tea like I do every day." Dorothy was completely unaware.

"Use your magic. You're never going to get control of it if you don't use it."

Dorothy blushed and started back down the step stool.

"Let me get that for you." Brian lifted her from the last step with his hands at her waist and then procured the tea in the colorful tin from the third shelf with a wave of his hand.

Olivia slapped a spectral hand to her forehead and shook her head at me. "I don't think this is going to work, Molly. Everyone does everything for her—especially *him*."

I knew Olivia's biggest problem with Brian had nothing to do with witchcraft and everything to do with losing her daughter to a man—especially this man. But I agreed with her about his interference in Dorothy's training. She had such a sweet personality that everyone wanted to help her. In this case, helping her was actually hurting her.

"Brian, you have to let Dorothy use her magic," Elsie said before I could.

"She wasn't using magic," he pointed out. "What difference does it make?"

"I think the difference is that *I'm* supposed to be using magic." Dorothy smiled. "Sorry. I keep forgetting and doing things the other way."

Brian still had his arm around Dorothy's waist. They exchanged a few murmured words, and he let her go.

Olivia came in close to me at the table. "Say something about him keeping his hands to himself too."

"I'm not getting involved in that unless there's a problem between them," I whispered.

"I can't say anything, Molly. It sounds like sour grapes if I complain, and it makes me very uncomfortable."

"I'm sorry it happened this way, Olivia. But my concern is for Dorothy's progress as a witch. I'm not her chaperone. You're going to have to look the other way."

She huffed loudly and fled to the ceiling, where she got entangled with the old ceiling fan. Elsie laughed when she saw Olivia going around and around with it.

The tea was ready. Elsie had used the old copper spoon to measure out the exact amount into each of our cups. My cup was the goldfish. Elsie's had flamingos on it. Olivia's cup was star-shaped, and Dorothy's had a tree for her earth magic. We'd recently purchased a cup for Brian too—stars and a dog staring at the moon. It had seemed appropriate for him, but I couldn't tell if he liked it or not.

The scent of chamomile and mint filled the shop. We sat down at the small table together a little awkwardly after years of it only being the three of us. Olivia hovered above us, unable to drink the tea from her cup. She said she enjoyed looking at it and being part of our old ritual anyway.

"Should we put up some extra spells on the shop?" Elsie asked. "For the witch killers coming our way, I mean."

I gazed around Smuggler's Arcane. It held an extensive library of magic books, charms, herbs, potions and other amenities for local witches. It was also our sanctuary from the rest of the world. When we had problems, we came here to solve them. It had become the center of our witching lives.

"That's probably a good idea," I said. "Harper is here full-time now that Olivia is gone. I don't like the idea of someone sneaking up on him."

"I'm not gone," Olivia remarked. "I'm right here and you know it, Molly. Don't you start with that ghost-abuse stuff."

"I'm sorry, but you know what I meant. I had hoped Harper would go back to your house once Dorothy moved there with you, but I guess he's put off by Hemlock being there."

"You know two familiars don't like to be together in the same house," Elsie said.

"It was just a thought." I bent down to stroke Harper's silver-blue fur. He'd been much friendlier to us recently. I'd thought he was getting over Olivia's death very well, but he wouldn't go home.

"You shouldn't bother doing extra protection spells on this place," Brian said. "You could sell all this stuff on eBay and make a fortune. You don't even need the building. Come into the twenty-first century."

He didn't realize how important the physical presence of Smuggler's Arcane was to us. The shop wasn't just about making money—good thing, because we'd never made much. It was important to us, and it was a hub for other witches in Wilmington. They came here for supplies and gossip, not to mention for a place to feel safe and welcome. We couldn't do that on the Internet.

"I like you, Brian," Elsie said. "But don't ever say anything like that again or I'll decapitate you with my sword."

"I'm not worried about your sword," he mocked. "I have a wand."

"And good luck using it once I chop it to bits with my sword." Elsie held her large sword in the air.

"Let's just agree to strengthen our protection spells here, and at our houses," I said. "Cassandra gave us a heads-up. Let's use it appropriately."

We agreed on that—Brian more reluctantly than the rest of us.

"I expect a large crowd here today, stocking up for the

full moon festival," Elsie said. "I wish it wasn't such a bad time for Larry. He could come too."

"A *bad* time?" Olivia sniped. "A werewolf during a full moon is more than a bad time."

"You know he's vegetarian and hasn't killed or eaten anyone in over twenty years." Elsie defended her new boyfriend. "That means something to most people."

"I think you're right about there being a big crowd today," I intervened before the discussion got out of hand. "We have ninety minutes before we're supposed to open. I suggest we visit each of our houses before then, do a thorough blessing and strengthen the protection spells already there. Then we can come back here and do the same between customers."

"I like that idea," Dorothy agreed. "Brian, do you have your new place set up yet?"

Brian had decided to quit Cape Fear Community College and move out of the apartment he'd shared with a few other students.

He wasn't as forthcoming as the rest of us, so we didn't always know what was going on in his life. It was awkward not having a real commitment from him to be a member of our coven, not to mention not knowing how he felt about us. We didn't want to tell him to commit or leave—he might still decide to stay.

"My place is okay. I'm still working on it," he said. "But I don't need any blessings or extra protection spells. I'm good. I'll be glad to help you ladies with yours, if you'd like."

Dorothy's brown eyes gazed admiringly at him. "That would be *wonderful* of you, Brian. My magic has a long way to go to be as powerful as *yours*."

Elsie and Olivia both sighed. Heavily.

After raising a son, I was used to the young male ego. There was no point in antagonizing him. He wasn't committed to us—but he obviously enjoyed something about being here with us—hopefully not only Dorothy. I still had hopes that the bond would strengthen among us and he would become our second new witch.

"That sounds great." I glanced at my watch. "Let's get going. We'll start at Dorothy's."

As the words came out of my mouth, Joe texted me. Meet me at the house in ten?

My stomach was immediately in knots. That's the way it had been since the night he'd called me his little witch. I knew eventually that I'd feel safe again, but it was going to be a while.

I returned his text. See you there.

"Change of plans." I put away my cell phone. "Does anyone care if we start at my house?"

Dorothy had her own car but decided to ride with Brian in his Corvette. She asked me if Olivia could go with Elsie and me. Olivia went wherever her rune staff went. It didn't matter to me, but I knew Olivia wouldn't be pleased.

That was putting it mildly.

After Smuggler's Arcane was locked with key and magic, we got into my car. Elsie didn't drive. I put Olivia's staff in the backseat.

"This is just not fair, girls," our ghostly friend railed. "I've only had my daughter for a few months, and that *man* is trying to get between us."

Elsie rolled her eyes as she tried to lock her seat belt in place. "Welcome to having a child. You barely make it out of diapers and soccer games before they want to move out on their own. Of course, if you're lucky, you get grandchildren—but not always. In my case, you get a bitter child who lost her husband too young and had to move back in."

"I know I didn't get to be there for Dorothy as she was growing up, but you know I had no choice. If Drago had found her when she was young, he would have completely corrupted her and made her as evil as he is. At least that didn't happen."

I could see Olivia's pouting features in my rearview

mirror. "We know you had to protect her. And I'm sorry you might not have had much time alone with her, Olivia. You'll have to make the best of what you have."

I started the car and drove toward my house. It was drizzling. I hoped the weather would be better for the full moon festival. If not, we had a few witches with strong weather-magic abilities who lived in town. They might be able to help out.

"You know I love Brian," Olivia said. "But he hasn't committed to us. Why are we letting him hang around and complicate our lives?"

"Because he's the best shot we have at a second witch right now," Elsie answered. "He hasn't committed, but he's there all the time. He participates even though he has a snarky attitude. I like him. I hope he stays around."

"I agree with Elsie," I said with a look at Olivia's face. "Brian is unstable, but we could train him. And I think he likes us too."

"I just can't believe it." Olivia was outraged. "Are you choosing him over *me*?"

"He's a lot better looking." Elsie laughed. "Don't forget, you brought him into our lives. You're just upset because you had relations with him, and now he wants to do it with your daughter."

"Molly!" Olivia appealed to me. "Are you going to let her talk to me that way?"

"We both know she's right about how you feel." I tried to take the high road. "I know it's more than you possibly having a son-in-law that you had sex with, but it's the heart of the matter."

I pulled the car into my driveway. Joe's SUV was already there. I kept reminding myself that, if the council had heard him call me a witch, they would already have acted. I had to stop worrying about it all the time.

"You might as well take my staff and drop it in the Atlantic," Olivia moaned pitifully. "No one cares about me anymore now that I'm dead."

I was happy to get out of the car.

Joe walked out of the garage. He had a look on his handsome face that I knew so well. It said, *Something's wrong.*

I hugged him right away in case he was about to say anything that involved witchcraft before I could protect him. "Not here," I whispered close to his ear. "Not now."

He moved his head back to look into my face. His thick black hair was threaded with silver and his dark brown eyes were concerned. "Is something wrong?" he whispered back.

"Maybe. Is everything okay with you?"

"Something weird has happened. I wanted you to know about it right away."

I squared my shoulders, ready for the worst. "We'll handle it. I won't let them take you."

His brows knit together. "Molly, I think we're talking about different things. I brought my new partner home to meet you."

I saw the older woman approaching from behind him and felt a huge sense of relief. "Why didn't you say so?" I moved away from him and held out my hand to the other woman. "I'm Molly Renard. It's very nice to meet you."

The other woman grasped my hand in a firm grip. "Hi Molly. I'm Suzanne Renard. It's a pleasure to meet you too."

CHAPTER 3

Smoke of air and earth,
Cleanse and bless,
Chase away harm and fear.
May only good be here.

I admitted to being at a complete loss for words.

I recognized the name—Suzanne was Joe's first wife.

They had divorced thirty-one years ago, give or take. He'd only been married to her a short time. We'd never met, because she'd been out of his life before he and I were a couple.

How was this possible?

Joe laughed nervously. I could feel Elsie, Olivia, Brian and Dorothy at my back. I knew they were all wondering what was going on. I couldn't remember if I'd shared Suzanne's name with Olivia and Elsie. She'd only been a small blip on my radar, and it had been so long ago.

"Hi." Joe smiled at my friends. "Would you mind if I take Molly into the house for a minute so we can talk?"

"Not at all," Elsie said. "We'll just talk to your new partner. What did you say your name was? You know how older people don't always remember things."

Joe's new partner raised her voice. "Suzanne. I'm Suzanne Renard."

I guess I'd told Olivia and Elsie about Joe's ex-wife. I could tell from Elsie's voice that she knew who Suzanne was. That only left Brian and Dorothy in confusion.

Joe grabbed my hand and we went inside. As soon as the door was closed, I didn't hold back. "Why is *she* here?"

"See, that's the weird thing," he explained. "Suzanne was with the Wilmington police when we met. You knew that. She got a new job in Charleston for a while, and finally ended up in Savannah."

"You're right. This is weird." *That's putting it mildly.* "And now?"

"We're working on a possible serial homicide case. The killer seems to be slowly moving up the coast, killing young men. We had a possible death from this killer two days ago, right here. Because the murders started in Savannah, the police commissioner there loaned us someone familiar with the case— Suzanne. I don't have a partner right now. I was the obvious choice to work with her while we solve this. Weird, huh?"

"'Weird' isn't the word I'd use." *Ridiculous. Stupid. Impossible.* "Doesn't the department have a policy against relatives working together?"

"Suzanne and I aren't technically relatives, since we've been divorced a long time. Captain Phillips doesn't think there'll be a problem, because I assured him there wouldn't be." He put his arms around me. "Come on, Molly. I don't even know her anymore. I've spent most of my life with you."

Sometimes it still rankled that I'd known he was the one for me the moment I'd met him, but he'd married Suzanne first. I had to remind myself that I was a witch, and Joe wasn't. He wasn't as attuned to nature as I was.

"I'll be fine," I said in my old schoolteacher's voice. I used the tone sometimes when my emotions were in turmoil.

"Hey." He put his hand under my chin. "Don't use 'the voice' on me. This is only for a short time. I know you're not worried about anything happening between Suzanne and me, right?"

I smiled, pleased that he knew me well enough to hear how I sounded. "Really, Joe. I'll be fine. Just be careful out there with a serial killer on the loose. Wilmington doesn't see much of that."

"Lucky for me this serial killer only seems interested in young men in their twenties. It's a very specific group of people who are being targeted. I'll be fine as long as you are." He kissed me lightly. "Was there something you needed to tell me?"

"Not here. Later. We'll have to talk tonight."

"Okay. Suzanne and I have to go to a joint task force meeting about the killings. There's more than one law enforcement group involved. It's kind of stupid really, because we don't know for sure that it's the same person committing these murders."

"What makes them think it's a serial killer?" I thought about what Cassandra had told us at the shop. I hoped the two problems weren't the same. People like Joe and Suzanne, who didn't possess magic, didn't do well against people who did.

"It's complicated. I don't want to keep your friends waiting while I explain. I'll see you later, and we'll talk about all of it, okay?"

"Sure. Will you be home for dinner?" I was in the habit of asking, even though I knew he wouldn't know until right before he headed home.

"Maybe." He shrugged. "I'll let you know. I love you, Molly."

I hugged him hard. "I love you too."

He started out the door, looking at the people waiting for us in the driveway before going out. "Molly, don't I know that young man from somewhere? My Spidey senses are tingling looking at him."

"You've met him. He dated Olivia for a while." *He was a murder suspect for a short time too.* "He's spending some time with us at the shop."

"Just be careful who you get involved with right now. A good con man can take advantage of a situation like this."

"Thanks." I smiled at his concern. "I'll be careful."

We went back outside together.

Suzanne grasped my hand again. "Molly, I know how strange this must be for you. It's strange for me too. I wouldn't be here if it wasn't really important. And I'll be a good partner for Joe. I'll make sure nothing happens to him."

Olivia, Elsie, Dorothy, Brian and I watched as Joe and Suzanne climbed into the SUV and left. It was so quiet for a moment that I could hear birds chirping in the backyard plum tree.

Then the dam burst. "What in the world was that all about, Molly?" Olivia started first.

"Molly, isn't that woman Joe's *ex-wife*?" Elsie demanded.

"Wait!" Dorothy blinked. "Joe was married *before* Molly? But they've been married forever."

"Could we go ahead and get the spells done?" Brian asked. "I have an appointment this afternoon. I want to look my best for the full moon ceremony tomorrow."

"Let's go inside and talk about it." I glanced nervously around the yard. I never felt safe anymore.

Once we were in the house, Elsie insisted on making more tea, and that meant dragging out some orange cookies I'd made. I explained everything that Joe had told me. They absorbed it like the orange cookie absorbed the tea.

"You aren't going to let this happen, are you?" Olivia asked. "Those orange cookies smell so good. It's not fair that ghosts can't eat."

"You could pretend." Dorothy held up a cookie. "Just lean over like you're taking a bite. *Mmm*. Good, huh?"

"I'm sorry, honey. But it's just not the same. Thank you for thinking of me." Olivia managed a small air hug for her daughter.

"It sounds to me like Joe is talking about the same thing Cassandra warned us about today," Elsie said. "I hope someone else finds this killer before him. I suppose it would be all right if Suzanne finds him first. If she were dead, she couldn't come back and work with Joe again."

I patted Elsie on the shoulder. I knew she was only thinking of my happiness. Her late husband, Bill, had been a salesman and a cheat. He'd used every opportunity to sleep around. Elsie had known but had stayed with him for the sake of her daughter. Before she could divorce him, he'd died.

Joe wasn't like Bill. I knew that. Bill had even flirted with Olivia and me. Joe was steady and serious. I wasn't sure he had any idea what flirting was. I'd practically had to hit him over the head to get him to notice me thirty years ago. I believed him when he said that I didn't have to worry about Suzanne and him.

At least as far as *he* was concerned. I wasn't sure about Suzanne, not to mention a possible witch serial killer in town. What else could happen?

CHAPTER 4

I am the moon and stars,
I am the richness of the earth,
I am all that was and ever shall be,
I am mistress of the night.

We did a quick blessing and protection spell on my house. My familiar, Isabelle, wasn't comfortable with so many people being there. She knew everyone, but she never liked a crowd. Maybe it was because her spirit inside the large, long-haired gray cat was that of a witch from the 1600s who'd been burned at the stake. That seemed reason enough to be uncomfortable in a crowd to me.

Elsie had asked to borrow a purple velvet hat that I rarely wore. She wanted to wear it to the full moon celebration. Dorothy and Brian went on to meet us at her house—this time with Olivia in the car—despite Dorothy's pleas to leave her mother there with us.

A person could only handle so much in one day. I felt as though I were reaching my limits too.

I grabbed the purple hat off the shelf in the closet as Elsie drank the last of the tea and ate the last orange cookie in the kitchen. I turned to leave the bedroom, and the Bone Man of Oak Island was standing right in front of me.

I took a step back. I'd never seen him anywhere but on the island. Why was he here in my bedroom?

He didn't say anything—he didn't have to. His visage spoke for him. He was at least seven feet tall and as thin as a young tree. His joints stuck out all over. His head was too small for the rest of his body, and his empty black eyes stared right through me.

He wore dried bones around his neck and an old black suit of a fashion that had been popular two hundred years ago. I'd often wondered if he'd stolen it from one of the graves on the island.

Or was it his? No one was sure if the Bone Man was alive or dead.

His mouth was stained red. No one I'd ever spoken to knew why, and we were all afraid to ask. Witches frequently went to him to make trades or ask his advice. His secrets were those of a man caught between our world and the next.

There was disagreement about his status in the magic community. A witch knew when she was conversing with another witch or magical creature. The Bone Man was neither. While we all believed he had magic, none of us knew what kind of magic it was. He was respected and feared by all of us.

"Why are you here?" My voice shook, but I forced the words from my lips. "What do you want?"

He smiled—a ghastly experience—but didn't say a word. In another instant, he'd vanished.

I sat on the bed, my trembling hands covering my face. My heart was threatening to burst from my chest.

"Molly?" Elsie came into the bedroom. "Oh, thank goodness. I was afraid you'd left without me. And you found the purple hat. Thank you." She sat on the bed beside me. "Is something wrong?"

"I—I saw the Bone Man." The words scraped out of my throat.

"*What*? Have you recently visited Oak Island? You didn't say anything to me. Did you go alone?"

"That's just it. I haven't been to Oak Island since last year." I moved my hands from my face. "But he was here, in my bedroom. That's never happened before."

Elsie caught my hands in hers. Her green eyes were filled with the same fear I was sure she saw in mine. "Here? Why would he be here? We always go to Oak Island to see him. Are you *sure* it was him?"

I stared at her. "How could I mistake him for anyone else? He was standing here when I came out of the closet. I can't imagine why."

Elsie tried on the purple hat, tipping it to the right on her head. "It probably wasn't him. It was probably only a vision of him. I don't know why on earth he'd send you a vision. Or were you *thinking* of visiting him?"

"No. I haven't thought about him since the last time we went to the island. I can't imagine why he'd appear here."

But a fleeting thought suddenly filled my brain. It was Joe repeating the words he'd spoken before we'd gone to sleep that night six months ago. *Good night, little witch.*

Why had I thought of that?

I couldn't ask Elsie for her opinion. I hadn't told her that Joe knew I was a witch. We all knew it was bordering on suicidal to tell anyone we loved who didn't possess magic. Elsie had never confided in Bill or Aleese. Witches who were smart kept their secrets to themselves.

But I had been forced into a position that had made me worried about Joe's safety if I didn't tell him. Nothing less than his life would have made me confide that secret. I knew the consequences.

"Molly?" Elsie snapped her fingers in front of my face. "You're not seeing him now, are you?"

"No." I got to my feet. "I don't understand why I saw the Bone Man. I hope I never see him again, except on the island.

We'd better get over to Dorothy's house before Olivia drives her and Brian crazy."

"Maybe it's the stress of knowing Joe will be working with his ex-wife," Elsie conjectured as we went out to the car. "I could understand that. She's *very* well preserved, isn't she?"

I didn't reply. There were too many other things running through my head to even think about what Suzanne looked like—though I had to admit she was in good shape.

We got in the car and drove across town to the Historic District. Olivia's family home was on Third Street. At least one member of the Dunst family had lived here for more than two hundred years. We were all glad that Olivia had someone to pass her family's legacy to.

Brian's Corvette was in the drive with the silver Mercedes Olivia had left Dorothy. Dorothy still drove her Volkswagen Beetle most of the time. She said the Mercedes made her nervous.

The three of them were waiting inside the lovely old home for us. We'd managed to reconstruct most of the inside of the house, which had been trashed by Olivia's killer. There was still a lot of work to be done, but a spell we'd set in place kept everyone but witches from seeing the damage.

Elsie and I couldn't have done it without Brian and Dorothy. Their magic was very powerful together—when we could direct it.

Dorothy was holding her tuxedo cat, Hemlock. Brian was trying to stroke the cat's silky black fur. Hemlock wanted nothing to do with anyone except Dorothy, which was the way most familiars were.

"Maybe I need a cat," Brian said. "Now that I've got my own place, I could have one."

"I'd be glad to help you find one," Dorothy volunteered.

Olivia shook her head, a movement that left shadows behind, like a bad movie going from side-to-side for a few minutes. She came close to Elsie and me. "Can we get on with this, please? Spending too much time with Dorothy and Brian is upsetting my equilibrium."

"Talk about equilibrium—Molly just saw the Bone Man in her bedroom." Elsie chuckled as she enjoyed the look of distaste that crossed Olivia's still-pretty face.

"Why would he be in your bedroom?" Olivia asked. "He's a man with certain tastes that don't run to vanilla pudding, if you know what I mean."

"Are you saying I'm boring?" I asked.

"Not exactly." Olivia flew around the crystal chandelier above us, making it tinkle. "But he's definitely not your type."

"I don't think he was there to enjoy my company," I said delicately, though I had no idea why he'd been there. "Never mind. Let's get the blessing and protection spell done here before Brian has to leave. We still have to go to Elsie's house."

I wished I hadn't told Elsie what I'd seen, but at the time it had been so overwhelming. There were dozens of questions from Brian and Dorothy. It was hard to concentrate on the spell.

"I've never met the Bone Man," Brian said. "What's he like? I've known other witches who went out to the island to trade with him. They're terrified of him."

"Everyone is who has any good sense at all," Elsie said. "I would never want to see him again if I didn't absolutely have to. He's like a walking nightmare. You never know what he's going to do."

"I've never seen him either," Dorothy said. "He took my mother's ghost in exchange for information. That seems a little harsh."

Olivia laughed. "It wasn't a bit like that. He was just lonely. We had a good time together—at least as far as I can recall. The whole incident is blurry for me."

"Maybe you need the equivalent of rosemary for ghosts," Elsie said. "It could help with your failing memory."

"Can we please focus and finish the blessing?" I wished

the subject would go away. I was already worried I'd see the Bone Man in my bedroom again when I got home.

Everyone agreed to finish what we'd started, and in no time at all, we were ready to move on to Elsie's house. It was an especially good opportunity for us to work a protection spell, since her daughter, Aleese, would be at work.

Dorothy opened the heavy front door to the house she now shared with Olivia. It was carved with magic runes that glowed when she touched it. She was immediately confronted by a man and woman.

It was clear to all of us that the pair were witches. She was tall and stately with thick black hair and blue eyes that matched the sapphires around her neck. Her white dress was stunning against her dark skin, but the expression on her face was hardly welcoming.

"Good day. We're sorry to interrupt, but we've come to take our son home."

CHAPTER 5

Willow wand and herb of sage,
Cleanse the air. Fire, rage.
Velvet cloak and silver coin,
Take this dream and make it mine.

"Mom." Brian stepped forward. "Dad. What are you doing here?"

"I think your mother was clear on that point," the man said.

Brian's father was tall and a perfect match for the woman. His gray suit was expensive, probably handmade. His brown hair and blue eyes reminded me of Brian. Between them, it was easy to see where he'd gotten his good looks.

"Excuse me." Brian stepped to one side. "Elsie, Molly, Dorothy and Olivia—these are my parents, Schadt and Yuriza. Mom, Dad, these are my friends."

I could see the anger and distance in Yuriza's wonderful blue eyes. She didn't like the crowd her son had fallen in with. Cassandra had probably told them about seeing us together at the cave. We weren't exactly the cream of the witch world.

"I can't believe you are with these people, Brian—and one of the undead. What are you thinking?" she demanded in a powerful voice. "Come with us this instant."

Brian stepped back and grabbed Dorothy's hand. "I'm

not going anywhere with you. You ignore me for years and only come to find me so you can look down on my friends. Go home, Mom. Leave me alone."

Schadt shook his head, his thick hair moving like a lion's mane on his head. "You'll either come with us now, Brian, or you'll find yourself without family or money in the future, do you understand?"

"I get it." Brian raised his chin and stared down his father. "I've been without family for a long time. As far as money is concerned, I'll just sell the gifts you've given me to make up for actually spending time with me. Thanks for the heads-up."

Without another word, Schadt and Yuriza abruptly vanished.

"Can you do that, Brian?" Elsie asked him. "If so, can you teach me?"

Brian shook himself. "It's not something teachable. Some of the families pay a premium to the council for the extra magic it takes. It's convenient—charms and spells, that kind of thing. I know you don't do it, but lots of other witches do. Are you guys ready to go now? Let's finish this."

Elsie and I, with Olivia and her staff, led the way to Elsie's house on Grace Street in my car. Of course we discussed the unfairness of being able to purchase more magic on the way there. None of us had even known it was possible to purchase more magic.

"So that's why some witches are able to keep their magic for hundreds of years." Elsie nodded, the purple velvet hat covering her faded red curls. "It makes sense to me now. Why should the witching world be any fairer than the normal world?"

"I guess that's what made Dorothy's father so powerful and vital when I met him, even though he was a thousand years old." Olivia sighed. "I had no idea you could pay for extra magic. I wonder what it costs."

"Probably more than any of us have," Elsie said. "And let's

not forget that Dorothy's father was so evil that you had to hide her from him all these years."

"I don't see where one has anything to do with the other," Olivia argued. "Besides, I am quite well-to-do."

"And you're also quite dead. Having enough money to buy more magic doesn't seem to be in your future." Elsie smugly smiled.

"I could buy extra magic for Dorothy." Olivia shrugged. "Well, *she* could buy extra magic with my money."

"I'm not sure if Brian can really stand up to his parents." I changed the subject. "If they want him back badly enough, they'll probably just take him."

"Maybe it would be just as well for Dorothy," Olivia said.

"For Dorothy?" Elsie asked. "Please."

We were finally at Elsie's house. It was a lovely place that was surrounded by tall, old trees and green shrubs. It wasn't historic, like Dorothy and Olivia's house, but it was very nice. Bill had provided a good income while he'd been alive. Elsie had taught school until she'd retired.

Dorothy and Brian were standing in the cobblestone driveway with their heads together—literally—his head against hers. Their fingers were entwined.

"Aren't they cute?" Elsie giggled. "I don't know how you can *not* want to see them together, Olivia. You might even have grandchildren."

"Grandchildren?" Olivia slid from the car like hot smoke. "I'm not old enough to be a grandmother. I suppose I never will be now."

"You've got a hundred years before you move on," I reminded her. "You should fill them as carefully as you did your house when you were alive."

She bit her lip and floated away. It was an emotional subject for her.

Elsie opened the front door to her house, and we filed in

after her. It wasn't as grand or filled with antiques, but it had a nice homey feel to it that I'd always enjoyed.

"I guess the foyer is as good a place as any for the spell." She took out several red candles that had been in a bureau to the left side of the door. "We can set them right here."

To my surprise, as Elsie touched each candle, it burst brightly into flame.

"How in the world did I do that?" She was as puzzled by it as the rest of us. She hadn't been able to quick-start a candle in years.

"You are one hot mama." Brian grinned as he came near her. "Good job, Elsie."

We were about to start the blessing when Aleese came downstairs. "What's going on, Mother? I smelled the candles. Are you trying to burn the house down?"

Aleese was a very nice, practical sort of accountant, whose husband had died, leaving her nothing. She'd moved in with Elsie to survive, and was nearly the spitting image of her mother years before, with her bright copper red curls and petite build. Only the eyes were different. Aleese had inherited her father's brown eyes instead of her mother's magical green eyes.

"It's just a few candles," Elsie told her. "Why are you home? I thought you'd be working."

"I wasn't feeling well. I guess that's why you felt free to bring your friends here instead of meeting them at that awful shop."

Elsie stopped smiling. "I felt free to bring my friends here because this is my home. Go back upstairs, Aleese. We won't be long."

Instead of listening to her mother, Aleese kept coming until she'd reached the foyer. She looked at us as though we were specimens in a jar. "Mother, this isn't a good idea."

Brian smiled and touched her, muttering a spell under his breath.

Aleese stopped moving as she took on all the attributes of

a statue. It was an old spell, not difficult to do. Elsie had managed it on her own recently—mostly by accident, of course.

But it was different since Brian had done it to her daughter. "What are you doing?" Elsie demanded. "Take that spell off her. She doesn't know about magic. I'd like to keep it that way."

Brian shrugged. "Let's get the protection spell done, and I'll take it from her. I can't handle any other family interference today. I guess it doesn't matter if it's from parents or kids. It's just annoying."

"Is he talking about *me*?" Olivia demanded. "I'm not annoying. I'm just worried about Dorothy's future. That's all."

Elsie's hands glowed red as she approached Brian. "Get that spell off my daughter now, punk."

"Look at that!" Dorothy was amazed at seeing Elsie use her magic so effectively. "I didn't know that was possible."

"Fire witches can be deadly," Elsie hissed. "Brian, this is your last warning."

"Okay." He touched Aleese and muttered the counter spell.

Aleese moved as though she were sleepwalking. It would take a few minutes to get over the effects of the spell. "What happened? Why am I down here? Mother? W-what's going on?"

Elsie helped her daughter back upstairs, reassuring her that everything was fine despite her confusion.

"I'm out of here," Brian said. "This is stupid. I'm sorry, Dorothy. Can you catch a ride back with them?"

Before Dorothy could answer, Brian walked out the door. He didn't disappear as his parents had. The Corvette's engine revved, and he was gone with a squeal of tires.

"What happened?" Dorothy blinked away the tears that had gathered in her big brown eyes.

"Oh, he'll be back," Olivia said. "It's just a tantrum."

I put my arm around Dorothy's shoulders. "If you could wait another ten years to fall in love, it's more likely that you'll find a man mature enough to handle it. Brian is just having issues. I'm sure he'll be fine."

Elsie returned without Aleese. We whispered the protection spell and blessing on the house with the three of us holding hands. When it was over, Elsie decided to stay with Aleese until she made sure her daughter was all right. She was still very angry with Brian.

I took Dorothy and Olivia back to Smuggler's Arcane. It was just in time for the shop to open. We had a busy day ahead of us, but we were going to have to handle it without Elsie or Brian.

CHAPTER 6

Love, elusive and free,
Bring him back to me,
Touch his eyes and make him see,
Bind his heart to me.

The day was as busy as I had expected it to be. Witches we knew, and some we didn't, came in for supplies to celebrate the full moon. We almost sold out of candles and silver knives. I knew the organized event in Wilmington was going to be well attended. I hadn't realized how many smaller events were going on around us too.

That was good news for us as witches as well as for Smuggler's Arcane. The Council of Witches always worried about losing witches without gaining new ones. One might be born a witch without knowing it, like Dorothy. Or one could be a witch and choose to ignore it. Either way was bad for the propagation of witchcraft in the new century. A strong base meant a better chance of survival.

I didn't worry about the survival of witchcraft overly much, but the council continuing to bring it up had left me worried. I was glad to see new faces at the shop.

Many of our customers were not witches at all. Some of them wanted to observe our customs, while others were simply curious. I handled all of them the same. It was a blessing to have people interested in the old ways.

Phoebe came in from Atlantic Beach and filled a tote bag with everything from herbs to a new cauldron. She was a regular customer, and a practicing witch.

"Have you all heard the news yet about the deaths of the witches from Savannah and Charleston?" she whispered as she paid for her haul. "I've heard there has been another death right here in the Wilmington area."

"Yes." I finished running her MasterCard and gave her a receipt. "I've heard that too. Cassandra is supposed to be at the celebration tomorrow night. I hope she has more news on that front."

"It's the beginning of a new purge," Phoebe said. "There are too many witches now, and we're too open about what we do. Do you know how many witchcraft pages there are on Facebook?"

"No. I don't get on Facebook much."

"I counted one hundred and fifty," she confided. "That's why they want to do away with us."

Being a witch didn't preclude being paranoid from time to time. With the history of our craft, it wasn't surprising.

"That sounds like a lot," I agreed. "I don't think we can take back the knowledge that we exist now."

"The council could take it back. They could erase the memory of us from all the non-magic people in the world. Then we'd be protected. I have a petition right here that I'm planning to present to them." She rummaged in her large handbag and pulled out a petition that was written on a scroll. "Will you sign it, Molly?"

Since I was fighting not to have Joe's memory of witches erased, I could hardly sign her well-meant petition. As I glanced up for a diversion that could allow me to escape from behind the counter without hurting Phoebe's feelings, a large bag of lemon balm fell to the old wood floor.

Olivia smiled and shrugged.

"Excuse me, Phoebe." I smiled at her. She was a very good customer and an old friend. "I have to clean up this mess."

"Oh!" Dorothy noticed the bag of lemon balm. "I can do that for you, Molly."

"Kay needs your help choosing a new robe for the celebration," I told her.

We had brought in a few new robes, dresses and other elaborate apparel for the event. Not dozens of them, since they were expensive, but I hoped to sell them all.

"Sorry. Sure." Dorothy went to help Kay, who was from Wrightsville Beach.

I still had to sweep up the spilled herb. Phoebe waited for a few minutes, and then one of her friends came into the shop and claimed her attention.

"Sorry, Molly," Olivia said. "It was all I could think to do on the spur of the moment, and then it almost didn't work. What does Phoebe think she's going to accomplish with that petition? All she's going to do is rile up the council."

"I guess if you're afraid or worried enough it doesn't matter." I swept up the mess and went to dump the dustpan into the trash container in the supply closet. When I opened the door, the Bone Man was standing there, grinning at me.

I dropped the dustpan and the broom. What was it with him and closets?

"Will you speak to me now?" I asked in a low voice, not wanting to attract attention.

But it was as though he were nothing but a shadow. He stood there without moving or speaking for a moment and then disappeared again.

"Do you need help with that?" Dorothy came up behind me. "I think Kay found a robe she wants. I'm not sure how to work the cash register, with or without magic."

"Yes." I took a deep breath and gathered my scattered wits.

What did it mean? Why was the Bone Man haunting my closets?

I rang up Kay's purchase of a beautiful sea green robe. She was very excited about the big celebration. It was the first of its kind in Wilmington. Usually witches met privately and kept their activities secret.

In recent years, the council had encouraged us to go out and celebrate the full moon and other important events more openly in the hope that other witches would join in. It seemed to be working, as there appeared to be more witches in the city, where they had once hanged our kind.

"It's going to be a good strong moon too," Kay said. "I'm very excited."

"So am I." I bagged her purchase and handed it to her. "I hope to see you there. Blessed Be, my friend."

Portia de Winter came in with a lovely, warm smile for everyone. She was in charge of getting the full moon celebration going. The council had tasked her with the responsibility of making our events more visible.

She was a beautiful, older witch with long silver hair and sharp, blue eyes. She dressed well, always wearing a colorful ankle-length skirt. She was ready for the full moon in a gorgeous silver cotton that almost matched the color of her hair.

I couldn't think of a better choice for a witch who had to go out among other witches and spread the word. Witches could be clannish and, sometimes, rude to strangers. Portia had a way about her. She was friendly and appealing.

She nodded to the witches she knew as she came into the shop, and shook hands with those she didn't know, introducing herself to everyone in Smuggler's Arcane.

"Good afternoon, Molly." Portia came up and took my hand. "I can see you're very busy. I hope a lot of this is for the celebration."

"I'm sure it is."

Dorothy was finished cleaning up the lemon balm I'd dropped. She eagerly shook hands with Portia. "How are you? I'm so looking forward to my first full moon celebration. I can't believe I missed out all these years."

"We'll just have to make up for that by having the best celebration ever," Portia responded with excitement in her blue eyes. She was a water witch, like me, but with much stronger magic.

"Great! I can't wait."

Portia worked for the council, and was also the only council representative we'd met who didn't immediately spurn Olivia's presence. "Hello, Olivia. How are you today?"

"I'm just fine, except for a growing feeling of loss regarding my magic. My own familiar, Barnabas, refuses to come back home. I still feel like a witch, but I'm reviled by my own kind. It's very difficult being a ghost. No wonder witches usually move on right away."

"Olivia, take heart," Portia counselled. "Things will change. They always do. At some point, ghost witches may even be able to use their magic again. Don't give up. Remember— you're here for your daughter. I can't think of a worthier cause."

Elsie came in while Portia was still there. She stowed her large purple bag behind the counter. "I'm sorry, Molly. I was just so upset seeing Aleese that way. I overreacted. I guess I owe Brian an apology too. I don't even know how long it's been since I got that hot—literally. I didn't even know it was possible anymore."

"It's not a big deal," I told her. "I know how you felt. We tried all our lives to protect our families from magic. It's hard when it comes right into our homes. I think Brian was embarrassed by the whole situation with his parents and then with Aleese. He isn't used to dealing with those kinds of issues."

"He'd probably be better off if he was more interactive with his family—although they seemed like twits to me. The emotion would have been good for him. He's all brain and knowledge, but there's very little heart in his magic."

"I know." I told her about seeing the Bone Man again in the supply closet. "I don't know what to think about it. He's not exactly the person you want to have visions of."

She knit her red brows together. "Maybe he's trying to contact you. Maybe he needs help."

I gazed at her with complete disbelief. "First of all, why would the Bone Man need help? He's an entity unto himself. And second, why would he contact *me*? It's not like we're friends or something. I'm as terrified of him as you are."

She shrugged as two more witches came up to pay for their purchases. "I don't know. Olivia had some kind of relationship with him that I'd rather not think about. Maybe she could pop out there and talk to him. You should ask her when things get quiet."

But the shop was even busier after Portia got there. We made tea for her, and she sat at our table drinking it and talking with friends. It was always a pleasure having her there. We all wished she'd become a member of the council.

Dorothy was getting familiar with the merchandise, but was still unsure of many things, which meant that Elsie and I had to talk her through dozens of purchases. I thought she did an exceptional job for her first big day there. I couldn't have asked for more.

Around five P.M., people slowly stopped coming in. We helped those who were already there and got ready to close for the day. I'd convinced one woman who believed she was being visited by a demon that it probably wasn't so. She wasn't a witch but had created what she considered a perfect lover from her fantasies. I assured her that demons didn't really make good lovers, despite present day fiction, and sent her home with some Valerian root so she could get a good night's sleep.

"Girls, I think this may be the busiest I have ever seen our shop." Olivia was smiling, although sometimes her ghostly facial expressions were difficult to decipher. "I'm so glad I was here to be part of it."

"I'm glad you were here too, Mom," Dorothy added.

"I wish I could join in tomorrow at the full moon celebration, but I'm afraid some of the others might be mean to me. I hate to miss it."

"Let's think about it." I had no real goal in mind. I knew how most witches felt about ghosts, even ghosts of witches. "Maybe we can think of some way to hide you."

Portia had gone, and Dorothy saw the last customer out of the shop before she locked the door and put out the closed sign. We were intent on closing up, giving Barnabas food and water, and then going home.

I was particularly anxious to talk with Joe about his new case—and his new partner.

"Did you ask Olivia what she thinks about the Bone Man appearing out of nowhere?" Elsie put on her purple hat and picked up her bag.

"What about the Bone Man?" Olivia's whole body shuddered. "He wasn't so bad. I just don't ever want to go out there again."

"I'm not planning on going out there," I assured her. "I've been seeing him here."

The expression on Olivia's face was simple this time—horror. "Molly, I can't believe he's your type. And what about Joe? This is too much."

Dorothy frowned at me. "Is that a good idea? I mean, I haven't met the Bone Man, but Joe is such a nice person. And what about Mike? How is he going to take this?"

I ignored her question about my son and what he'd think about the Bone Man. "I'm not dating him. I saw him in my bedroom this morning after coming out of the closet. I saw him here in the supply closet. That's why I dropped the dustpan."

"You mean he's *appearing* to you?" Olivia asked. "That's odd. I've never heard of him reaching out to anyone. Have you, Elsie?"

"No. Never." Elsie adjusted her bag on her shoulder.

"Maybe it has something to do with your mother's amulet that you started wearing. You remember, he was very keen on it when we were out there last time."

I fingered the amulet. "Maybe that's it."

"Or maybe he's in trouble," Olivia said. "Maybe you should check on him, Molly. What if he needs help and you're the only one he can connect with?"

"I think *you* should go, Olivia. You know him so well," I suggested.

"No. Not me. He hasn't been appearing to me anyway, Molly. I think he wants *you*."

"This is the Bone Man we're talking about," I reminded her. "We don't randomly stop in at Oak Island with a Bundt cake and ask him how he's doing."

"But what if Mom is right?" Dorothy added. "If he were anyone else, you'd help him."

Elsie giggled. "Sounds like a road trip."

CHAPTER 7

Teach me what I need to know,
Show me truth and light.
I fear no evil—no remorse.
Gird me for the fight.

Dorothy was excited by the idea of finally meeting the Bone Man. That was only because she'd never met him. I felt sure she'd be as frightened of him as the rest of us once she laid eyes on him.

"I'll just wait at the house tomorrow until you girls come back." Olivia went out the door with Dorothy, who was carrying her staff. "I've spent all the time I want out there. Just be careful. We know the Bone Man can be tricky. Don't let him take your amulet with some kind of shady deal, Molly."

"I'm not entirely convinced this is the right thing to do." I locked the shop door behind us, and we headed to our cars. "How would we approach him? The only reason witches visit him is to trade for knowledge or items we need for spells."

"Why can't we just say we're checking on him because you had visions of him?" Dorothy unlocked her brown Beetle.

"I can't imagine saying that to him." Elsie shrugged as

she got into my car. "But Molly was pretty good with him last time—except for letting him have Olivia."

"Don't remind me," Olivia called out. "Dorothy, make sure you leave my staff at home when you go."

Elsie laughed. "I thought you had a good time with him, Olivia."

"I dated a weredragon once too," Olivia said. "We don't want to go into all my mistakes."

"I'm sure we'll think of something," Dorothy decided cheerfully. "Should I bring my magic stone?"

"Not unless you want him to trick you out of it," Olivia replied. "I don't know, girls. Maybe Dorothy is too green to go out to Oak Island."

"I think she'll be fine," Elsie said. "She's bound to go out there with us sometime. It might as well be tomorrow."

I sighed as I got behind the wheel. Elsie and Dorothy seemed very sure it was the right thing to do. Olivia did too—she just didn't want to be part of it.

As we drove back to Elsie's house, I prepared her for the fact that I might decide not to go to the island tomorrow. "There's so much to do. I don't know if there's time for the ferry trip and to get ready for the full moon celebration. Maybe we should wait a few days."

"Not afraid, are you, Molly?" Elsie asked.

"Yes. All of us are—except for Dorothy, who doesn't know any better. I don't know what kind of magic the Bone Man has, but I know he's a lot more powerful than the three of us. The only times we've gone out there, we were desperate. I don't feel desperate enough to allow my fear to overwhelm my common sense."

"I don't like him either, but he has helped us many times. Remember that one time we were trying to help that poor Selkie who'd lost her skin? He was the only one with a workable solution."

"Solution? You mean the time we all had the fillings in our teeth removed so we could give them to him," I reminded her.

"Oh, yes." She frowned. "I'd forgotten about that part. But we did help the Selkie. Is she still around Wilmington?"

"I see her almost every day down by the docks with her easel and paints." I pulled in front of Elsie's house. "That was different, don't you think? We were trying to help someone who couldn't help herself."

Elsie stared at me with emerald green eyes. "We don't know we aren't trying to help someone this time, do we?"

"You mean the Bone Man?" I shook my head. "It's hard for me to believe he needs our help. Maybe that's uncharitable, but usually association with him comes at a price."

"Well, give me a call in the morning if you change your mind." She smiled. "I'll change it back for you with a major guilt trip from all the stories I can remember of the times he helped us. Good night, Molly."

I watched her walk slowly into her house before I drove away.

Joe was home when I got there. I wished I could explain to him about the Bone Man. I felt sure he'd agree with me about not going to the island. It would've been nice to have someone in my corner.

But the only way we could discuss witchcraft was inside an enchanted bubble to protect us from the prying eyes and ears of the council. The enchantment didn't last long. Certainly not enough time to explain my fears and trepidation about seeing the Bone Man again.

I walked in the door to the smell of Joe's peppers and onions sizzling on the stove. He'd also made veggies with meatballs and marinara to go on hoagie rolls.

"Hi, Molly." He grinned as he stirred the peppers and onions in the skillet so they wouldn't burn.

"I didn't expect you to be home, since you're working on a homicide." I put my bag on a chair. Isabelle came up and nudged me with her head, reminding me how much she disliked the smell of peppers and onions. She wanted her food so she could take a nice long nap while we ate.

"The task force is still trying to decide if the young man who died in Southport is part of the homicides we're tracking."

"What did he die from?"

"That's unclear. Some people think it was a drug overdose. There are no wounds on the body. Suzanne and I can't do anything until we get all the information. I thought you and I could have dinner together before this whole thing becomes a rock rolling downhill."

I wanted to talk to him as much as he could about the case before we had to discuss its portents of witchcraft in the bubble. I was never quiet sure how long I could hold on to that magic. The amulet had increased my abilities, but I still felt uncertain. When you try something enough times and it doesn't work, it makes you feel insecure.

Joe told me what he could about the possible serial killer. "It's been the same story since Savannah. The numbers change in each town, but the deaths all look the same. No apparent wounds that could cause death. No poisons. No reason these healthy, young men should be dead at all. That's one of the reasons everyone has hesitated to label these murders as the work of a serial killer. We can't figure out what's happening."

I tried to imagine how this could fit in with what Cassandra had said. It was possible for a witch to kill without leaving a mark on the victim. But that would mean we were dealing with a witch killing his or her own instead of a non–magic user killing witches.

Cassandra hadn't mentioned witch-on-witch deaths being involved in this. Perhaps she'd just neglected to include that information until her big reveal tomorrow night at the full moon celebration. She had a strong flair for the dramatic.

"Can you put that aside for a few minutes so we can go into the bedroom?" I tried to make it sound suggestive, as though I'd missed him and needed time to cuddle.

He smiled, moved the pans from the stove and turned off the heat. "Sure thing."

The bedroom seemed like the best place to use magic to escape detection. We'd made our past visits to the bubble seem like romantic interludes in case anyone was watching and listening.

We went into the bedroom. Joe immediately took me in his arms and began kissing me. I put my arms around him and then muttered the enchantment for the bubble.

"Oh." He glanced at the opaque covering around us. "I thought we were *really* going to fool around."

"I need to talk to you about these deaths. All the victims are witches. I don't know if the killer is a witch yet. I might find out tomorrow night."

"How do you know that, Molly? Does someone keep up with that kind of thing?"

"Yes—the same people who make this enchanted bubble necessary. We got word this afternoon that witches are dying. That was right before you told me about your case."

He shook his head. "Any chance your witches' council would like to share information?"

"None whatsoever. I'm giving you a heads-up. Witches can kill leaving no mark behind. You'd never be able to use forensic science to discover the killer. If I find out there's a witch killing other witches, you need to think of a good reason not to be part of this investigation."

"You know that's not going to happen." He frowned, still holding me close. "I can't just drop a case because my wife is a witch and she's afraid for me to go toe-to-toe with another witch. We'll figure it out. Have some faith. No telling how many witch killings I've worked on and didn't even know it."

"Witches don't normally kill other witches. The council would handle it if they did." I stared into his beautiful eyes. "I know this is hard for you to understand, but if there *is* a witch killing these young men, anyone standing in the way could die too. And you wouldn't even have the protection these young witches had."

He kissed me again. "I love you, Molly. But I'm not going to quit my job because you've told me there's real magic in the world. I would appreciate any updates you get."

Joe had always been stubborn. I loved him anyway. I knew I might have to come up with a plan to protect him despite himself.

I could feel the enchantment wearing off and smell the peppers and onions waiting for dinner in the kitchen. That was all the time we had to discuss what was happening on his case. I hoped it was enough to make him more aware while he was looking for the killer.

"Supper smells really good." I smiled as we started out of the bedroom. "I didn't realize how hungry I was."

The doorbell rang. Joe suddenly got a guilty expression on his face.

"I'm sorry, Molly. With everything going on—I forgot to tell you that Suzanne needs a place to stay—until she's set up at the hotel that's been approved by her police department back home. I thought it wouldn't be a big deal if she stays in Mike's room for tonight."

CHAPTER 8

Keep my loved one from harm,
Take my fear from me,
Light his way through dark and storm.
One, two, three—So mote it be.

I didn't make a big deal out of sharing dinner, or the bottle of wine Suzanne had brought with her. We sat around talking for a while after the meal—mostly Suzanne and Joe talked about the old days and what they'd been doing since then.

I sat with them for an hour and then went into Mike's room to change the sheets on the bed for our guest.

Isabelle jumped squarely on the bed and faced me. She couldn't believe I was welcoming this woman into my home. My cat had decided that this was crossing certain personal lines that shouldn't be crossed. But then, Isabelle had the spirit of a woman. I was sure Joe would never understand.

I didn't try to explain. I smoothed the sheets as Isabelle offered a spell that would make Suzanne itchy all night. I thanked her for it, but didn't use the spell. I knew plenty of spells that could do the job if it came down to it.

After that was done, I went into the garden. The moon was bright and pink-hued as it rose over the horizon. A spring moon. Tomorrow would be the full moon celebration. I toyed with the idea of using the moon for a spell to make sure Joe and I would be strong together.

But in my heart, I knew we were all right. Joe thought of this as a kindness to a fellow officer who just happened to be his ex-wife. He would've also extended the courtesy if the Savannah police had sent a man he'd never met. It was part of who he was, and I loved him for it. I didn't want him to be any other way.

So far I hadn't received any kind of vibe from Suzanne that she thought of Joe as anything more than her temporary partner. If I received that feeling, I could always resort to strong measures to deter her. She wasn't a witch, and even though the council frowned on using magic against people who had none, it went on every day.

As I sat in the garden with the moonlight bathing me, my amulet began to glow. I looked inside it and saw movement in the active blue stone. It was as though the tides were trapped inside, restless and waiting.

It reminded me that there was something else we needed to concentrate on during the full moon celebration—our missing spell book.

We'd used magic to search for it after it had been stolen. I had tried not to make a big deal of it, since I knew Olivia blamed herself for its loss. Not that she could have done anything to prevent it from being stolen. She had already been dead when it happened.

I thought about her funeral six months ago. She'd cried more than anyone else gathered at her graveside. Only the witches present could hear and see her. The flowers had been beautiful, and the service sweet, with bagpipes playing, just as she'd requested.

It was the oddest funeral I'd ever been to.

Still, it was nice knowing she really wasn't in that deep pit in the ground. Maybe other witches didn't like it, but I didn't care. It was wonderful still having her here with us each day.

But it had left us uneasy where discussing our missing spell book was concerned.

We'd tried locator spells with Brian's help, but there had been no sign of it. We'd given up, as Dorothy's training had begun and other matters had taken our attention.

We couldn't forget that our spell book was important. It held all the spells that had been written by our families for several generations. We had incorporated the spells we'd used too. I didn't like the idea that it was out there being used by someone else. Despite Olivia's sad feelings about remembering that time, we had to talk about it again and get it back.

I stared into the cool orb above me. The moon could reveal important matters and secret things. Whoever had stolen our spell book had it hidden. The magic was powerful enough to keep us from finding it easily.

I needed to talk with Dorothy and Elsie before we went to the celebration tomorrow. If we all focused our energy on a spell, perhaps the location of our spell book would be revealed. We needed it if Elsie and I ever planned to retire. It would be handed to Dorothy as the leader of the new coven. I hoped she would be the oldest and strongest witch of the three we needed to find.

I breathed in the sweet smells of spring, feeling the new life surrounding me. I thought about Brian and his importance to us. He was still an unknown factor. Without commitment, no magic was strong. He had been elusive and cagey about wanting to be part of the group. I didn't mind him being around. He was very helpful. But there would come a time when he would either have to commit to us or we would have to ask him to leave.

It was easy to see that the idea of commitment was alien to him. His life was fractured with no real meaning. Even his training—despite the fact that he came from a powerful bloodline—had been neglected. I didn't understand what his parents were thinking, sending a young witch into the world with too much money and so little emphasis on the responsibility to his magic.

Not that it was my place to question. I only knew what sort of witch worked well for a coven, and Brian wasn't that witch, at least right now. I hoped he would be in the near future and that he would commit to us. That would leave us with only one more witch to find as a replacement for the three of us.

Joe was retiring from the police department soon. I hoped to be able to "retire" at the same time—and convince him that we should move to Boca. It wasn't something we'd talked about yet.

I hoped that wasn't asking for too much in the next few years.

"Molly?" Joe walked out into the garden. "Suzanne has gone to bed. Are you about ready? I have an early day tomorrow."

"Yes. I'm ready." We put our arms around each other as we walked to the house.

"Nice moon." He looked up. "Isn't this the harvest moon or something?"

"No. It's spring. This would be the planting moon."

"My grandmother used to keep up with all that stuff. She knew every phase of the moon and how it affected gardening. I looked at the *Old Farmer's Almanac* with her when I was a kid. It was fascinating."

"How the moon affects us is important," I agreed. "It subtly influences many aspects of our lives and shows us hidden places inside ourselves."

He opened the door into the house. "That's not part of the *other* stuff, right?"

"No. That's folklore and the *Old Farmer's Almanac*." I hadn't said anything to him about his mistake in calling me his little witch. We'd met in the enchanted bubble once a week or so to talk about things. I warned him each time. There was no point rubbing his nose in it. No one was perfect.

"I hope you're okay with me letting Suze stay here over-night."

Suze? "It's fine, though I wish you would've called or texted me to let me know so I could be prepared. She walked in as you told me."

He locked the outside door and ran a hand around the back of his neck. "I'm sorry, Molly. You're right. I guess I dreaded telling you."

Maybe he was figuring it out. "Why?"

"I don't know. The whole ex-wife thing, I guess." He smiled. "Thanks for being so understanding."

We got ready for bed and turned out the lights. It was an odd feeling knowing Suzanne was asleep in our son's room. Not that we hadn't had friends or relatives spend the night in that room before. It was knowing who she *had been* that made me uneasy.

Isabelle confessed to having the same feeling and vowed to spend the night watching Suzanne in case she made any threatening moves. She promised to sleep outside Suzanne's door in case she needed to alert me to her activities.

I stroked her soft fur and thanked her for looking after me.

It was a little after midnight the last time I looked at the clock. The full moon brings dreams with it, and I dreamed about being at Oak Island again.

It was clearly during a time when the English colony had still been there. I walked through the sandy lanes and rough houses. Children were crying, and women were carrying bundles of clothes to be washed in the Atlantic surf.

This was long before the lighthouse had been built to provide safe passage past the rough rocks and dangerous shoals. The people in the colony hadn't survived, much like other early settlements. These were difficult situations, where desperation and fear took their toll on the hardy souls who'd ventured here.

I heard shouting from a distance and then a woman was

dragged into the center of the village. Three men dressed in black tied her hands to a pole and began heaping wood around her feet.

She was very lovely. The sun shone on her auburn hair. Above her gagged mouth, crystal blue eyes beseeched her captors to release her. Other members of the village began spilling out of their houses.

"Do not look into her eyes," one of the men warned. "Her heart is black with evil magic. She will enslave you to do her bidding. Stay away, lest ye be taken."

The villagers crossed themselves, and only the men remained to see a fire lighted in the branches around the woman's feet.

"Thou shalt not suffer a witch to live," the man who'd spoken said. "Fire cleanses all. Our village will grow and prosper once the witch is dead."

It was played out in my dream as it had been in real life so many times during that era and before. As Phoebe had said at the shop, we were fortunate to live in a more enlightened time. Witches weren't routinely killed in the name of superstition. Yet the terrible history of our past remained.

In my dream, a sudden wind blew up from the sea. The waves rose up, crashing louder on the shore. It took only moments for the village to be swamped with seawater, houses and people washing away.

The fire no longer burned at the feet of the witch, but she hung, lifeless, from the pole.

Another man, naked, his black hair hanging to his shoulders, was mostly covered with seaweed. He approached the woman with measured strides, cut her down and cradled her in his arms. The sea continued to rise, gray and green, around them. He didn't move, ignoring the rising waters. In a few moments there was nothing but ocean where the village had been.

I woke with a start, feeling that woman's pain as though it were my own. It had been so *real*. My heart was racing and my hands shook. I pressed myself against Joe and listened to his steady heartbeat. He put his arm around me and murmured sleepy words of assurance.

Smiling, I looked into his face to kiss him.

It was the face of the Bone Man.

I screamed and jumped out of bed—or tried to. My foot got caught on the sheet and I fell face first on the carpet. Joe yelled and knocked over the bedside table lamp. It shattered against the wall. He grabbed his revolver from the bedside table where he always kept it.

"Molly?" Joe was breathing hard.

"Just a bad dream." I pulled myself up from the floor. I didn't want to explain my recent Bone Man sightings to Joe. "Sorry."

He turned on the overhead light, came around the side of the bed and examined my face. "Are you okay?"

"Better than the lamp. These are the ones your mother gave us."

Joe hugged me and put away his gun. "I never liked them anyway. Let's go back to sleep."

But there was no way I could get back to sleep that night. I was going to have to find out why the Bone Man kept coming to see me.

CHAPTER 9

Calling on the craft of old,
Show me secrets—now unfold.

"But you said yourself, there's so much to get ready for the celebration tonight," Elsie said. "Are you sure there's time to run out to Oak Island and back?"

"We might be a little late for the celebration. But I'm going out there today. It's one thing to see the Bone Man in the closet—it's another thing to wake up with him in my *bed*."

"*Eww.*" Dorothy may never have seen him, but it was bad enough to hear his description. "I think this is the best thing to do. Get it out of the way. Get it over with. How bad can it be?"

"Never ask that question." Elsie righted her large pink hat. "I can't believe I forgot my hat pins. Of course, Molly called me at five A.M. to tell me we had to do this today. I think it threw me off."

We were already halfway to the ferry that would take us to Oak Island. I wasn't spending another day wondering what the Bone Man wanted from me. I didn't want to know what the next step would be in him trying to get my attention.

He'd been there in my bed. Even though he'd vanished when I'd screamed, his image was engraved in my mind forever.

I had never screamed in my life—except for a few tricks Olivia had played on me when we were children. I had understood when Suzanne ran into the bedroom last night, partially dressed, her gun drawn. It had been enough to give a more anxious person a heart attack.

I'd explained again that I'd had a particularly bad dream. Suzanne had glanced at Joe and then gone back to bed. Isabelle had been a little snarky when I'd explained my dream to her. She was more upset about the witch being burned at the stake than about me having seen the Bone Man in my bed.

"What do you think the dream meant?" Dorothy asked. "Do you think that was one of your incarnations as a witch?"

"No. I was definitely an outsider. It was as though I were watching a movie."

"A particularly troubling movie," Elsie said. "Did I mention that I baked my poppy seed rolls for tonight? They're always a big hit."

"Was I supposed to bake?" Dorothy asked. "I'm not very good at baking."

"No. Of course not," I told her. "We each bring food for the feast. The more seasonal, the better. It's spring. Some nice wild greens would be appropriate or early fruit. I like to bring some flowers too. Sometimes we bring some dandelion wine that we've made in past years."

"Dandelion wine." Elsie licked her lips. "Wish we had some mead. I love mead."

Dorothy was writing everything we said in her notebook. It had a black cat on the cover, and she'd written *Witch's Notebook* on it. She took it everywhere with her. "So, lighter fare than there would be at the harvest moon festival?"

"Exactly." Elsie pointed out Fort Fisher as we passed the old historical monument. "We're almost there."

I talked to them about the spell book. It was a good time for it, since Olivia wasn't there. Each of us gave a deep sigh as we thought of it. It seemed almost impossible to get it back after it had been gone so long.

I gave them the same pep talk I'd given myself. "I know it's hard, but we need to find it."

"Hard?" Elsie made a *humph*ing sound in her throat. "It's impossible! We worked on it a long time. It's hidden somewhere, Molly. I don't think we can find it."

"What about asking the Bone Man?" Dorothy asked.

"Usually you can only make one deal at a time with him," I explained. "We'll see how it goes, since he summoned me. There might be some wiggle room."

"What about the seer?" Dorothy suggested. "Didn't you say she could find anything?"

"It's not about finding with her," Elsie began in her old teacher's voice. "It's more about if she can see what it is. It's difficult to explain."

"I was thinking we could use our magic tonight with the full moon to uncover the secret place the spell book is hidden," I intervened. "Moonlight is good for discovering secrets. We could make this our joint priority instead of making individual requests."

"That's a good idea," Elsie said. "I don't think it will work, but the only thing I was going to ask for was a boyfriend for Aleese. I think she'd be more hospitable with Larry if she had a boyfriend over for supper too. I could always do a love spell later."

"That's fine with me," Dorothy said. "I don't have a boyfriend, but I have a new house and more money than I know what to do with, not to mention a Mercedes. What more could a girl want?"

Her emotions gave her words away. They screamed out how disappointed she was that Brian had left after our tiff yesterday. Obviously she hadn't heard from him.

Elsie reached around to the backseat and patted Dorothy's hand. "Don't worry. He'll be back. Brian likes you. It might be why he's hung around so long—though I'd like to think it was partially our company too."

Dorothy smiled. "It's okay. I don't really expect someone like Brian to want to be with someone like me."

"Why ever not?" Elsie demanded.

"Well, he's got money, and he's interesting, not to mention that he's hot. Those type guys don't date girls like me."

"That's ridiculous." I pulled into the parking area for the ferry. "You're a beautiful young witch with strong gifts of magic. I'm sure Elsie is right and he likes you a lot, Dorothy. I think we should consider giving him a little nudge tonight. Everyone dresses up. We should find you something to wear that will knock him down."

"Because we have nothing else to do between now and then, so we can go shopping," Elsie muttered.

"I'm sure there will be plenty of time," I assured her. "Let's make sure Brian knows what he's going to lose if he doesn't shape up."

Dorothy's soft brown eyes were hopeful as we got out of the car. "You really believe that, Molly?"

I hugged her. "Yes I do. Now let's get this over with so we can get ready for tonight. I know Brian will be at the celebration. Even if he's not looking for us, let's make sure he notices *you*."

We paid for our tickets to the island. It was early in the season, so there weren't any other people waiting to take the ferry. Elsie and Dorothy had to visit the ladies' room before we left. I got on the ferry, watching the activity of the workers and the captain as the crew got ready to depart.

There was a sudden *thump* as though something had hit the ferry from beneath. It raised the boat high enough that it lost its moorings and began to drift into the channel of water between the mainland and the island.

I thought the ferry would simply go back, but it seemed it was only a few moments until it was time to leave. If they went back, it would wreck their schedule.

The captain shook my hand and apologized. "I'm sorry, ma'am. Occasionally this happens. There's a swell pushing the ferry toward the island. Rest assured your money will be refunded on the other two tickets you purchased—unless your friends want to take a later ferry."

I saw Dorothy and Elsie come out of the tiny bathroom. They watched the ferry leaving and began to hurry toward it. Elsie gave up right away and waved to me. Dorothy ran all the way to the dock before she stopped. I could only imagine their distress. My cell phone had no coverage either, so I couldn't explain.

I knew I could turn around and take the return ferry as soon as I reached the island, but that wouldn't solve my problem. Intuition—part and parcel of a witch's life—told me this was no accident.

I had felt the magic as it released the ferry from the dock. I couldn't identify it or where it had come from. Everyone had always said that the Bone Man had no magic of his own. Yet it was suspicious that he'd only contacted *me*, and now I was the only one going to the island.

The mainland receded farther and farther until I couldn't see it. I looked down into the water that splashed against the side of the ferry. I breathed in the sea air. This was where my magic was strongest. I didn't like the idea of seeing the Bone Man by myself, but I was glad I had this time on the water to renew and refresh my energies.

I held my mother's amulet in my hand. I could feel that the water inside was in tune with the sea. The amulet was warm to the touch despite the cool nature of a water witch's magic.

Despite the strange start to my journey, I gathered my

wits before confronting the Bone Man. His appearance alone was enough to make many witches faint at his feet. Dealing with him was difficult too. He was sharp and ready to take advantage—as he had with Olivia's staff. We'd come to trade other items that day for the help we'd needed, but he'd soon taken the one thing he really wanted. He'd given us information in return, but I hadn't felt as though it was worth the price we'd paid.

We got Olivia and her staff back again, but it wasn't because of anything we'd done. The Bone Man had released her. We couldn't have stopped him from keeping her out here forever.

This time, I had to be better than that. Sharper. Smarter.

He wanted something from me. I remembered his keen interest in the amulet when we'd been here last time. He'd promised to show me how to use it if I came back again. I wouldn't make that trade. I would learn to use it myself.

I wished I'd put on the amulet when my mother had first given it to me. But it was gaudy, and at the time I'd considered it ugly, something only my mother would wear. I wasn't impressed by her stories of how many other witches in our family line had worn it, or that it had been a gift from a sea god whose name no one could remember.

My feelings were very different now. When I came upon it in my jewelry box last year, I was surprised to feel the power emanating from it. I put it on and had worn it ever since—despite Cassandra's demand that I give it to the council for safekeeping.

Or perhaps because *of her request.*

I tried to frame in my mind what I was going to say to the Bone Man when I saw him. I could ask him why he'd contacted me. Or I could just wait for him to tell me. Words might get in the way. Mostly I wanted to know why he'd been in my bed, and then I wanted to hurry home for the moon celebration.

If he was in some kind of trouble, as Olivia seemed to think he might be, I'd ask what it was about and what was in it for me if I helped him. It sounded coldblooded, but it was best not to get personal with him. He could easily turn anything I said against me.

I hardly noticed as the ferry bumped into the dock at Oak Island. The captain shook my hand and apologized again for what had happened. I told him not to worry. My friends could accompany me next time.

"That old swell cut off a lot of time for us." He glanced at his watch. "But we'll keep the same schedule for the return trip. Enjoy your visit."

I left the ferry and walked past the old lighthouse. I didn't see anyone visiting that day. It looked forlorn and lonely in this time of electronic devices that guided ships at sea. And yet the beacon from its lamp still shone out over the water every night beginning at sunset and ending at dawn. It was part of a network of lighthouses that stretched along the North Carolina coast to keep ships from foundering in the Graveyard of the Atlantic.

But I wasn't there for a mental history of the lighthouse, I reminded myself. I turned and started the short walk to the old cemetery that was hidden in the trees. Not many came this way, and yet the sandy path was always clear of debris. The Bone Man lived in the cemetery, which had sheltered the dead from the first settlement.

I wondered if the witch that had been in my dream was buried there. Or was she real at all?

My purpose was clear, and I had been calm about following it right up until I began to see the small headstones that marked the cemetery. It suddenly hit me that I was going to visit the Bone Man *alone*. My heart started racing and the logical part of my brain screamed at me to leave while I could. My whole body trembled in terror at what I was about to do.

"This is crazy," I muttered to myself in the silence. "I should go back and get Elsie and Dorothy. I can't do this alone."

But before I could turn from the path into the cemetery, there he was. The Bone Man rose up from behind a tombstone with his red mouth and terrible smile.

"Welcome back, Molly."

CHAPTER 10

Spirits of the moon, fly close,
Mark this spot where we do host.
Water clear,
Soil damp,
Time to dance,
Light the lamp.

The Bone Man knew my name.

I had never heard him call anyone by his or her name before. It was terrifying to think that he knew who I was, where I lived and where Smuggler's Arcane was located. I was frozen to the spot as I considered what that meant. My mind raced as I gazed at him.

I always thought I was imagining his height and countenance when I hadn't seen him for a while. But each time I was wrong.

He was impossibly tall and thin. There were normal humans who were seven feet tall, but they weighed enough that their bones weren't so prominent. He was a horror poster for starvation. The joints in his arms, hands and legs stuck out with only a thin layer of skin covering them. His head was barely more than a skull under a black top hat. There were black eyes in the skull sockets. The wind from the sea shook the dried bones that hung around his throat. He wore a tattered black suit covered in dirt as though he'd dug it from a grave. His hands and feet were large and prominent, with no shoes or gloves to cover them.

He had a visage no living person should have to see—especially alone.

The island wind whipped around me as he waited for me to reply to his greeting. It took a moment or two for me to recover enough to speak. All my preparation on the ferry was blown away by the sight of him.

"Hello." My voice cracked and squeaked.

"It's very nice to see you again. I *thought* it would happen sooner after I saw you wearing the amulet, but you are a very stubborn lady, aren't you?"

He laughed and I shivered.

"I'm not really that stubborn. Why would I come to see you?"

"Because you want to make a trade for knowledge about the amulet." He rubbed his hands together in anticipation. "What have you got for me?"

This was not a question I had anticipated. I hadn't planned on trading anything for knowledge of the amulet. I wasn't desperate enough to explore its abilities by coming out here to see him.

What should I say that won't make him angry? "I'm just letting it come to me naturally. Thanks anyway. I don't want to trade for that knowledge."

He moved closer. I caught my breath as he towered over me, skeletal face staring down, red-stained mouth open.

"It won't just *come*, Molly. You must be taught to use it. The magic in the amulet is old magic—not even magic at all the way you understand it. I can show you what to do."

This was something new. The Bone Man seemed determined to convince me into learning about the amulet from him. Usually we were in the opposite position of seeking something from him.

What does he want from me? I gulped as my brain raced to decide what to do. It must have shown in my face.

He laughed again. "You are very transparent, Molly. You understand why you're here, don't you? The Bone Man wants you to do him a favor."

A favor? That was nearly enough to send me running back the other way. I knew many witches who'd reacted to him in that way the first time they'd seen him. If Olivia, Elsie and I hadn't been so determined to get what we needed when we'd first come here, we would have done the same.

"You want *me* to do *you* a favor?" I had to make sure I understood the situation so as to decrease the chance of trickery.

"Yes."

"And in exchange, you'll show me how to use the amulet?"

"Yes." His smile stretched hideously across his face. "You catch on quickly."

"Suppose I don't want to trade knowledge of the amulet for the favor you're asking of me?"

He actually pondered that question for a moment, one bony hand to his chin. "Then I suppose you might have something else you would like me to do in exchange. You have something you need that I can supply?"

I considered his words again. I couldn't believe I was negotiating with him. As I saw it, I was in the position of power on this. Maybe I was wrong—I hadn't heard the favor he was asking yet.

"I see you twisting the marriage ring on your finger. Could you be having marriage problems? Perhaps we have a deal."

"What? I didn't ask for anything. We don't have a deal." I knew he'd try to trick me. I couldn't let that happen.

He closed his eyes. "You want protection for your husband and son from the Council of Witches, no?" He laughed again, almost upsetting the top hat on his head. "I heard the tiny whisper of knowledge from your husband after he'd learned that you are a witch. We both know what the council is capable of."

"Yes," I whispered the fear that had gathered in my heart since that night, hating that he knew it too.

"I can do this for you, Molly—if you will grant my request."

Could he really keep the council from hearing Joe's possible slips in the future? I couldn't do it. I didn't know anyone who could. How could he protect Joe?

"You have no magic." I said it as flatly as I'd thought it.

"You're right. At least I don't have magic that you or your *kind* understand. But I can protect your family from the council. They will never learn your secret."

"I don't believe you." What I really couldn't believe was that I'd said those words out loud. "No one can do what you're promising. It's one of your tricks."

His face—what there was of it—twisted. I thought for an instant that he might kill me. Or curse me. Who knew what? I was terrified. I don't know what kept me from running away.

Then he laughed again. "You want me to prove myself to you, eh? I don't think anyone has asked that of me in a very long time. You are a brave woman, Molly Addison."

I started to correct him. Addison was my maiden name. I had been a Renard for longer than I'd been an Addison. I decided not to press my luck. I'd come this far on sheer audacity. I would wait to see what his next move was.

I could see the choppy gray ocean through the trees. He stared at it for a moment and raised his hand.

Immediately, the waves that beat against the rocky shore began to grow. I could hear shouting from the area of the lighthouse. The voices were raised in alarm as the Atlantic rose higher, lapping at the base of the old structure.

The Bone Man hadn't moved. His hand was still outstretched, his black eyes fixed on the water. I could see the ocean coming closer. Water was already filling the sand between the old headstones. It kept rising, as it had in my dream about the witch in the old colony. The soles of my shoes were getting wet.

"You're a *water* witch?" I dared to ask, though no water witch I'd ever known was powerful enough to raise the sea.

The Bone Man lowered his arm and looked back at me. "Understand it as you will. Never doubt that I can do what I say."

He'd convinced me. I was sure the sea had risen this far on other occasions, during hurricanes or floods, but not on demand and not on a clear, sunny day.

"It was you, wasn't it?" I dared to ask. "You caused the ferry to leave without Dorothy and Elsie. You caused the swell that brought the ferry here faster."

He bowed. "You recognize my hand in this."

I was completely blown away by the information. He had magic I couldn't explain or hope to duplicate. I was amazed and, for some odd reason, less afraid. Maybe it was our kinship to the water or maybe I finally understood something about him. I wasn't sure. But when I searched his black eyes again, I was more at ease.

"Why did you visit me at home and at the shop?"

"I thought I had made that clear. I need a boon from you."

"But why *me*? There are other more powerful water witches in this area. Why not call one of them?"

"You do yourself a disservice. And the choice was mine to make."

"It's the amulet, isn't it?" I smiled at his discomfort. "You chose me because you know I have the amulet. What is it about it that you find so interesting? Did you know that the Council of Witches wanted me to surrender it to them?"

His face contorted again. "Never give the amulet to them or anyone else. It only belongs to you now that you are the last of your line."

"I won't." I touched the amulet and didn't ask how he knew I was the last witch in my family.

"And now that you are finished with trying to understand me, do we have a deal? Are you willing to trade the safety of your husband and son for my request?"

What else could I say? "Yes." I took a deep breath, hoping the favor he wanted wasn't something beyond my limited abilities. "What do you want me to do?"

"I want you to find my wife."

The words were plain and simple, yet I had a difficult time understanding what he was asking. "You mean you want me to find someone willing to marry you?"

"No. I have loved the same woman for hundreds of years. I need you to find her and bring her to me."

"Really? With all the power you have, you can't find her yourself?"

"Do you agree to this trade or not?" His black eyes looked impatiently through me.

"Sure." I thought quickly. "Where is she? How will I know her?"

"You will know with this." His hand grasped mine and there was a burning sensation in my palm. "Find her, Molly. Bring her to me."

I found a rune etched on my hand. It didn't hurt anymore, but it was clearly marked, red and purple, in the skin.

I started to ask at least another dozen questions, but he slowly sank behind one of the larger tombstones. That was it. The deal was struck. I'd made an impossible trade and now had to find a way to keep my part of the bargain so he would keep his.

I wished I had some idea how to accomplish that.

CHAPTER 11

Sweet moon of spring,
Turn your face to me,
Favor all I do,
Grant me love and bounty.

I could barely wait to get back to the mainland and tell Dorothy and Elsie what had happened. The swell that had brought me to Oak Island was absent on the return journey, so the trip seemed to take forever, but in reality it was the normal amount of time.

My mind was buzzing. How would I know if the Bone Man would keep his word about protecting Joe and Mike? It wasn't like we could try it out and see if it worked. The risk was too great.

Maybe he knew that, I thought gazing back at the island. Maybe he was asking for a favor without really giving me anything in return. How would I know? I felt gullible and silly. Had he tricked me again?

The ferry bumped against the protective barrier on the dock. Dorothy and Elsie got out of the car, and I ran to them, hugging each of them. "You aren't going to believe what happened."

I explained everything on the way back to Wilmington. My friends were as astonished as I had been.

"What a story to share at the celebration tonight," Elsie said. "Molly Renard bests the Bone Man."

"But did I?" I held up my hand so they could see the rune drawn there. "This is what he gave me to find his wife with. Have you ever seen anything like it?"

Elsie examined it close up. "Nope. I've seen a lot of runes but never this one—at least not that I can remember. You should show it to Olivia. She's always been hot for the runes."

"Molly, I thought the Bone Man didn't have magic." Dorothy sat forward between the seats to look at my hand. "How did he do all this without magic? And what is he going to do in return for you finding his wife?"

It was difficult to answer, since I hadn't told them that Joe knew I was a witch. I thought it was asking for more trouble if they knew too. I knew Elsie would certainly frown on it. She'd never told her husband or Aleese. We both knew how serious the punishment from the council would be.

"I think he has magic," I told them. "Water magic. We can't sense it from him because he's not a witch. I don't know what he is, but it's not something we've encountered."

"And I missed it." Dorothy shook her head. "It was probably the best Bone Man visit *ever*."

"What about the other part, Molly?" Elsie picked up on Dorothy's question. "What's he trading for this?"

I fingered my amulet. "He's going to help me with the amulet." It was a small lie, but one that wouldn't involve them in case the Bone Man didn't hold up his part of the deal. I couldn't tell them about Joe until I was sure he was protected.

We talked about what the Bone Man's wife might look like. Was she a witch? Was that why he thought I could find her? Would she go willingly with me to see him? If she'd been alive as long as he implied, there was every chance she was more powerful than the three of us combined. We probably couldn't force her to go.

"Maybe that's what the rune does," Elsie conjectured.

"Maybe it's an entrapment spell. You show it to her and she has to go with you."

"What if she's not a witch and doesn't live in Wilmington?" Dorothy asked. "You said the Bone Man is tricky."

"I don't think he would've bothered asking me do this if he didn't think I could find her. I think she's probably a witch—a water witch—and that's why he asked me to trade him for this favor."

"That would make sense," Elsie said. "Now let's talk about what's *really* important—what are you wearing to the celebration tonight?"

We decided to check out Elsie's attic, which was like a vintage clothing store. I didn't think any woman in her family had ever thrown anything away. There were hundreds of old dresses in every style for the past hundred years, all colors and sizes. There were hats of every kind imaginable with bags, gloves and shoes to match.

Every so often we raided her stash for different clothes to wear to various celebrations. It was fun romping through a history of clothes in the attic with dust, lit by sunbeams, floating in the air.

"Look at this!" Dorothy held up a beautiful green satin dress that was ankle-length and formfitting. It had a large, stand-up collar that was studded with sequins and rhinestone stars. "Do you think it would fit me?"

"Try it on," Elsie encouraged. "If it doesn't, we'll fix it."

"Would we have time to get it altered? Is there a witch's tailor shop?"

Elsie and I laughed.

"Just try it on," I said. "Let's see."

I was looking at a black velvet gown that was shot through with bright blue threads. "I feel guilty doing this without Olivia."

Elsie put down the red blouse she was holding. "I do too. But I think she might feel worse being here and not being able to try things on, don't you?"

"I do. I just hate ignoring her because she's a ghost."

Barnabas meowed loudly.

"Pipe down," Elsie told him. "He thinks ghosts shouldn't hang around—like the council. Or maybe he's jealous that we don't have one here. Who knows?"

Barnabas hissed and ran down the attic stairs. His spirit, encased in an orange-tabby body, was that of a preacher from the 1700s who had been mistakenly hanged for witch-craft. Like Isabelle, he could be a little sullen. Old souls were sometimes that way.

Dorothy came out of the closet looking radiant. Green was certainly her color. The dress was a little large for her, but combining our magic, Elsie and I were able to tailor it until it fit like a glove.

"What do you think?" She twirled around like a child. "How do I look?"

"You look amazing," I said. "I'll bet there are shoes and a bag that go with that."

We searched around until we found them and then took everything downstairs.

Elsie was going to wear the beautiful embroidered red blouse she'd pulled out of one of her aunt Cecilia's boxes with a matching flounced red skirt. "Aunt Cecilia was a fire witch too. I remember her wearing this outfit. Now there was a witch who knew how to party."

"I have some shoes that will match this gown perfectly." I held the black gown up against me. "Your attic is like a treasure trove. It seems that, no matter how often we go up there, we always find something new."

"That's what comes of having a family of hoarders." She laughed. "You two better go home and finish getting ready. Are you picking me up, Molly?"

"Let me drive tonight," Dorothy volunteered.

Elsie and I exchanged frowns. Neither one of us wanted to ride in her tiny brown Beetle.

Dorothy laughed. "In the Mercedes, ladies. I know that would please Mom. She's wanted me to drive it for months. What are we going to do about her? Can we sneak her into the celebration with no one noticing?"

"I'm afraid that's not possible," I told her. "You can see how the other witches feel about ghosts. I don't know what to do."

"There's no disguise for a ghost that I've ever heard of," Elsie said. "I wish it could be different. Olivia always enjoyed a good party."

"What about ghosts going into other people's bodies?" Dorothy stared at us. "I mean, is that a real thing or just something in movies?"

"I'm not really sure." I peered at Elsie. "Do you know anything about that?"

Elsie's red brows knit together. "I remember an old spell to put a ghost into a cat. I don't know where I remember it from, or how to do it. We could ask around."

"What a great idea," Dorothy said. "How do you think Harper would feel about it? He'd be the natural choice."

"I don't know. I guess we'd have to talk to him first and then talk to Olivia. I'm not sure how she'd feel about being in a cat's body, even for a short time." I grabbed my dress. "We can't do it tonight, unfortunately. It would take some advance planning. It would help if we could find the spell book. I'm sure that's where Elsie saw the spell. Let's remember to keep this in the forefront of our minds at the celebration. We need the spell book."

"So is that a yes about me driving tonight?" Dorothy asked. "If so, I'll pick you both up."

Elsie and I were fine with that. I dropped Dorothy off at her house and then went home. I could hear laughing and talking coming from inside as I opened the door. Joe and Suzanne were eating lunch. I closed the door hard behind me—just so they'd hear it.

"Hey, Molly." Joe got to his feet. "I've got plenty of Chinese chicken for you too. Let me get a plate."

"No, thanks. I'm on my way out." I stared at them—Joe normally didn't come home for lunch. I tried not to feel weird about it. They were working together. Partners did that kind of thing.

Isabelle followed me into the bedroom to help put the dress away. She told me all about Joe and Suzanne, how long they'd been there and what they'd talked about. It was as innocent and work-related as I'd thought.

I wished I could share what had happened with the Bone Man. But I was still uncertain about the pact I'd made and unwilling to risk it.

"I have to get ready for the celebration tonight," I told Isabelle. "You don't have to worry about Joe and Suzanne. I'm not worried."

She called me a fool and sauntered back into the kitchen to continue her eavesdropping.

I went into the kitchen to see what I needed for food that night. Joe and Suzanne were gathering their plates and silverware together. "You don't have to leave on my account."

Joe kissed my cheek quickly. "We just got word on the Southport, Molly. The ME has confirmed that it's the work of the same killer."

CHAPTER 12

Protect my love,
Keep him from harm,
Use this charm.
North. South. East. West.

There was no time for further conversation. Joe and Suzanne left. I didn't have time to brood over how I could protect Joe if he came across the killer witch. I closed my eyes and whispered a protection blessing for him, got the list of supplies I needed and headed for the store.

I won't say that everyone attending the celebration tried to outdo everyone else, but we were all excited about the event. I knew there would be witches who'd spent huge amounts of money on new, flashy clothes and expensive food.

It wasn't in keeping with the spirit of the moon celebration— giving thanks for the passing of the winter and showing gratitude for the coming season of growth. But witches were only human after all, and sometimes we showed it more than others.

By seven P.M., my food was ready to go, packed away in containers that would be easy to carry. I'd made a fresh strawberry salad with wild greens and a tangy vinaigrette. I'd found some baby asparagus and tiny red potatoes that I'd made into a casserole. For a sweet, I stuck by the old favorite that had served me well through the years—chocolate sin cake.

Dorothy was beautiful in her green dress when she came for me. She got out of the Mercedes and spun around again. Her makeup was perfect, as was the antique emerald necklace and earrings she wore. I knew they had belonged to Olivia.

"Doesn't she look scrumptious?" Olivia seeped out of the partially opened car window. "The emeralds are fantastic on her, yes? What a good idea to spend time in Elsie's attic. I wish my ancestors had saved something besides expensive jewelry and priceless antiques."

"You look lovely." I smiled at Dorothy before I addressed Olivia. "Are you going to the celebration?"

"Of course. I've never missed one."

"You might get some flak from the witches," I pointed out, though it broke my heart to say it. It was better for me to hurt her feelings than for someone at the event to.

"I don't care. If someone doesn't like it, they can just kiss my behind. I want to see my daughter shine at her first full moon celebration."

"I don't blame you. I just wanted to make sure you'd thought it through."

"I'm tougher than that, Molly." She wrinkled her nose. "I can handle it."

I didn't think she could, but the decision was hers. She could always leave the celebration and stay in the car until we were ready to go.

"What was Dorothy talking about—putting me into Harper's body?"

"Elsie mentioned a spell she recalled. I don't know yet. How do you feel about it? It would only be temporary."

"I know how those spells work. Witches have always been able to mingle with animals when they needed a disguise. I'm not sure how Harper would feel about it. He's a little prudish when it comes to magic. He's not like Isabelle or Barnabas, who understand how it works. He only has the spirit of a British sailor in him."

"I know." I shrugged as we got into the silver Mercedes—Olivia calling shotgun. "It's something to think about for the future. One hundred years as a ghost is a long time."

"I think he might go along with the idea if I ask him the right way."

"It's worth a try," Dorothy said. "Show her the rune, Molly."

I turned to reach my hand between the seats so Olivia could look at the rune. I didn't need to, because Olivia simply stuck her head *through* the car seat and stared at it.

"That's something." She traced the mark with her finger. "Dorothy told me what happened with the Bone Man. You must've been scared out of your mind."

"I was at first," I admitted. "But later I felt comfortable with him. Did you feel that way too?"

She giggled. "I don't know if I'd say *comfortable*, but I wasn't scared of him anymore. You know, it's kind of funny—I remember being there with him and all the things we did—but it's really hazy. More like a dream than something that really happened."

"Maybe that's because you're dead," I suggested.

Olivia's eyes widened. "I'd expect something like that from Elsie, but not from you, Molly. Dead people have feelings too. I remember other things that have happened since I died that don't have that gauzy quality to them. I think the Bone Man may have cast some sort of spell on me. Now that we know he has magic, it's possible."

I didn't want to get any further into that discussion, which might include Olivia relating everything she'd done with the Bone Man. Instead, I went back to the rune on my palm. "Any ideas what this could be?"

"I've never seen anything like it." She continued to study

it. "I take that back. Once when I was in Ireland to buy crystal, I saw an Irish rune that looked similar to this one. It's hard to say now if it was the same thing. I can look it up for you."

I glanced at Dorothy, who was watching us in the rearview mirror as she drove to Elsie's house. I didn't want to hurt Olivia's feelings again by suggesting she couldn't look things up anymore.

"She's still a whiz with the books," Dorothy confirmed. "She can't do anything on a computer."

"She couldn't do anything with a computer when she was alive," I said.

"Hello? Still here," Olivia said. "I was talking about looking in some of my older rune books. They wouldn't have something like that on the Internet anyway. I'd take my old books over that stuff anytime."

I smiled at her. "Thank you for offering to look it up. Elsie said you know runes better than anyone, and I agree."

"Well, thank you for that, Molly." Olivia went back to the front seat. "People think ghosts aren't good for anything. There's still a lot we can do. They don't let us stay here for a hundred years for nothing."

We pulled into Elsie's driveway. She was already waiting, a bunch of flowers in one hand and a box of food at her feet. Dorothy jumped out to help her.

"Isn't it wonderful having so much energy?" Olivia asked as Dorothy and Elsie got everything into the trunk. "I just love watching her."

"It's nice having her around. I'm glad you found her again."

"So am I. I wish I hadn't been so afraid after I found out I was pregnant with Drago's baby. You can't imagine how scared I was that he would take her and make her like him. Or maybe you can after your private meeting with the Bone Man."

"I'm sure it was nothing like fearing for your child's life."

Olivia looked through the seat at me again. "There's something you're not telling us about this, isn't there? I can *feel* it."

I didn't deny it. "Leave it alone for now. Maybe I can explain later."

Dorothy helped Elsie into the car, and we were off again.

All the conversation was excited talk about the celebration. I looked out at the full moon, which sailed in the dark sky above us like a schooner in calm seas. I could feel its power reflected in the amulet. It helped that we were so near the Cape Fear River. The celebration was taking place at a park that was beside the water.

Was I a fool not to take advantage of the Bone Man's offer to show me how to use the amulet?

I might never know for sure. But believing that he could keep Joe and Mike safe would be a load off my mind. Of course, I would have to believe it first—and that would mean finding a way to prove it without taking a chance with Joe's memory. It was something I would have to think carefully about.

We arrived at the crowded park—who knew there would be so many witches coming for the celebration? Normally we only saw a few dozen. It looked like Portia had done a good job letting everyone know about the event. The council would be pleased.

Dorothy found a place to park, and we lugged everything we'd brought with us to the first available picnic table. Before doing anything else, we lit some candles and joined hands to bless the table and the event. Elsie had brought a beautiful rose-colored linen tablecloth that enhanced the table.

We put out our food to share with everyone. Each of us carried our magic tool in one form or another. I had added my tiny silver cauldron around my neck, along with the amulet, as my mark of being a water witch.

Elsie carried her sword in a gorgeous satin sheath with a shoulder strap. Dorothy had surprised us all and had a setting made for her emerald cull so she could wear it around her neck.

"I was afraid I'd lose it if I kept dragging it around in my pocket." She blushed at our compliments on the unusual and beautiful setting she'd had created for it.

"That's my daughter." Olivia smiled. "She's a chip of the old block. I've always had exquisite taste. But you girls know that."

Elsie smiled but kept her comment to herself.

"Good evening, ladies." Brian made a gallant bow to us. He was extremely handsome in black velvet pants and black satin shirt. His brown hair was carefully combed away from his face. A bright blue scarf around his neck mirrored the color of his eyes.

I glanced at Dorothy. She was mesmerized.

"Good evening, sir." Elsie tried to do an elaborate curtsy and almost fell on the damp ground.

Brian rushed to her rescue and tucked her hand into the crook of his arm. "Let's take a walk and see who's here."

I poked Dorothy. She hadn't said a word.

Brian smiled at Dorothy and offered his opposite arm. She smiled back. The deal was sealed.

I stayed behind with Olivia, who'd agreed to remain there with me after significant glances in their direction. "Aren't they cute together?"

"I suppose so." She sighed. "I'm having a hard time letting go of her, Molly. It's too soon. We're just getting to know each other."

"Even if she dates Brian—even if she marries him—she's going to stay in your life. She has a lot to learn from you."

"You really think so?"

"Yes. This is her home. She loves the house and her new life with you. She's going to be a great witch one day. And her children will love you too."

Olivia had no tears to cry anymore, but something streamed down her face like tears. "But what about you and Elsie? If I stay here with Dorothy and the two of you move to Boca, I'll never see you."

"We'll see each other. I don't expect Mike to move to Boca. I think that means frequent trips up here to see him and his family, and you and your family."

"That makes me feel so much better, Molly. Thank you."
Olivia put her arms out and tried to hug me. It was a strange
feeling since there was *something* there, but it wasn't a warm
body.

Two young witches who I didn't recognize strolled up.
They saw Olivia, of course, and made a few rude comments
about ghosts at the full moon festival.

"Ignore them," I told Olivia. "We don't care what they
think."

As soon as the words came out of my mouth, the rune in
my palm began itching and burning. I looked at the two
witches. Was one of them the Bone Man's wife? How would I
know for sure?

I coaxed Olivia into leaving the picnic table so I could follow the witches. I had to get a better idea of how this worked.
Would the rune change if I confronted the Bone Man's wife?

When the two young witches stopped to chat with another group, I pretended they'd dropped something on the
ground and tried to get them to face me.

"It's the freak with the ghost," one of them said.

"What do you want?" the other asked, as they walked
away. "I'm not talking to you with that *thing* hanging
around. We're not supposed to have the undead here."

"Why you . . ." Olivia was angry. She rushed through
both witches, leaving a cold, clammy sensation behind. I'd
experienced it before. It was distinctly unpleasant.

Both witches crossed their arms on their chests, shiver-
ing. They ran into the darkness, scared.

"Not a good idea," I muttered, looking around to see if
anyone else had noticed.

"I'm sorry. I couldn't help it. I'm tired of being treated
like a third-class citizen. I have every right to be here too."

The burning and itching didn't go away with the witches.
My hand was already red and raw from it. I looked around the
crowded riverside park. There were no other witches close to

us. I couldn't confront every witch who was there. I definitely needed something more specific.

There was a series of sparks and shooting flames in the middle of the new green of the park. The fireworks were followed by changing purple, red and green smoke.

Everyone applauded. I saw Brian, Elsie and Dorothy near the front of the display. I wanted to join them, but I didn't think it was a good idea to have Olivia up there. We stayed at the back of the crowd that had gathered.

Portia de Winter arose from the colored smoke and extended her arms to every witch there. "Merry Meet, fellow witches. Welcome to the moon celebration."

CHAPTER 13

Merry Meet we join together,
Wind and rain, friends forever.

Portia talked about how wonderful it was to see such a large crowd gathered in the park. She talked about the power of the full moon and hoped we all had important ideas in mind for our spells.

She was only the center of attention for a few moments before there was another large blast of sparks and flames. Cassandra was there, raised above us by a flaming platform.

She was dressed in black silk that caught the moonlight, which shimmered in the material. Her hair danced around her, caressed by unseen wind currents.

Even if you didn't like her—as many there didn't—you had to admit it was an incredible entrance.

"Hear me, sisters! I bring you warning of a terrible threat that has come to the Wilmington area. Someone is killing our young men, leaving behind little of their bodies. Protect yourselves. Use stronger spells. So far the deaths have only been male witches, but this could change. The Grand Council of Witches is here for you. We are investigating these deaths and hope to have the culprit taken shortly."

There was a moment of stark silence that followed her announcement. It immediately ended with dozens of questions about the threat against us. All the witches were frightened and unsure if their protection spells were strong enough to handle the danger.

"Farewell. Blessed Be!" Cassandra left without answering a single query. She disappeared in the same flame that had brought her.

"What a waste of a perfectly good dress," Olivia said. "I'm sure that wasn't off the rack either."

After all the excitement was over, Olivia and I headed back to our picnic table. Brian, Dorothy and Elsie joined us soon after.

"Can you believe that about witches being killed?" Elsie asked.

"Cassandra told us about it at the shop, remember?" I replied.

"That's right. I knew I'd heard it somewhere."

Brian brought his food—store-bought chicken and potato salad—to our table and took a seat beside Dorothy. "I just want to apologize to all of you for losing it while we were blessing the houses. My parents make me crazy. And I didn't mean to do anything to your daughter, Elsie."

She smiled and patted his hand. "I understand. Family can be excruciating. Have some of this macaroni salad I made. I even baked fresh bread and cookies."

"Cookies!" Dorothy squealed. "I love eating dessert first, like Bill Clinton."

We all laughed at that as we passed around the food. Other witches stopped at our table to share blessings and food with us. It was a beautiful night on the river.

I would have enjoyed it more without the rune on my palm. The constant itching and burning was annoying. It made me long for some aloe to ease it, even though that would be defeating the purpose.

"I think the deaths of these witches are part of the same case Joe is working on," I said. "When he and Suzanne were at the house for lunch today, they got confirmation of a death in Southport being linked to the other killings."

Elsie blinked as she bit into a cucumber. "Joe and his ex-wife were having lunch at your house today?"

"They were waiting to hear about the murder." I picked up one of Elsie's delicious chocolate fudge cookies.

"Were they already there when you got home?" Dorothy nibbled the edge off a cherry tart. "Awkward."

"It wasn't awkward at all," I told her, even though it had been. "They're partners. Partners eat lunch together."

"But usually partners aren't people who were formerly married," Olivia added. "Don't tell me that doesn't bother you, Molly."

"You're looking at this the wrong way," I said.

"I agree with Molly," Brian added. "Just because Joe is at her house with his ex-wife doesn't mean something ugly is going on. They're working together. Men can work with a woman without thinking of her as a sexual object."

Elsie and Olivia burst out laughing.

"Not in *my* experience," Olivia said.

"Certainly not in my late husband's experience," Elsie said.

"Forget I brought it up," I finally said. "We should be focusing our moon energy on finding our spell book anyway."

"I have a new locator spell if you want to try it," Brian offered.

We agreed, and held hands around the table, concentrating on our spell book. Olivia hovered near us to feel like she was part of the coven. We each held a silver coin to draw moon energy to our cause.

After a few minutes, we sat back and released our hands.

"I hope one of us will have a dream later that shows where the spell book is hidden," Brian said. "That's the way this works. If you have a place where you can sleep in the moonlight, it will be even stronger."

"Good evening, ladies. Brian."

I looked up, surprised to see Abdon Fuller standing beside us. He was Brian's grandfather and one of the most powerful witches on the council.

"Granddad." Brian tried to get to his feet but was hampered by the picnic table. "I didn't expect to see you here tonight."

"Isn't *that* the truth?" Elsie muttered before swallowing a gulp of sweet tea.

It was a surprise for us too. I'd seen him at various large witch functions a few times since I was a child, but I had never talked to him. I'd never seen him so close.

He didn't resemble Brian at all. He had blunt features, a crooked nose and a twisted mouth. He had a large scar on one cheek that gave him a pirate look. I wondered why such a powerful witch would keep a scar like that when he could easily remove it.

"Mr. Fuller." Dorothy scooted off the bench to allow Brian to get up. She stuck out her trembling hand to Abdon.

He looked the other way. "Brian, if I may have a word alone with you."

"I know what you have to say, Granddad. Mom and Dad already said it."

Abdon lifted one corner of his lip in an attempt to smile. It only made him appear to snarl. "I'm sure you'd rather not hear what I have to say in front of your new *friends*."

The way he said "friends" sounded like the way someone else would say "trash." Elsie tried to get to her feet. I was glad the picnic table still held her hostage. Abdon Fuller would laugh at a witch with her limited abilities.

Brian glanced at us. "All right. But I'll be back." He bent

his head and kissed Dorothy full on the mouth. "Don't go anywhere."

The look of disgust on Abdon's face was apparent even in the dim light. He turned his back and began to walk away. Brian caught up with him, and the two disappeared into the darkness.

"I've never met anyone ruder than that man," Olivia said.

"I thought about turning his head into a watermelon," Elsie said. "I couldn't get up from this stupid bench. He was lucky tonight."

I smiled but hid it behind my hand. Elsie was lucky she couldn't confront him. It could have meant serious consequences for her—and for the rest of us, as we wouldn't have stood still and watched her be abused.

"Are you sure you want to get involved with this messed-up family?" Olivia asked Dorothy.

"A person doesn't get to choose her family," Dorothy replied. "I was just lucky that I could be with the three of you. Brian wasn't so lucky."

Brian came back a few minutes later. He was oddly quiet the rest of the time we were there. We didn't leave the park until after midnight. There was very little food to pack up by then. I was happy not to take anything home.

"It was a good celebration." Elsie yawned. "I'm ready to go to bed now."

Brian said good night. I sensed an awful sadness and finality in his tone. He didn't kiss Dorothy good-bye. I hoped he'd be all right.

The burning and itching in my palm went away as soon as we left the park. It had to mean that the Bone Man's wife was a witch and that she had been at the celebration. But which of possibly hundreds of witches was she? Was she new to the area or had she lived here for a long time? Maybe I'd known her forever without realizing who she was.

We got back to Elsie's house quickly, since there was no traffic on the streets. I was ready to get out and help her.

She put her hand on my arm to stop me. "Tell us right now what happened with the Bone Man's deal, Molly, before we get in too deep."

"I'll have to use an enchanted bubble." I gave in to the inevitable. I'd hidden the problem with Joe for a long time. It would be good to share it with my friends.

"How will that work with me?" Olivia asked.

None of us had the answer. She was the first ghost we'd ever tried to share with.

"Let's just do it and see what happens," Dorothy said. "I mean, when you're ready. I don't know how to make an enchanted bubble."

"It's a good time for you to learn," Elsie decided. "The spell is pretty easy. I think I did my first bubble when I was eight or nine."

I waited to see if she was going to do the bubble. Elsie glanced at me. I knew she either couldn't remember or didn't feel up to it.

"All right." I bent my head and muttered the incantation.

CHAPTER 14

Shield us now from hurt and fear,
Keep the silence round us here.
Words of anger, words of pain,
Never to be heard again.

"Cool!" Dorothy said. "It's like the whole car is surrounded by gray slime."

I opened my eyes. She was right about the whole car being involved. Olivia was in the car, too, so it included her.

"And that's how we make an enchanted bubble," I said. "Once you're inside the bubble, no one can hear you outside—including the council. How long it will last depends on how much magic you put into it. I've seen them last for a day before, but usually you only conjure one for a short conversation. Anything more draws attention."

"Well, let's get to it before the bubble is gone," Elsie said. "Tell us, Molly."

I explained about finding it necessary to tell Joe about magic. There was a group gasp at that. "I didn't have any choice. I was afraid he might be killed. I decided that I would rather lose his memories than lose him."

"Quite a risk, and a debatable question," Elsie declared. "So he's kept it to himself?"

"Except for one night right before we were going to sleep. But that was a while ago. Nothing happened."

"And then you started seeing the Bone Man," Olivia reminded me. "How can you be sure it wasn't just a council trick to get you to admit it?"

"Again, nothing has happened. The Bone Man offered to tell me how to use the magic in this amulet in exchange for finding his wife. I changed the trade. He promised to protect Joe and Mike from the council."

Elsie slapped her hand to her forehead. "You've got to be kidding me! One little demonstration of water magic and you were willing to risk your family's lives? I can't believe it, Molly."

"You weren't there," I argued. "I don't know what kind of magic he has, but I don't know a water witch who can raise the ocean at will, do you?"

Everyone had to admit that it didn't seem like a parlor trick.

"So what happens now?" Dorothy asked.

"I find the Bone Man's wife for him, and take her to Oak Island. He protects Joe and Mike in case Joe makes a mistake. Mike doesn't know. The Bone Man has never gone back on a pledge to one of us. His deals are always true. I have no reason to think this won't be the same."

Elsie tapped her chin. "How do you plan to convince the Bone Man's wife to go back to him? If she lives around here, it's not like she doesn't know where he is. It must be a conscious effort on her part to stay away from him."

"That's true, Molly," Olivia agreed. "And is the Bone Man protecting Joe right now—or is he waiting until you fulfill your end of the bargain?"

I shrugged, tired and uncertain. "I don't know. I didn't think to ask him that. I don't want to go back out there right now. I'll warn Joe to be extra careful for a while. I guess I'll look for the Bone Man's wife and deal with her not wanting to go back when I get there."

The enchanted bubble began slipping away. It took only another moment before we could clearly see Elsie's porch light and the big moon above us.

Elsie shook herself and began getting out of the car. "A discussion for another day. Good night, sisters. Blessed Be."

After Elsie was inside the house,, Dorothy drove me home. Joe's black SUV wasn't in the drive. I knew he must be working late on the case.

"Good night, Molly," Dorothy said. "Do you need help getting things inside?"

"No. I'm fine. How did you like your first full moon celebration?"

"It was wonderful—except for the part about Brian's grandfather. What makes his family so angry and rude?"

"Wealth, I suppose," Olivia said. "And an impeccable lineage."

I squeezed her hand. "Try not to worry about it. It's all up to Brian. He'll have to decide how he wants to live his life. I'll see you both tomorrow."

"I'll look up that rune tonight, Molly," Olivia said. "I'll let you know what I find in the morning."

They waved to me and were gone. Tired but not sleepy, I looked up at the moon. I decided to go out into the garden for a while and enjoy the moonlight.

After everything from the celebration was put away or in the dishwasher, I changed into my nightgown and went out. I spent a lot of time out here, regardless of the season. Most witches are renewed when they are close to nature.

The moon was reflected in the surface of the water in my birdbath. I noticed that it bounced from the water to my amulet. The colors danced in the center of it. I took it off to peer inside, always wondering if it was a trick of the light that made it look so alive. It had to be a stone of some sort, my rational mind argued. But I was sure it was something different, something I couldn't define.

Like the Bone Man.

What was he? He wasn't a witch. He didn't fit as any of the supernatural creatures that I'd met—including were-wolves and a cranky old vampire who lived on First Street.

I knew Georgia, the Selkie. I had also met a mermaid or two. Georgia was pleasant and very nearly human. Mermaids, on the other hand, were not human at all. They were also extremely rude and could be dangerous. I'd known a witch who'd almost lost her hand to one.

I sat in my chair near the birdbath and let the magic moonlight bathe me. There was a small altar, between my chair and the other two, which had been blessed. We'd used it for many years.

I put the amulet on the altar. For a moment, nothing happened. Then the moon caught it and a thousand lights flared from it, like from a diamond. The lights moved and swayed. Mesmerized, I watched them.

It was as though I fell into a trance watching them. I saw the dead witches who had been killed in the past few months. I clearly envisioned their faces and even the places where they had been killed. It was amazing and frightening at the same time.

The front door closed, and I snapped out of it. Joe called my name. I grabbed my amulet, thanked the moon for being so gracious and went inside.

"There you are." Joe smiled as he put his gun and badge away. "How was your party?"

"It was very nice. Anything new on the murder front?"

He sank into a chair in the TV room. "Almost too much to take in. There are eleven official deaths now that are part of the investigation, including the one in Southport. A new one took place near the river last night. The killer is moving pretty fast."

"Can I get you something? Are you hungry?"

"No. They brought in pizza at the station since we were all working late."

I sat in a chair opposite him. "Can you tell me what makes them think these killings are related?"

"Sure. There's too much similarity between the deaths. There are no wounds anywhere on the body. The victims look as though they drowned, but there is no water in the lungs. Cause of death is still undetermined. Each victim has been found with seaweed and sand on their clothes and in his hair."

I thought about what he'd said. "Since each of them came from a town near the water, I suppose you'd expect something like that."

"But not on our victim that was found near the river, and not a few of the others who were found near lakes and rivers. Yes, they were all in coastal towns, but the seaweed and sand is from the ocean."

"Maybe the murderer killed them at the ocean and then left them near the other bodies of water."

"Maybe. But what about what killed them?" He glanced at me significantly.

I knew he was wondering if I had any ideas from a witch's point of view.

What could I say without going into the enchanted bubble? "I have heard a rumor that all the victims were of the same *religion*."

"Same religion?" He nodded. "Oh. Okay. I get it. Do you think the killer might be of that religious persuasion too?"

"I don't know. I've heard it's hard to sneak up on someone who follows that religion, but it can be done by someone *also* of that religion."

"I'll keep that in mind." He ran his hand through his hair. "Have you heard if people from that religion are doing their own investigation into the deaths?"

"I'm sure they're looking into it. They'd definitely act if they found out who the killer is."

"Okay. I'll see how that works into our investigation." He yawned. "Suzanne got her voucher to stay at a hotel. She already picked up her stuff. It's weird working with her again."

"*Again?*"

"Maybe I didn't tell you that we were partners when she was here in Wilmington."

"You mean when you were married? I don't think so." *I'd have remembered that.*

"Well, it's kind of a strange story. We met on the job. A lot of people said it wasn't a good idea for the two of us to get together. We got married anyway, and they wouldn't let us work together—it's a rule. I guess they were right. She moved right after we got divorced. She was a good officer. She's a good detective too."

What's strange about it? I waited for the punch line. It never came.

"Great." I got to my feet. "I think I'm going to bed. Are you staying up?"

"For a while." He stood and kissed me good night before turning on the TV.

"See you in the morning."

I climbed into bed. The conversation we'd had may have been stilted, but I had gotten the idea and so had he.

It was clear to me that the killer was a water witch.

It made sense. A water witch would choose to kill, or do anything else important, close to water, where she was most powerful. Considering how the deaths laid out geographically, I considered that she had begun her spree in Savannah and would probably head up the coast until whatever motivated her to begin killing had ended.

There was no way to know how many victims that could include.

But why? Why would a witch kill another witch? It was completely against our beliefs to take life of any kind.

I thought the sand and seaweed might be a cover for how the real deaths occurred, possibly to throw off investigators from the Council of Witches. It would be easy to fool the police. They would never consider magic as a weapon.

I thought of a few ways I might be able to help. It was important that the council figure out who was doing this to save Joe from getting caught in the middle. As terrible as it sounded, sending Cassandra out to warn everyone that they could be in danger might be as close as the council got to being part of the investigation.

They needed a nudge in the right direction. It looked as though I might have to be that nudge.

CHAPTER 15

Uncloud my path,
Show me the way,
Make blackest night
As light as day.

Dorothy had to work at the downtown branch of the New Hanover County Library on Chestnut Street the next day. I volunteered to help her bring the children's books that were going to be discarded to Smuggler's Arcane. She said she thought two cars would be enough to handle them.

I called Elsie to let her know that I'd pick her up around noon when Dorothy was finished for the day. There wouldn't be many customers after the rush that had built up to the full moon celebration. She said she had tomatoes to plant in her garden anyway and welcomed the time at home.

Though Elsie was a fire witch, she had a wonderful green thumb. Her plants were always bigger and produced more fruit, flowers and vegetables than anyone else's. It would be interesting to see how Dorothy's earth magic stacked up next to Elsie's fire. Dorothy was planting a small garden in her backyard too.

Olivia, being an air witch, had never grown a plant in her

life. All the greenery around her house had been carefully installed and maintained by landscape services. But she was also excited to see what her daughter could do with her innate abilities.

My garden managed despite the fact that I frequently over-watered. Elsie had always helped with me that. I suspected Dorothy would too.

While I waited for Dorothy, I looked up information about the killings on the library's computer. The local newspapers were full of the story too. Nothing like a series of murders to get people's attention. Between the two sources, I learned that the images I'd seen while gazing at my amulet in the garden last night had been accurate. I was surprised to say the least. My skills as a scryer had never been strong. The amulet was enhancing that magic too.

"What are you so intent about over here?" Olivia joined me. She'd been hovering around the library. "You have the worst frown on your face, Molly. You have to stop that before you start looking that way all the time. Our faces don't like wrinkles as we age."

There was another woman looking up information on a computer one chair away from mine. It would be impossible to discuss this with Olivia since the other woman was so close.

I grabbed my bag, smiled at the other woman and retreated to a comfortable chair in a corner near the window. Olivia accompanied me.

"I had a vision last night after I went home. I saw the faces of the eleven people murdered since Savannah, and the places they were killed."

"I though you were looking for the Bone Man's wife. Why are you looking at dead people? Aren't all the victims young men?"

"Yes. They're certainly *not* the Bone Man's wife. But you know the council isn't going to do much more than give us a warning. Joe is working on this case. He knows another 'religion' is involved, but he won't be able to stop the killer."

"Another religion?" Olivia looked confused. "What are you talking about?"

I sighed. I should have realized that she wouldn't get what Joe got last night.

"Oh. You mean witches. Magic. Joe knows about your magic, but you can't help him."

We both put our hands to our mouths as she finished speaking. She knew exactly what she'd said, but it was too late to take it back. I had to hope the Bone Man was sincere about protecting Joe. And I hoped he wasn't waiting until after I'd found his wife.

"Sorry," Olivia whispered as she glanced around us. "I'm so sorry, Molly. It's hard not saying it now that I know."

"Maybe it's okay. Nothing's happened so far." My heart was still pounding. Despite my words, there was no way of knowing when the council might pop up and say that I had violated one of our most sacred trusts.

We waited a few more minutes—nothing happened.

"Anyway," I continued. "I recognized all of their faces from my vision. You know how odd that is for me."

"You think it's your mother's amulet, right? I'd agree, since the Bone Man mentioned it twice *and* the council wanted it. Whatever power is in the amulet must be really strong. I've noticed your magic has been better lately."

"I know."

"I looked up that rune on your hand last night. I don't sleep, you know. It's nice to have something to do while everyone else is sleeping. Dorothy didn't get to bed until almost three A.M. because of her crazy cat telling her stories about his past."

"What about Hemlock's past?"

"It seems he was a Greek scholar who studied with Plato and witnessed the volcano erupting at Pompeii. He was a wise man and a prophet who foresaw the end of Greek civilization. Blah blah blah. You know how cats talk."

I laughed, sympathizing. Isabelle could spin a good yarn too. "What about the rune?"

"Yes. I couldn't find one exactly like it, but I found one that was close. Let me take a look at your palm again."

I found a way to hold my hand palm-up so she could view it without people thinking I was a crazy person.

"That's what I thought. It has something to do with the sea. I found it as part of other runes mentioned frequently in Irish lore. It's definitely Irish, probably back from before what we think of as Ireland today, possibly from the Tuatha de Danaan."

I caught my breath. "The faery folk?"

"Yes. I think it may have been used in conjunction with other things—such as sea nymphs, sea dragons, sea horses. You get the idea."

"After the Bone Man's display of water magic, I'm not surprised. Thank you for looking it up. Elsie's right. No one knows runes like you."

"Thank *you*, Molly. It's the first time I've felt useful since I died. People feel bad about getting old—they should try being dead. Nobody needs you or wants you when you're dead."

I wished I could truly hug my old friend. I could tell she needed it. I had to settle for praising her and reminding her how lucky she was to be able to spend time with Dorothy.

That revived her, and we talked again about the Bone Man's wife.

"She has to be a witch, doesn't she?" Olivia asked. "The rune stopped bothering you right away after we left the park last night. But how are you going to figure out which witch she is?"

We both laughed at that. A few library patrons turned and stared. I ignored them.

"I don't know. Maybe the rune will get even *more* uncomfortable if I get closer to her." I shook my head. "That sounds like fun. The Bone Man didn't explain much when he put it on me."

"I wouldn't want to be stuck on that little island all the time either."

"I guess I'll cross that bridge when I figure out who she is."

"You'd better put your time into that instead of trying to figure out who this witch killer is, Molly. The Bone Man is serious about his deals. You know that. How many witches have we known who have tried to go back on a deal with him? It never ends well."

I remembered that happening only a few times. The Bone Man's deals could be difficult to fulfill. Some witches had boasted that they would beat him because they had his trade already and had no intention of doing what he'd asked them to do.

"I can't remember ever hearing from one of those witches again, can you?" I shivered in the cool library.

"That's exactly what I mean. Who knows what happened to those poor souls?"

I didn't want to think about it. I was going to find the Bone Man's wife and somehow convince her to go back to the island with me. What happened after that would be between the two of them.

But I also couldn't stop thinking about the young men who'd been killed. One of them had been my son's age, in his second year of college, according to Joe. Another had been Brian's age. Someone had to stop this from happening again.

Even if I could only come up with possibilities to pass on to Joe, it would be better than nothing. Whatever information I could find would help keep him safe too. Not that I had any intention of him facing the witch that was killing these young men. When the suspect was clear, I would summon Cassandra. She and the council could do their part. A witch didn't belong in a non-magic prison.

It was finally time for Dorothy to be done working. I was glad, since I'd skipped breakfast and was starving. I thought we could pick up something to eat on the way to Smuggler's Arcane. Elsie was always willing to eat.

We lugged the boxes of books from inside the library to our cars. There were twelve large boxes—more books than I'd thought. I wasn't sure what we would do with them at the shop yet. Space was tight for what we already carried. We might have to put out one box at a time. At least the books would escape the trash heap.

"That's it." Dorothy was breathing hard. "Thanks for your help, Molly. I was hoping I wouldn't have to do it alone."

I was breathing twice as hard—there was a big age difference. I remembered an incantation from our spell book that would have moved the boxes for us, but there were too many people going into and out of the library to try using it. I'd have to remember to teach Dorothy that spell for the future.

It occurred to me that we might have to start a new spell book. I still hoped to find the old one, but in the meantime, we needed to write these spells down for Dorothy and whoever joined the coven in the future. We could always merge the two later.

Creating and sealing a witch's spell book was a difficult process. It required layers of protection and spells to keep the magic. That was one reason why witches passed their spell books on to people who came after them. Some witches had spell books that were thousands of years old.

Our spell book was only about a hundred and fifty years old. The spells weren't particularly powerful, but they had been left to us by the many witches in our families. They were more than just a repository of magic. They were also memories of our past.

Thinking about the new spell book, I waved to Dorothy and got into my car. I dropped the keys on the floor and bent to retrieve them. When I looked up, the Bone Man was riding shotgun.

CHAPTER 16

Secrets dark and secrets light,
Reveal yourself on this night.

"What are you doing here?" I tried to catch my breath as I put my hand to my chest to still my rapidly beating heart.

"Why didn't you take her last night? The rune told me you were near her."

"Is that what it does? Because I thought it was supposed to guide *me* to her. If you're going to pop in and out of Wilmington, maybe you should get her yourself."

It was audacious to speak to him that way, but he'd scared me. *Again.* I could only take so much.

"If that were possible, I should not have made the deal with you, Molly." There was no expression in his voice or bony face. "That would adversely affect our trade, would it not? If that were the case, the council would certainly have come for you and your husband today."

"Are you listening in on my conversations? I didn't agree to that."

"You are fortunate that I heard and blocked your ghostly friend's remark. She would be wise to move on through this world. You would be wise to stop telling others of your mistake in enlightening your husband."

"I know I agreed to help you find your wife in exchange for your protection. That doesn't mean you can tell me how to live my life."

"I understand your distress. Do not think to blame it on me or our trade. Fulfill your part of our bargain. Find my wife and return her to me."

"You could tell me how to use the rune to do that."

"You knew you were close last night. Don't act the fool with me. When the rune bleeds, you will know you have found her."

"*Bleeds?* But—"

It didn't matter. He was gone.

Dorothy had stopped in the alley and come back to knock on my window. "Are you okay, Molly? You looked like you were having a stroke or something."

"It was the Bone Man again. I guess, since I made the deal with him, that gives him the opportunity to stop by whenever he feels like it." I took a deep breath and tried to center myself. Being angry with him wouldn't help.

"Oh my goodness! This is exactly what I was afraid of," Olivia said. "He's going to be in your life forever now. You'll never get rid of him."

"He'll go away when this is over," I told her with absolutely no idea if I was right. "Let's go on to the shop. I'll get Elsie and meet you there. What sounds good for lunch?"

When I got there, Elsie was ready to go, dressed in royal purple with matching hat, gloves and shoes. She got in the car and I helped her fasten her seat belt. I told her about my visit from the Bone Man.

"I have a bad feeling about this, Molly. He's taking too much for granted, and there's still a lot you don't understand."

"I know. But it's too late. I can't get out of the trade with him now that I've made it. I'll just have to use the rune to find his wife and find a way to get her out there."

"A bleeding rune sounds really nasty." She shuddered as she adjusted her hat, which had been thrown off-kilter when she got into the car. "I know you're right. Maybe we could do a spell to find her. With Brian and Dorothy's help that sounds possible, doesn't it?"

"Maybe. We don't know who we're looking for—no clue at all. We could talk about it. Maybe Brian has some ideas."

We stopped and got Chinese food from a small place close to the river. It was another beautiful day. Dozens of colorful sailboats were on the water. Gulls swooped around them. Tourists watching the water traffic littered the docks. At Smuggler's Arcane, we decided to eat outside to take advantage of the weather.

"A spell might be possible to locate the Bone Man's wife." Olivia sat above her chair on the tiny porch. She had a small plate containing sweet and sour chicken on the table before her. She liked looking at the food even though she couldn't eat it.

"We'd need help." Elsie drank her tea. "Where's Brian today?"

"I haven't heard from him," Dorothy admitted. She hadn't even tasted her vegetables and noodles. "Maybe his grandfather really had the final say in what he's going to do."

"Brian doesn't strike me as that kind of young man," Olivia said. "He's been on his own for a long time. His parents and his grandfather haven't paid any attention to him. I'd hardly call them a family."

"That might be all the more reason for him to want to be with them now." Elsie said. "I'm sorry, Dorothy. I hope that isn't the case."

"Let's talk about creating a new spell book." I finished my egg roll and changed the subject. "I really think we should do this to preserve any new spells that we create. We could also add any old spells that we can remember. I know it wouldn't be the same, but I think it's important to the coven."

Elsie clapped her hands, the sound muted because of her elbow-length purple gloves. "I adore the idea, Molly. A new spell book. Like a new chapter in our lives."

Olivia wasn't so sure. "I won't have any new spells in this one. I want our old spell book back. It's not just our spells, but the combined knowledge of our mothers, grandmothers and great-grandmothers in that book. It's our heritage. We can't just give it up."

"I'm not suggesting we give up the old one." I tried to calm her. "We should find the old one, but so far our efforts haven't been fruitful in that direction."

"What do you think, Dorothy?" Olivia asked her. "Do you think we should forget about my important spells that I created over fifty years of my life?"

"Of course I don't think we should forget the old spells, Mom. But I agree with Molly and Elsie that we shouldn't lose the new ones while we're looking for the old spell book. And I'd like to see a new book created. How often does that happen in a witch's lifetime?"

Elsie and I exchanged glances.

"It's never happened in our lifetimes," I told her. "The spell book that was stolen was created before we were born."

Dorothy smiled. "Then I definitely vote to do a new spell book. Is that right? Is it a vote?"

"It's good enough," I told her.

We pored through catalogues from Elder Magics, a company in Germany from which we purchased most of our important magic items. They had been in business for hundreds of years.

"Oh, I like that one." Olivia pointed to a heavily runed book with a leather cover.

"Of course you do," Elsie remarked. "It has runes on it."

"Could we look for one that doesn't have a leather cover?"

Dorothy winced. "They had to kill something to get that leather."

"There are some very nice cloth spell books," I said.

"But you know our spell book wouldn't have lasted so many years if it had been made of cloth," Elsie added. "That's why the best ones are made of leather."

"I'm sorry, Dorothy." Olivia smiled at her. "I have to go with Elsie on this. It should be leather."

"Maybe they have some kind of space-age material that will be good for hundreds of years but nothing died to make it." Dorothy bent her head over one of the catalogues.

The door to the shop opened with a little chime, and Brian staggered in.

"Brian!" Dorothy got to her feet and ran to him.

"He looks awful," Elsie muttered as the couple embraced.

"He's probably had a bad night, poor darling," Olivia sympathized. "I wish I could take him in my arms and hold him tight."

"That might be awkward in more than one way right now," I added.

Elsie chuckled. "Like TV-talk-show awkward. I don't think Dorothy would like her mother holding her boyfriend in her arms to comfort him."

"Oh, you have such a dirty mind for such an old woman," Olivia retorted. "I only meant to hold him as one would a child."

"Sure you did." Elsie finished her tea and sat back to watch.

"Would you like some tea?" Dorothy asked Brian. "Or some Chinese food? I can run out and get something else if that doesn't sound good."

"Dorothy." Brian put his hands on her shoulders. His eyes were brighter than they should have been, burning in his face as though he had a fever. There were dark circles around them and his lips were white. "I've met the most wonderful woman."

CHAPTER 17

A little spell to ease my pain.
Start over.
Begin again.

"What?" Dorothy faltered like a young doe before a hunter. "What do you mean? I thought we had something—something important."

He grinned like a mad man and swung her around. "We *did* have something. We had something—but nothing like *this*. She's amazing. You wouldn't believe the pleasure she gives me."

"I know a little about pleasure." Olivia smiled. "But you look like death. I think this particular pleasure may be bad for you."

Elsie and I locked eyes across the table.

"Are you thinking what I'm thinking, Molly?" she whispered.

"The witch that's killing young male witches." I nodded. "This may be a break for us. The chances are good that the witch would ensnare her victim before killing him. It makes sense. You can't sneak up on most witches, but you can spell them when they aren't looking."

"What are you two mumbling about?" Olivia asked. "Say something to Brian. He's making a terrible mistake."

Dorothy managed to get him to the table. "Do you think a vampire bit him or something?"

"He's pale enough," Elsie said. "But I can't smell any blood on him, can you?"

"No." Dorothy had a keen sense of smell, as one would expect with an earth witch. "What else could it be? Look at him."

"I know you're disappointed that I can't be here with you," Brian explained. His whole body was jerking and shaking like he was an addict. "If you could just meet her, you'd understand."

"We'd like to meet her." I took him up on his offer. "Why don't you bring her around? We could have tea and cakes this afternoon."

"That's a great idea. I'm sure she'd love to meet you too." He jumped to his feet. "Let's do that."

Before we could do or say anything else, he was gone again. Dorothy was sniffling and Olivia was outraged.

"Don't cry, Dorothy." Elsie took her hand. "The boy is bewitched. He can't help himself. It has nothing to do with you."

"You mean someone can just put a spell on him and take him away from me?"

"I'm afraid so." I thought it was best for her to understand what she was up against. "He needs our help. Brian is very strong. To do this to him means the witch who cast the spell was at least as strong or stronger."

Dorothy wiped her eyes. "What can we do? Is there a spell that can free him?"

"It might be more complicated than that," Elsie told her. "Molly and I both think it could be the witch killer."

"Oh no!" Olivia came closer to the table. "We can't let her kill Brian too. We have to do something, girls. Maybe we should contact Cassandra."

None of us liked that idea, but for Brian's sake, we were willing to give it a try.

We went into the cave under Smuggler's Arcane. The

flame under the cauldron got hotter and brighter with Elsie's presence.

"Did you see that?" she asked proudly. "I've still got it."

"Do we need a spell to call Cassandra?" Dorothy asked.

"No. It's usually easier than that." I closed my eyes and gripped the amulet as I called the herald's name. "Cassandra! We have need of you."

There was no immediate response. We waited in the cave for thirty minutes and nothing happened. Elsie was snoring when I decided we should give up. Cassandra would come when she was ready.

"Let's get those books out of the cars," I suggested. "She can contact us just as well outside."

"All right," Dorothy agreed. "But I wish she'd hurry. What if he dies before we can save him?"

"A cheerful thought," Elsie said.

"You shouldn't be so attached to him anyway," Olivia scolded. "You're too young to be serious about Brian. You should take this opportunity to go out and live. Go places. See things. Meet other men. Take me with you, of course. I can be a big help when it comes to choosing good men."

Elsie cleared her throat. "Says the ghost woman who chose to have a baby with a thousand-year-old evil witch."

"Oh, hush about that." Olivia stuck out her chin.

"Let's get the books," I said again. "It doesn't matter if Dorothy is in love with Brian or not. Brian is still our friend, and we should help him."

"Not to mention that he's another possible replacement for one of us," Elsie said.

"We can't just get the books, Molly!" Olivia said. Brian may be in serious trouble. We have to do something!"

I agreed as I opened the front door. "The sooner we get the books out of the cars, the sooner we can figure out what to do."

Dorothy sighed. "All right! I learned a spell for displacement. That should make it faster."

"It's a spell from our old spell book that I remembered," Olivia said. "She's very good at it. A natural—just like her mother."

Elsie rolled her eyes but didn't say anything. "What do you need us to do?"

"Just hold the door and stand back." Dorothy put her hand on the emerald cull around her neck. She closed her eyes and muttered her spell.

"Holy Hannah!" Elsie cried out as the car trunks opened and all the boxes of books began flying in from the parking lot.

"Mom explained that it's all about displacing the air around the boxes. They aren't really moving at all. It's the air and molecules around them."

I was standing on the small porch, which was enclosed by an iron railing, as the books began their journey into the shop.

The woman next door ran a small bookstore called Two Sisters. She watched in horror as the boxes rushed past me, and looked around to see if anyone else had noticed. When she didn't see anyone, she ducked quickly into her shop.

"You have to be careful when using magic out in the open," I cautioned. "The council could strip that woman of her memories if they'd seen you."

"Sorry." Dorothy shrugged. "I thought of that at the library. That's why I didn't use the spell there. I didn't see her."

"We'd better come up with a plausible excuse in case she comes to see us. I'd hate to be responsible for the council removing her memories," Elsie said. "Maybe we could say we have a conveyer belt."

"I don't understand why the council doesn't want anyone to know," Dorothy said as the last box of books came up the stairs. "Why not let everyone know that magic is real? I think it would be great."

"It comes from the past," Elsie explained. "I'm not saying I agree with taking people's memories away. But there were too many witches hanged and burned right here in Wilmington.

Keeping those memories out of the mainstream probably saved lives."

None of us could argue with that. While I knew Joe would keep my secret, what about the woman at Two Sisters? Would she understand, or would she be the person who posted on Facebook that she saw boxes magically moving into our shop?

Dorothy closed the door. The boxes had stacked themselves in a corner.

"Thank you," I said to her. "Well done. Let's make sure we put that spell into the new spell book."

"With an addendum to use it after dark." Elsie smiled at her.

As I'd thought, there weren't many customers at the shop that day. Many of the witches who'd attended the celebration were still at home sleeping it off. The few that straggled in for supplies were filled with fear that they might know the next witches killed.

When it was quiet, we selected a new spell book and ordered it from Elder Magics. It wasn't leather, but it had runes on it. That made everyone happy.

"Maybe we should do a finding spell for the old spell book while the moon energy is still strong," Dorothy suggested.

"Good idea," Elsie agreed. "We've tried all the finding spells I knew. Can anyone think of another one?"

"There was one that Drago taught me," Olivia said. "It's very strong and takes a lot of magic to do it. I was terrified that he'd use it to find me. Maybe, with combined magic, we could get it to work. It would've been better with Brian helping us, but who knows if that will happen?"

I wasn't sure about using a spell from an evil witch who could have taken Dorothy from Olivia. "If Drago has any enchantment attached to the spell or if it's something he created, we could be drawing him here by using it."

"Molly's right," Elsie agreed with me. "We certainly don't want that to happen."

"Why doesn't anyone ever agree with *me*?" Olivia asked. "It's because I'm a ghost now, isn't it? I understand. I'm not a witch anymore. No one cares what I have to say."

"I don't think that's what they meant, Mom," Dorothy tried to smooth her ruffled feathers. "You worked really hard keeping me hidden from my dad. It might be better to use a different spell that has nothing to do with him."

"Oh, fine. Find your own spell then. There's probably not enough magic between us to make it work anyway."

"What about a different kind of spell?" Elsie suggested. "We've tried all the finder and locator spells we can remember. What about an attraction spell?"

"How would that work?" I asked.

"I was thinking we could find something that belonged to each of our mothers and grandmothers and bring it to the cave tonight. We could cast a spell to attract anything that belonged to them. That would include the spell book. We could use the moon energy for finding hidden items for it."

"That's a wonderful idea, Elsie," I congratulated her. "That's what we need—some original thinking."

"I'm so glad you can *still* come up with original ideas," Olivia drawled.

"Good. What do we do for the spell?" Dorothy asked.

We sat at the table and tried to remember what each of us still owned from our mothers and grandmothers.

"You've got plenty of clothing," Olivia told Elsie. "Can you recall what dress belongs to each person?"

"My grandmother used to tat lace. I know there are some lace cuffs and collars she made that are still in the attic."

"That's the best energy of all," I commended. "The spell would be stronger with items that were handmade."

"I have some jewelry that I know belonged to my mother and Meemaw," Olivia said. "Oh you would've loved your great-grandmother, Meemaw," she added for Dorothy. "She was a party girl."

"What about you, Molly?" Dorothy asked. "Did that amulet belong to your grandmother and your mother?"

"Yes." I fingered the cool stone. "But I have some other items that I would be more comfortable using in a spell. I'm not sure about the amulet."

"But you're wearing it," Olivia reminded me. "I'm a ghost, and I can feel the power from it. You should use it."

"I'm not happy with that idea—"

"Come on, Molly. It's settled." Elsie smiled. "We meet back here at midnight. Mind you, dress appropriately. Bring the items with you. We'll see if we can *attract* the spell book."

"What will happen if we do?" Dorothy wondered. "Would it come and knock on the door or something?"

"Unlikely," I told her. "We'll take the big mirror into the cave with us, and hopefully we'll see where the spell book is."

"What about Brian?" Olivia peered at the clock on the wall. It was approaching five P.M. with no sign of him. "Should we call him?"

"We can try." I patted Dorothy's hand. "Do you want to do the honors?"

"Yes. I'm worried about him." She took out her phone and called him. There was no answer. She left him a voice mail and then texted him before tweeting him a message and leaving something for him on Facebook.

"That should cover it," Elsie said. "Let's see if we hear back from him."

We were getting our things ready to leave the shop when Cassandra appeared, dramatically draped in front of the door. "Not leaving so soon after summoning me, are you?"

CHAPTER 18

May my magic protect
from all who would harm me.

"We've been here all day," Elsie told her. "We thought you were too busy to care if we found the killer witch's new victim."

Cassandra, dressed in flaming red satin, bestowed a sweet smile upon her—the kind annoying young people at restaurants give to older people before they call them "sweetie."

"I am the herald for the Council of Witches," she said. "I am quite busy. But for you ladies, I'm always ready to lend a hand. What makes you think you know who the next victim is?"

We told her about Brian and the way he'd been that day. She took it all in and then patted Dorothy's shoulder. "I'm *so* sorry. It's a difficult lesson to learn when you're young, but as they say in the movies—he's just not that into you."

"Why you—" Olivia flew at her.

Cassandra held up one graceful hand and pinned her to the wall. "Keep your ghost under control or I'll bring it to the council for extinction. You know you shouldn't keep dead things around."

"This isn't just a matter of Dorothy's feelings toward Brian," I tried to explain. "You could see he was under a spell."

She turned black eyes on me. "Must I remind you that his family is very powerful and they don't approve of him and our new witch? No doubt this is a geas they put on him to break them up."

"So they take no part in his life normally, but since he might have a chance to be happy, they spoil it?" Tears spilled down Dorothy's cheeks. "That's horrible."

"That's life, little one. Try to get over it and move on. There's nothing worse than a whiny witch."

I could see the fury and hurt building in Dorothy's face. I wasn't sure what she'd do, so I moved to step between her and Cassandra. Being a thousand-year-old witch, Cassandra could hurt Dorothy. I didn't want that to happen.

Before I could put my good intention into reality, Dorothy raised her hand, much as Cassandra had, and muttered a banishing spell. To my astonishment, Cassandra disappeared. I could tell by the look on the herald's face before she disappeared that she'd been completely surprised and unprepared for Dorothy's magic.

Olivia slid down the wall and flew over to us. "What did you do?"

Dorothy blinked. "I don't know. I just muttered a spell I'd read to get rid of her. What happened?"

"She left, baby." Olivia glanced at Elsie and me. "Let's go home."

"Okay. Let me get the rest of my noodles out of the refrigerator." Dorothy seemed happy to go. "What was that?" Elsie whispered as we huddled together near the front door. "She shouldn't have been able to do that."

"I told you that she could be very powerful from her father's side, but not necessarily in a good way," Olivia murmured.

"Did you teach her that spell?" I asked quietly.

"No. I don't know that spell," Olivia said. "We have to

keep an eye on her, girls. We can't let Drago's bloodline take hold of her. We might never get her back."

"Here it is." Dorothy had the small white box in her hand. "I'm ready now. I guess we'll see you tonight. I'm very excited about doing this new spell. I wonder what else we could attract."

"Let's see if we can make it work for the spell book first," I said. "We'll see you later."

When Elsie and I got out to the car, she was very upset about Dorothy banishing Cassandra. "I hope the herald won't take revenge."

"She didn't take revenge on you when you turned her into pottery," I reminded her.

"That's true. I hope she's as lenient with Dorothy. We need to teach our young pupil some anger management."

We waved good-bye to Olivia and Dorothy before leaving the parking lot of Smuggler's Arcane.

"What are you going to do about finding the Bone Man's wife?" Elsie asked. "I'm more worried about him than Cassandra."

"I'm in a business that caters to witches. It wasn't like there was a time frame agreed on or anything. His wife will probably come to me. I'll wait until the rune starts bleeding and I'll know she's in the shop." I wasn't looking forward to that event.

"I don't know if he's going to be happy with that, Molly. What if he starts following you around all the time? It could be very annoying."

I agreed with her, but it wasn't like I could walk up and down the streets looking for the Bone Man's wife. It seemed to me that I had no choice but to wait for her to come to me.

We passed Georgia the Selkie as she sat painting at the docks in her small chair. It occurred to me that she might have some idea who the Bone Man's wife was because of her connection to the sea. She was very old and probably knew things that we didn't understand.

Whether she'd share those things with me was another

story. She owed us a debt we had never collected, but Selkies—creatures that could shed their sealskins and become human—were notoriously difficult to get along with. That was one reason we'd never grown chummier with her.

I pulled the car off the road and into a parking space. Elsie stared at me. "What's up? Did you forget something at the shop?"

"No. I see Georgia out here almost every day. I was thinking she might know something about the Bone Man's wife."

Elsie's green eyes widened. "Seriously? She's not exactly the most pleasant person in the world."

"You wouldn't be either if people were always attempting to enslave you and keep you from your home. I think she'll talk to me—she owes us for finding her skin. You have to admit that she's been around a long time. She might know something about the Bone Man that could be helpful."

"Molly, are you sure? I'm going to be late for dinner. You know how I hate being late. Plus, we're doing the attraction spell tonight, and I have to get ready."

"I can take you home first."

She sighed. "No. That's fine. I don't want you to see her alone. She might decide to jump in the river with you and I'd never see you again. Let's go."

Because the day had been so clear and sunny, there were dozens of painters and photographers near the docks. We walked right up to Georgia where she sat facing the river with her easel and paints.

"Hello, Georgia!" I smiled as though I had been looking for her. "What a lovely day for painting, and what a wonderful job you've done capturing the river."

I'd never seen anything else except the river on her canvas as I passed her.

"What do you want?" she snarled back.

Elsie sighed and shook her head, sitting on a bench behind us.

"I have a small problem I thought you might be able to help me with," I continued in a pleasant tone.

"Why?"

"Because you've been around a long time and you're a magical water creature." I didn't want to play the you-owe-me card until I had to.

"I can't help you. Go away."

She didn't even look up from her scene on the canvas. Her fingers were covered with paint. There was a smear on her cheek too. Her dark hair was wild and uncombed, hanging down her back and ending in rat's tails. Her clothes were grubby and torn. She wore the same outfit every day, but never any shoes.

"Could you at least *listen* to my question before you decide you can't help me?"

"No. Go away."

I glanced at Elsie, who shrugged and focused on the river traffic.

"We found your skin and gave it back to you so you could be free from that fisherman who'd trapped you."

"So?"

"So you could repay me by telling me what you know about the Bone Man and his wife."

Finally Georgia looked up at me. "The Bone Man? Why did you have to go and mess with him? You're a witch, aren't you? Why didn't you use your own magic?"

Now maybe we were getting somewhere.

"He asked me for a favor. He wants me to find his wife and return her to Oak Island."

She grunted but didn't reply.

"I made a trade with him so he'd protect my family. But I don't know how to find his wife." I held up my hand so she could see the rune. "Can you help me?"

"No one can help you now, witch. You shouldn't have made that trade. Why do you think he didn't find her himself? You people are all the same. You always want what you can't have."

I was starting to get angry. If she didn't know anything—fine. But she didn't have to be so rude about it.

"I can tell you a story," she said. "Maybe it will help you. Maybe it won't. That's all I can do—and you're darn lucky to get that from me. I didn't ask you to find my skin. That was *your* doing. Don't expect any thanks from me."

"And the story?"

CHAPTER 19

Words of anger, words of hate,
Words of tomorrow, seal your fate.
From your heart, from your soul,
Let these words make you whole.

"There was once a beautiful young maiden with hair of auburn fire and eyes of blue crystal. She had fire inside her as well. Her favorite place to get away from the strict rules of her family and village was the ocean." Georgia kept painting as she spoke.

"If I'd known there were going to be fairy tales, I'd have brought my teddy bear," Elsie quipped.

"*Shh!*" I gave her a hard look. She knew how easy it was to distract the Selkie.

Georgia glared at us but kept going. "This young maiden gained favor with the Irish god of the sea—a lesser god, to be sure. As he passed her playing in the waves, the sun on her hair, he instantly fell in love with her. She felt the same for him when they met, and they spent many golden hours together in the water. One can only imagine the wonders he was able to show her."

Several toots from a loud boat horn interrupted the story for a moment. Georgia used her finger to remove some of the brown paint she'd added to the base of the river in her painting.

When she didn't resume the tale, I urged, "Is there more?"

"Of course there's more," she snapped. "What sort of tale would end that way?"

Elsie chuckled. "You'd be surprised."

Georgia wiped the paint from her finger into her hair. "Well, it's not the end of this tale. Tell your witch friend to be quiet."

I raised my brows at Elsie. She shrugged and settled back against the bench.

"As all good things do, the romance ended. It was winter, and the girl couldn't visit the sea god in the cold. She yearned for him and stood for hours looking out over the water, growing thinner and less able to handle her real life. She held a token he'd given her, never letting it out of her sight. Until one day."

"Why does she keep stopping?" Elsie whispered.

"*Shh!*"

Georgia took a deep breath and focused on the water. "Another young man from the village loved this girl. But when she spurned his attentions for the sea god, hate began to grow in him. He had seen her with the man from the sea. He wanted revenge for the girl not loving him. A common enough story."

I waited patiently. I could feel there was knowledge in this tale. I wondered if it related to the dream I'd had. It sounded similar.

"The man from the village struck. He stole the girl's amulet and accused her of witchcraft before the village elders. She was tried and convicted of using magic and cavorting with demons. The sentence was death by fire. They dragged her to the stake and tied her to it as she called out for the sea god to save her."

I noticed that Elsie had sat forward and was listening intently.

"But the sea god was far away. He heard her cries for help and rushed to her side. Alas, the fire had already consumed her. All that remained was his revenge on the folks who had killed her. He drowned everyone in the village, his wrath coming as a wall of water that wiped the sand clean."

My heart was beating fast with the story. I touched my amulet; it was warm. I could almost feel it pulsing with the magic in her words. Was my amulet the one in the story? Was that even possible?

"What happened next?" Elsie asked.

Georgia shrugged her rounded shoulders. "As you can imagine, the sea god did not want the girl to die. Some say he gave her new life in the water. Some say she turned to coral and is still wearing the amulet with seaweed and conch shells woven into her long tresses as she sits on a throne many hundreds of feet beneath the waves."

"So you're saying this girl is the Bone Man's wife?" I asked.

"I'm telling you a tale I heard from my mother. It may be true. It may not. Take from it what you will. Now, go away, both of you."

I thanked her for the story. Georgia didn't speak or look my way again.

Elsie and I went back to the car and got inside.

"Whew!" Elsie was shaking after hearing the story. "I've never heard a fairy tale that seemed so real."

"I think she was talking about my amulet—the gift the sea god gave the girl. I can't explain why, except for the dream I had. I saw the auburn-haired girl at the stake and the tall, black-haired man came on shore and drowned the village. It was so real in my dream—but even more real hearing Georgia tell it."

"Well, she *is* a magical sea creature," Elsie reminded me. "She has a way with a yarn. She should be doing that instead of painting those terrible pictures."

"You know she doesn't do it for money. She doesn't care what they look like."

Elsie stared at me. "I'm not sure I understand. How would your great-great-whatever come to have that amulet?"

"My mother told me it was a gift from a lesser sea god

to one of our ancestors. I suppose that would fit with the story. But if the girl in the story is the Bone Man's wife—does that make the Bone Man a sea god?"

"We've always said we thought he had different magic that didn't come from being a witch. Didn't you just experience the same thing, with the ocean rising at his command?"

"So the Bone Man's wife is already dead. He wants me to find a dead woman and bring her to him."

"Even worse, Molly. She was at the celebration, according to the rune on your hand. Wait!" Elsie put her hand to her mouth. "Didn't Olivia say the rune was Irish and had something to do with the sea? Maybe the Bone Man *is* a lesser Irish sea god."

I searched my brain for information about Irish mythology. "In the *Mabinogion*, they mention a sea god by the name of Manannan MacLir. But why would an Irish sea god live in the cemetery on Oak Island?"

"They did say he was a *lesser* sea god," Elsie quipped with a smile. "Maybe that was the best gig he could get."

CHAPTER 20

A water witch I was born to be,
A water witch I shall always be

I dropped Elsie off at her home. It had been a very exciting day.

Joe's SUV was in the drive when I got to my house. I couldn't wait to tell him about my amulet—even though it was still only a theory. What Georgia had said hit close enough to home to make me feel it was real.

First I'd have to explain about Selkies, and the Bone Man. I hoped Joe was ready for that conversation.

But it didn't matter. Suzanne was there with him. They were going over aspects of the serial murder case they were working on as they finished a late lunch.

I was disappointed. I'd looked forward to sharing these things with Joe, since he knew I was a witch. I couldn't make an enchanted bubble with Suzanne there. Maybe it was safe without it, but I wasn't secure with that yet.

"Molly!" He called out as he got to his feet. "I'm glad you got home before I have to leave again. We have some new evidence on the killer. We're hoping to follow up while the leads are still fresh."

"Good news," I agreed with a smile that hid my disappointment at not finding him alone. "I have a meeting tonight. I guess I'll see you in the morning."

I didn't do as good a job hiding the way I felt as I'd thought. Joe followed me into the bedroom and closed the door behind us. "Let's do this. You've got something to say, right?"

"What about Suzanne?" I asked.

"Is that what's bothering you?" He put his arms around me. "It's okay, Molly. Really. You don't have to worry. This will be over soon and she'll be gone."

"I'm not worried about Suzanne and you." I searched my heart and realized it was true. She'd been gone a long time. I knew Joe didn't have any feelings for her. Seeing her had produced a crazy jealous reaction on my part, but common sense had prevailed.

"What, then?" he asked. "Is it that other thing?"

"Yes." I smiled and kissed him. "We can't talk about it now. I'll be fine. We'll talk later. What about this new lead?"

"Someone saw our suspect when the victim was killed in Southport. We've convinced him to come forward. He's looking through mug shots right now. I think this is going to be our big break."

I hated to disappoint him. "The chances are good the killer isn't in one of your mug books. He or she is a member of my *club*." I emphasized the word "club" with my eyebrows. "You understand?"

"I know, but even members of your *club* could be picked up from time to time by the police, right? We could get lucky."

"Maybe," I finally agreed. This was what he knew. It was what he'd done for more than thirty years. I couldn't expect him to understand right away. I hoped for the sake of the witness that the killer didn't find out that he or she had been observed. It could mean another death, if that was the case. "Be careful with your witness. Members of my *club* can be dangerous."

"We'll keep that in mind." He kissed me. "I love you, Molly. I'll see you later."

When Joe and Suzanne were gone, I took a quick shower, cleansing my body for the ritual to come. I dressed carefully in a blue gown that I liked to wear for spell casting. It was the color of the sea on a sunny day. The amulet around my neck seemed to like the color too. A thousand lights danced inside it.

My hair was damp from the shower. I piled it on my head and secured it with a silver comb that had been a gift from my father. He hadn't been a witch either, like Joe. I wondered if he'd understood what was going on. My mother had never told me that she'd taken my father into her confidence about being a witch, but it was possible.

When I was done dressing, I looked around for as many pieces of my history as I could find. There was Great-Aunt Mary's shell bracelet. She had several spells in the book. I had a beautiful coral necklace that had belonged to my great-grandmother. I brought my mother's wedding band, which had a dolphin carved into the gold. I also found a blue scarf that had belonged to my Aunt Sylvia. I added my grandmother's wristwatch to the blue velvet jewelry bag, and I was ready to go.

I slipped my feet into sandals in case accomplishing the spell required taking my shoes off or getting my feet wet some other way. I looked at myself in the mirror and wondered again about Georgia's story.

If it hadn't mimicked the dream I'd had, I might have ignored it. But I could feel its truth in my soul. I believed the first person to wear this amulet had been the auburn-haired woman who'd been the sea god's lover. He must have passed the amulet to my early ancestor, whose name had been lost in time.

If that had all happened on Oak Island—which would explain the abrupt loss of the early colony there four hundred years ago—that would mean the Bone Man had stayed there after the loss of his wife. I didn't understand what would have kept him there, but it felt true to me.

I had a few minutes to look up Manannan MacLir in my Welsh book of mythology. The book said he was the son of Lir and rode in a chariot that surfed the waves. He was always accompanied by dozens of white horses that swam through the water behind him.

I looked up and tried to imagine the Bone Man being this sea god. What had happened to him? Maybe it was involved with him being trapped or for some other reason stuck on the island instead of returning to his native Ireland. Maybe it was some kind of karma for wiping out the colony.

Looking closely at the amulet, I wondered if he'd loved my ancestor who'd first owned the amulet. It seemed a little secondhand to give it to someone else after she was dead. I decided to find that missing ancestor no one could recall.

I put the book away and loaded everything into the car. It was still early, so I baked some brownies and got them ready to go. Elsie called and said that she was too excited to wait to go to Smuggler's Arcane and was wondering if I was ready to go.

I had a text from my son, who had run out of money—again. I added some to his bank account. Normally we would have had a discussion about it. I didn't like him to use up everything he had before the end of the month. I understood that this was different—he'd had car problems. A car could break down out of the blue but it wasn't a completely unexpected expense.

The calendar was circled for his next visit home. I sighed, missing him like always, and then went on to Elsie's house.

"I wasn't sure how much to bring," she said as we hauled two boxes of her personal possessions out to the car. "I'm assuming we'll need part of each thing to do the attraction spell. I didn't want to bring anything that might be destroyed by the spell. I hope I have enough."

"I'm sure you do." I closed the trunk and we got in the car.

"Joe says he has a witness in the death that happened in Southport."

"I hope you told him to be careful. A witness like that could end up dead."

"Exactly what I told him. The witch is getting careless if she let herself be seen killing someone. Not that I'd wish this on anyone, but I wish she'd move on to the next town. Hopefully it will be one with a larger police force."

"Not that the size of the police force matters. They won't catch a witch no matter what."

"I'm afraid you're right." We passed the empty docks. I thought about Georgia, back in her sealskin and swimming free in the river. The transformation from woman to seal had been amazing.

"You're thinking about the seal woman and her story again, aren't you?" Elsie asked. "Me too. I've hardly thought of anything else since we heard it. Do you still think it really happened, Molly?"

"Yes. I can feel it. You must too. I'm sure it's part of the amulet. It's been very active since we heard the story."

"It's affected you, the amulet. Your magic is better. You hardly ever make a mistake anymore. I'm worried that it really came from the Bone Man. No wonder he offered to help you use it. His magic probably created it. Does that bother you?"

I steered the car down the empty street. "Not really. I didn't bargain for it. It was a gift freely given, I assume. But no wonder the council wanted it. We may not understand the magic, but it's powerful."

Elsie giggled when she saw Dorothy's brown Beetle in the parking lot at Smuggler's Arcane. "I guess we weren't the only ones excited about tonight."

I parked next to the car and smiled. "I'm glad she's been able to get into the excitement of creating a new spell book and looking for the old one. At least it's something to take her mind off Brian."

Elsie and I grappled with our accumulated ancestors' wares. When they were out of the trunk, I decided to test my amulet's magic by moving everything into the shop. It was a good time to do it, since it was dark and all the other shops in the Cotton Exchange were closed.

"Do you think you should?" she asked with a worried expression. "What if you try to move them with magic and they fly out all over town?"

"Let's hope that doesn't happen." I closed my eyes and muttered the spell Dorothy had used yesterday to bring the books into the shop. I could feel the magic pumping through the amulet and into my spell.

"It's working!" Elsie clapped her hands. "Good show, Molly."

As if on cue, Dorothy opened the door to the shop. Elsie's boxes flew in through the doorway, barely missing her head. I brought my jewelry bag in with me, very pleased that the spell had worked.

"I hope we're ready to get this spell going and find our book," Elsie said as she strolled past Dorothy.

"About that," Dorothy said, twitching nervously. "I'm afraid something bad has happened, and I'm not sure what to do about it. I hope you can help."

I took her hand as I met her in the doorway. "What's wrong?" I glanced at the empty space around her. She was holding Olivia's staff. "Where's Olivia?"

"That's it." Tears were sliding down her cheeks. "Remember when we talked about putting her into Harper's body? Well, I kind of did that. But now I can't get her out."

CHAPTER 21

Wisdom I seek,
Bring it to me.
Wisdom I take,
So mote it be!

"That sounds bad," Elsie said. "Harper? Where are you, kitty? Or is that Olivia now? Here kitty-kitty."

Dorothy and I watched her try to locate Olivia's Russian blue cat. He wasn't very big, not like Barnabas or Isabelle. He also wasn't very friendly, even when no one had put a spell on him. He was still grieving for Olivia. That didn't help either.

"Any ideas?" Dorothy asked.

"Not right offhand," I admitted. "Let's find him first. Why did you try the spell alone?"

"I don't know. Moving the boxes went so well, I thought I could do this for my mother. You know she was uncomfortable at the celebration. If we could transform her when we needed to, it would be great, wouldn't it?"

"Transformation spells are extremely difficult," I told her. "It's very rare for a witch to manage one on her own. Glamour is one thing. Actually effecting a real transformation is another."

Dorothy started sobbing. "What if I can't get her out of

Harper? She might be stuck in him forever. I know she wouldn't like being a cat for a hundred years. Wait! Could she live that long as a cat? What would happen when Harper dies?"

"Here he is," Elsie called out from the supply closet. "He looks exactly the same."

I put my hand on Dorothy's shoulder. No point in going into how the change wouldn't be long and Olivia wouldn't remember being anything *but* a cat and would probably die for good when Harper passed. There was no reason to elaborate on how bad this could be. "Let's see what we can do."

We took Harper into the cave. Dorothy moved the boxes as Elsie and I checked out Harper.

"I'm looking in his eyes, but I don't see Olivia," Elsie whispered while Dorothy was busy. "Just Harper."

The cat agreed, and asked us not to get so personal.

I stared into Harper's blue eyes. With the proper concentration, it was possible to see elements of the soul that dwelled within the body. I concentrated as hard as I could, but I had to agree with Elsie. "There's no sign of her in there."

Elsie sat down hard in her chair near the fire. "What are we going to do, Molly? We can't get her out if she's not in there."

"She's not in Harper?" Dorothy asked. "Are you sure? I did the spell to transfer her energy into the cat. Shouldn't she be there?"

"As I said, transformation spells are tricky." I tried to remain calm even though I was sick at the thought of losing Olivia again. It had been so tragic to lose her, only to have her reappear as a ghost. I knew she was tied to Dorothy with a strong wish to remain on earth to help her daughter. I'd been so happy to have my old friend back again in any shape.

"What can we do?" Dorothy was a quivering wreck.

"What spell did you use?" Elsie took out her sword.

"I can get it for you. Mom and I came back and talked to Harper. He was happy to have her inside him. I found a spell upstairs in an old book. Mom looked at it and said it was a good one. I used it."

"Get it," Elsie commanded.

Dorothy scampered upstairs.

"Good grief." Elsie looked at her sword as she raised the fire under the cauldron. "Young magic can be as bad as old magic. I'm not sure there's anything we can do."

We were silent again as Dorothy brought the book.

"Here it is. Transform energy," she read aloud. "Do you want me to read the whole thing?"

"*No!*" Elsie and I both called out at the same time.

"Let's take a look at it without any more mishaps," I said. "Sit down, Dorothy. Hold Harper. He doesn't like it down here."

Elsie and I read the spell. It was an ordinary transformation spell. I noticed one important aspect of it at the bottom, in the fine print, and pointed it out to her.

"'Only transforms things to inanimate objects,'" Elsie read. "What?"

"Inanimate?" Dorothy hugged Harper close to her. "You mean she could be in anything in the shop? How are we going to find her?"

"It shouldn't be that general." I considered the possibilities. "The spell shouldn't have fanned out into the whole room. You're better than that. Otherwise you might have moved the cars into the shop with the boxes yesterday."

"I don't feel better than that. I feel horrible. How could I do this?"

"Feel bad later," Elsie suggested. "The consequences of putting a living spirit into an inanimate object are even worse than putting that spirit into an animal. At least Olivia would have been a cat. Now she might be a box or a piece of wood with no consciousness at all."

I frowned at her description even though it was accurate. "Let's think about this. Where were you when you did the spell?"

"I was right here. Mom said it would be better in the cave." Dorothy glanced around.

"All right." Elsie got up and started poking the sand and rocks that surrounded us. "Let me know if you hear anything."

I closed my eyes and held my amulet. At first all I felt was the rushing of water, millions of gallons of water. It reminded me of the night Joe had accidentally called me his little witch.

Then, suddenly, it came to me. I opened my eyes and went to examine the beautiful amber stone on the collar that Harper wore. I'd been with Olivia when she'd bought it at a bazaar in Istanbul.

"What about the stone?" I asked. "Olivia might be in the stone."

Dorothy yanked the collar from Harper's neck, which resulted in him scratching her, yowling madly and running upstairs. "Sorry!"

Harper didn't care about her apology. He just wanted to be left alone.

"Can you see her in the stone?" Dorothy asked.

"A stone isn't a living creature." Elsie stopped poking things with her sword and came back to us near the fire. "Let's try a spell to free her. Maybe there's one in that book. I didn't even know we *had* that book, did you, Molly?"

"We have hundreds of old books that we haven't touched in years." I separated the stone from the velvet collar. "Take a look, Dorothy. See what's in there."

There was no spell in the book that reversed or freed a spirit that had been transformed.

"Of course." Elsie sat down. "Isn't that always the way? Were those brownies I smelled in the car, Molly?"

"Let's try to focus," I suggested. "Maybe we could do something simple. It seems like I remember a small spell we learned when we were children. Maybe we could make that work."

I repeated the spell several times for Dorothy and Elsie. Then we repeated it together. I hoped that I remembered it correctly. I felt as though it might be our only shot to keep Olivia from being trapped in a rock forever.

We stood around the fire that burned under the cauldron. The amber stone was in my hand. After we'd repeated the spell together and I could feel the magic flowing, I dropped the amber into the fire.

I opened my eyes in time to see a flash of yellow light. Olivia's ghost sprang from it, flying to the ceiling of the cave before she looked down on us.

"That *hurt*. What were you girls thinking? You knew I was in there, and you threw it into the fire. Ghosts have feelings too."

We sank into the three chairs around the fire. Olivia was safe.

"Thank goodness you're back." Elsie used her sword to scratch her head. "I wouldn't know what to do without all that whining."

"Well, thank you too!" Olivia said.

"I'm so glad you're okay, Mom." Dorothy stopped crying. "I'm sorry. I thought I could do it."

"That's okay, baby. At least you tried." Olivia circled down like smoke from a chimney and pressed herself against Dorothy.

"I love you, Mom." Dorothy sniffled.

"There's a lesson to be learned here," I reminded them.

"How did I know you'd say that, Molly?" Olivia asked.

"You know what I mean. I can't believe you encouraged a new witch to try a transformation spell alone. What were you thinking?"

"I was thinking that I'm tired of people acting like I'm either not here or something that should have gone out with the garbage. I'd almost rather be trapped in that stone than go on this way."

Elsie chuckled. "You notice she said 'almost.'"

"I think we should break out a bottle of dandelion wine after all that," I said. "Let's go upstairs. I have brownies too, as Elsie mentioned."

We sat around the table eating brownies and drinking the potent dandelion wine we'd made a few years before. It was sweet and smelled of summer and flowers.

I related everything that had happened with Georgia, and with Joe. I could see everyone taking it in, even Olivia, who hovered above the table, refusing even to pretend to eat or drink.

"You think that story is real?" Dorothy asked. "Can you trust a Selkie? Not that I've ever met one or even knew they were real. She's not like the Bone Man?"

"No one is like the Bone Man," Elsie said. "You have to develop an instinct for what is true and what isn't. It's an important part of a witch's education. Can I have another brownie?"

"*May* I have another brownie?" I reminded her. It was hard to let go of being a teacher after so many years.

"You can have one too," Elsie replied. "It looks like there are three or four left."

"What are you going to do with the amulet now that you think you know where it came from?" Dorothy wondered. "Are you going to keep it?"

My hand automatically went to it in a protective gesture. "Of course I'm going to keep it. It's part of my birthright. I'm going to find out who in my family got it from the Bone Man. It would be good to know."

Olivia was still above us, not moving, not joining in as she usually did. There was a wistful expression on her face as it blurred.

I thought about how hard it must have been for her to give up everything that went with a corporeal form. I wasn't sure if she could make it the hundred years ghosts had allotted to them unless we could keep her connected. "What do you think, Olivia?" I asked her.

"I don't know, Molly." Her voice was weak and fragile.

"Dorothy, Elsie—would you excuse us for a moment?"

"Sure." Elsie's mouth was full of brownie.

Dorothy didn't look so sure. "What are you doing?"

"Olivia and I are going to step outside on the porch for a moment. We'll be right back." I smiled at her and touched her arm. She was still such a child in many ways.

"Why are we going outside, Molly?" Olivia asked as she followed me.

I closed the door behind us. The river was a large, black, glittering swath, except for a few lights on boats and barges. It was quiet too, as it never was during the day.

"Olivia, you can't go on this way. If you're serious about being here for Dorothy, you're going to have to overlook how people feel about you."

"That's easy for you to say. You know appearance is very important to me. I took care of myself and made sure everything I owned was either the best or at least very interesting. I was shallow in life, Molly. How can you expect more from me in death?"

"I thought you were here for Dorothy."

"I am, but—"

"You didn't even know where she was when she was growing up. You never got to play with her when she was a child. No teacher's conferences. No sniffles or skinned knees. I know you wanted all that, but you managed to hold on to your secret until you thought she was safe. She needs you now too. You can't give up yet."

"I don't want to, Molly. I really don't. I never thought it would be so hard not to be able to change clothes or put on perfume. Being in a cat wouldn't be any better, but I just don't know what to do."

"Maybe you need to live through Dorothy right now. I know she doesn't want to lose you. Neither do I. Find some way to make this work. We're depending on you."

She smiled. "I'll try it. But you have to promise me something too."

"What?"

"You have to promise to put that amulet back in the bottom of your jewelry box where it belongs."

CHAPTER 22

Witches fly
When the moon is high,
Across the trees,
Across the sky.

"I think your mother knew it wasn't a good thing. That's why she never wore it." Olivia made her case.

"I don't think that's true. Why would she give it to me?"

"If the Selkie's story is true and the amulet came from the Bone Man—or some Irish sea god—either way, it sounds like bad news to me."

"I'm not putting it back, Olivia," I said. "I'm going to do more research on it and learn how to use it."

"You're being stubborn about this. You know nothing good can come of it."

"What about the amulet renewing my magic? That seems good to me. How do we know all those older witches who have lived a thousand years don't possess something like it? And just because it came from the Bone Man doesn't make it bad. He's helped us with spells before. We didn't turn down what he'd given us then."

Olivia came right down in my face. "Think about it. I'm

worried about you. Don't let the amulet or the Bone Man own you."

She disappeared through the door after her dire warning. I took a deep breath of night air, fragrant with spring flowers and the scent of the river. I had no plans to set aside the amulet because of a story. My magic was stronger. I was making fewer mistakes. I couldn't see how that was a bad thing after the amulet had been in my family for so many years.

When I went inside, Dorothy and Elsie were comfortably sleeping with their heads on the table. It was almost two A.M. I decided the incantation for finding our spell book would have to wait.

"I can see me in her," Olivia whispered, studying Dorothy's sleeping face. "I think you're right, Molly. I have to refind myself in her. There are plenty of stories about ghosts becoming more human. I've met some of them too. If they can do it, I can do it. I just have to figure out how. It's not easy without magic."

"I know. I'll be glad to do anything I can to help."

"You know what I had to say on *that* matter."

"I'm not putting the amulet away, Olivia. Not without something more to prove that it's not a good thing."

We were at an impasse. It wasn't the first time, but our friendship had always seen us through. I knew it would this time too.

I woke Elsie and Dorothy. Dorothy awakened instantly and agreed that we should do the enchantment for the spell book later. Elsie was groggy, but agreed to postpone what we had intended for that night.

"Just don't forget about it," Olivia said as I locked and spelled the door to the shop behind us. "I don't like that someone else might be benefiting from all our hard work."

"Don't worry. We all want it back," I told her.

I waved to Dorothy, waiting to be sure her car started before I left the parking lot. Then I drove Elsie home and helped her inside. She'd slept all the way back.

After she was safely inside, I went home. I was tired and a little dispirited that Olivia thought the amulet was bad for me. I could take it off and put it away, but why would I? I couldn't imagine another witch who would after feeling its magic.

Except my mother.

Why had she chosen never to wear it? Why hadn't she told me about its history except as a passing thought?

I thought about my grandmother, Daisy. She and I had been very close. I loved her free spirit and curiosity. But I'd never seen her wear the amulet either.

I couldn't remember my great-grandmother well enough to know if she'd worn it.

Was there something to what Olivia had said about it? I didn't want to think so. I was enjoying my renewed magical energy. I wanted it to continue and grow.

Shedding my special clothes for the spell, I put on my lilac pajamas and sat in a comfy chair, reading everything I could find about Manannan MacLir. From what I could gather, he wasn't evil and hadn't done things to hurt people— except for the village he'd wiped away on Oak Island. I didn't know what I would've done in the same circumstances.

Isabelle heard Joe return before I did. She'd been asleep on my lap as I read but lifted her head to let me know we weren't alone.

"You're still up?" Joe yawned as he came in and locked the door behind him. "How was your *club* meeting?"

"A little unexpected, but good." I smiled and put my book away. "How did it go with the case tonight?"

"I think every branch of law enforcement was there to question and observe our witness. I would've been freaked out and run away if I were him. They're keeping him in a safe house with multiple guards. I was glad they didn't want me or Suzanne to watch him so I could come home. I might not have any choice later, though, if we can't get rid of this case."

"Did he give you a description of the killer?"

"Sure. He even helped a sketch artist with it. We've sent out the information to law enforcement up and down the Eastern seaboard. We don't know if the killer is finished in Wilmington and moving on or what. We can't take any chances."

"I'd like to see the sketch."

He produced a folded version of it from his pocket.

It could have been anyone. There was nothing unusual or distinctive about the killer. "And your witness is sure the killer is a man?"

"No doubt about it." Joe took the sketch back and put it in his pocket. "Do you have information to the contrary?"

"No. Not really. Members of my *club* can be male or female. But the killer could also be wearing a disguise."

He yawned. "Let's go to bed. Can I be a member of your *club* too?"

I turned out the lights as we walked to the bedroom. "I'm afraid not. You have to be born into it. I'm sorry."

He kissed me. "Probably better that only one of us is in this particular *club* anyway."

There were no bad dreams that night, even though I hadn't done anything about finding the Bone Man's wife. Joe and I had breakfast together the next morning. He went to meet Suzanne at the station, and let me know later that there had been no attempts to kill their witness during the night. There were also no reports of other murders.

But a witch would have known that he or she was being observed. Had the witch been wearing a disguise when the witness was there? Was that why the sketch was so nondescript?

I wished the killer would move on so the FBI, CIA and whoever else was involved in solving the case would move on too. That way Suzanne could go home, and the police department would find Joe a new, permanent partner.

I needed to focus on finding the Bone Man's wife and not on this killer witch. If Joe wasn't involved with the case, it would be easier to do. The police and the witches' council were working on finding the killer. They didn't need me to worry about it too.

Elsie was decked out in pink and white with a matching hat when I picked her up at her house. Her pink gloves were short today. Her attitude was pink too.

"I got an email from Larry last night. Now that the full moon has passed, he's starting for home. I'm looking forward to our happy reunion."

She was serious about her relationship with Larry the werewolf. I didn't have a problem with it. If he made her happy, I was happy for her, no matter what the council thought about it.

"Do you think I'm being old and silly about him?" she asked.

"Not at all. You're seventy-two, not dead. Why shouldn't you enjoy a romance with him?"

"Well, he's a lot younger, and a different species. I'm not sure how Aleese would feel if he turned one night at dinner."

I laughed at that. "I'm sure she'd be shocked and horrified. You should try to keep that from happening. Otherwise, you're both human with different magical attributes. As for him being younger—good for you. Maybe he can keep up."

She giggled. "Thank you, Molly. I've been excited about seeing him again, but also worried. I know the council won't like it."

"But they don't like much of anything."

"True."

"That was a silly mistake Dorothy made."

"Her magic is strong, but she's still learning. And don't forget, she banished Cassandra in an emotional moment. Magic is always stronger with emotion behind it."

"Yes. I suppose that's true." Elsie looked out the side

window. "What were you and Olivia talking about last night outside at the shop?"

"She needed a pep talk after being stuck in amber for a while. It's not going to be easy for her to stick around as a ghost. It's against everything we've ever been taught, and she doesn't like being ridiculed by other witches."

"I could see that. Olivia has always been very sensitive."

"And she told me I should give up the amulet, since we think we know where it came from." I waited for her reaction.

"You have to admit—having an amulet with the past Georgia hinted at is potentially a problem."

"Not you too?"

"I know you must have thought about why your mother didn't wear it. Don't tell me you didn't, Molly."

"I've wondered. I'm going to look through her journal and see if she mentions it. It's not like she gave me the amulet with some terrible words about it being cursed or something. She barely mentioned it. It was big and kind of ugly. I put it away. End of story."

"I wish you would do more research on it. What about this sea god?"

"Manannan MacLir. He's Irish, or at least mentioned in Irish mythology. He's not thought of as being evil. Except for knowing that he destroyed the settlement on the island, I can't find anything about him doing terrible deeds."

"Well, keep looking, just in case. I wouldn't turn away a magic pick-me-up amulet if my mother had left me one either. But it's good to know what jewelry you're wearing."

I agreed as we arrived at Smuggler's Arcane. Dorothy was just getting there too. She brought Olivia's staff out of the Beetle.

I could see right away that Dorothy had been crying again. She got out of the car and ran toward us, Olivia flying along behind her.

"We just came from Brian's apartment. He's gone."

CHAPTER 23

Turn the storm away,
Send me a rainbow.

"What do you mean gone?" I asked.

"I mean he hasn't been there," Dorothy explained. "I talked the superintendent into letting me inside. Brian's apartment was trashed. It looked like a hurricane had gone through it. I don't think he's been there since the full moon celebration. I think something terrible has happened to him, Molly."

"Slow down. Let's think about this. We know Brian was really upset about his grandfather coming to see him that night."

"What if Abdon took him away?" Dorothy asked tearfully.

"It's unlikely he'd leave anything behind," Elsie assured her. "Witches don't like to leave things behind."

Dorothy bit her lip. "Do you think Abdon hurt him?"

"Of course he didn't hurt him," I said. "Brian is his future. He may have talked him into going away to keep him from us, but he wouldn't do anything bad to him. Did you see his car in the garage?"

"I didn't think to look," she admitted. "You're better at this than I am, Molly."

"Was there any blood?" Elsie asked.

"No! I would've gone to the police right away if I'd seen *blood*." Dorothy wiped her eyes and blew her nose. "What can we do?"

I glanced at my watch. We had two hours before the shop was supposed to open. "Let's go back over there and do a thorough search. We might be able to figure it out."

"If not, can we use the attraction spell we were going to try for the spell book?" Dorothy asked eagerly. "There are plenty of his personal possessions around."

"We could do that. Let's get some candles and sage from inside and go to Brian's place."

I convinced Dorothy to ride with me. She seemed too distraught to drive safely. We got the sage and candles together and put a note on the shop door in case we weren't back at ten.

Brian's apartment house was very nice and upscale. It looked as though it had been built recently. It was outside the historic river district, going toward the newer section of the city.

"This looks like a place no self-respecting witch would live," Elsie commented as I parked the car. "Why didn't he find a nice historic spot? These apartments have no ambience at all."

"I imagine it's quite expensive to live here," Olivia observed. "Maybe Brian wanted something elegant."

"Let's go inside." I got out of the car and we walked to the door.

Brian's apartment was on the second floor. Dorothy had given back the key, but she had made a magical duplicate that opened easily when she used it.

"That's my girl." Olivia smiled. "She's so good, isn't she?"

Dorothy was right about the state of the apartment. It looked as though someone had gone wild in the place. Pillows, furniture—everything was thrown haphazardly throughout the three bedrooms, kitchen and living room.

"So we can grab something that belongs to him and use it to find him, right?" Dorothy asked.

"Yes." I put down the cotton tote bag that held our supplies. "But you're going to have to promise not to be disappointed if he doesn't want to be found."

She nodded. "I really thought we had something, Molly. Didn't you?"

"It's so hard to tell with a man like Brian," Olivia supplied. "He's a little wild and likes to have a good time. This could be the result of that."

"I've been here before, Mom. It didn't look like this. Brian was collecting things to make the place more his. Why would he trash it this way?"

Elsie, Olivia and I exchanged knowing glances. Dorothy had a lot to learn.

"Let's just say for the sake of argument that Brian is in some kind of trouble and we can find him and help him," I suggested.

"Here's his altar." Elsie pointed to a stone near the fireplace.

We examined it. The altar looked as though it had been used. There were burned smudge sticks and used candles on it.

"Look!" Dorothy grabbed something from under it. "It's Brian's wand. He wouldn't have left that here for anything. I knew something was wrong."

"Why don't you go down into the garage and try to spot Brian's car," I said. "We'll get started up here."

"I don't know. You might need my magic. I should wait."

"We won't start without you. The altar needs cleaning before we use it. I know looking for Brian's car isn't magic, but it could help us if we need to report this to the police," I told her.

"Okay," she agreed. "I'll be back."

After she was gone, Olivia thanked me for sending Dorothy away. "She's too emotional about this. Maybe you and Elsie could handle the spell."

"I agree. If Dorothy puts too much energy into it, the

spell won't work. Let's give it a try without her." I started cleaning the altar by removing the trash from it.

"You don't really think something happened to him, do you?" Olivia asked.

"He was kind of messed up when we saw him at the shop," Elsie added. "He looked like he could do something like this. I hope Dorothy doesn't get her hopes up on getting him back."

After the altar was cleaned, we used sage to clear the air. I put one of Brian's socks on the altar for something personal. I was concerned that his wand could throw everything off.

"All right. Let's try the attraction spell and see what happens."

Elsie and I joined hands and began to murmur the spell together. Olivia stayed close by and said the words too. I didn't think it would help the magic, but it couldn't have hurt.

Dorothy came in before we had a chance to work the spell. She immediately joined us. I could feel her emotional magic swirling through me. It was powerful and unfocused. I tried to keep us on track, but I lost control with the surge of Dorothy's worry and passion.

The altar cracked under the pressure, which drew our attention away from the spell. The door to the apartment blew open, and there stood Brian.

"What are you doing here?" he demanded.

"Trying to find *you*," Dorothy answered. "Where have you been?"

"I don't see where that's any of your business, and I don't appreciate being summoned."

If possible, he looked even worse than he had before. The circles were more pronounced around his bloodshot eyes. His skin had a yellow tinge to it. I could see the lack of vitality in him. He was fading away—or someone was draining him.

"Are you hanging out with that old vampire?" Elsie asked after noticing the same things I did.

"What are you talking about?" Brian stormed into the apartment. "You should get out of here now. Quit following me around. You old women don't have any idea how to have fun. Did you think I was going to hang around forever being bored out of my mind?"

"Don't talk to them that way," Dorothy said.

"What way? You're just as bad. You might not be old yet, but you're even *more* boring."

"Brian, you don't know what you're saying," Dorothy continued. "Stop now, before I get really angry."

His face scrunched up. "Are you threatening me? I could lay you out with my magic in two seconds. You don't even know what you're doing."

"Dorothy," Olivia tried to call her back from the brink.

"Don't do this, Dorothy," Elsie warned.

"Let it go," I said. "Take a deep breath."

It was too late. Brian was still in the doorway, but he was flat and solid.

CHAPTER 24

I transform this magic to be my own.
I transform this love to be mine.
I transform.

"Oh no!" Olivia said. "This is terrible."

"No." Elsie knocked on him. "He looks good this way, and he's not so argumentative." I put my arm around Dorothy's shoulders. She was crying as she stared at what she'd done.

"I'm sorry," she said. "I was so mad at Brian. It happened so fast."

"And of course, being an earth witch, you made him solid. I understand. But how did you do it? We haven't taught you anything that complex."

"I guess I got it from the book at the shop. There are a lot of spells in there." She sniffled. "I didn't even stop to think if it would work. I was so angry, I just did it. It was like the words from the spell came into my brain and *poof*!"

"All right." I made myself take a deep breath and calm down. This was bad, but we could probably reverse it. "Let's join hands and reverse this spell."

We tried every spell reversal we could think of. Even with Dorothy's potent magic, none of them worked.

"What do we do now?" Elsie knocked on him again. "It weighs as much as Brian."

"We can't leave it here," I said. "I don't know if he made this mess or if it was someone else. I don't want to wait around to find out. We'll have to take him to the shop. Maybe we can get rid of the spell there."

Everyone agreed, but Brian was too heavy to move. It was daylight, and the apartment building was crowded with people going in and out. We couldn't use the transport spell to move him. We had to get him downstairs.

Elsie thought of getting a hand truck. She felt sure the superintendent would have one, and she went down to borrow it from him.

Olivia was consoling Dorothy, but we had a real problem on our hands. Dorothy's emotional outbursts of magic would have to be curbed. She was so sweet, kind and gentle. It was hard to believe she could fly off the handle that way.

We were going to have to include some anger management with her training. I didn't like the path she was taking. We had to find a way to help her until she could curb her outbursts on her own.

"I guess Brian's car was still in the garage," I said as we waited for Elsie.

"Yes," Dorothy replied. "But it was like his apartment, really messed up, and he'd left his keys in it. Brian's proud of that car. He'd never do that."

"Well, I think we could clearly see he wasn't himself," Olivia said.

"What's happening to him?" Dorothy asked. "Is there anything we can do to help him?"

Olivia shook her head. She had no idea. I didn't either. I had never seen anything like it. We were going to have to do some research on the subject.

Elsie returned with the hand truck. "I told him I was Brian's mother. He said it was fine. Help me get him on here."

It was touch and go getting Brian's sturdy form on the hand truck. I thought for a moment that he might fall off on the green carpet. But we managed to keep him on the hand truck and get him into the elevator. It was another thing getting him into the car.

Dorothy offered to go back and get her car so Brian's one arm could stick out the window. Brian was six feet tall—and he wouldn't bend. We had to be careful not to break anything that might have to be repaired later.

"The problem as I see it," Elsie said, "is that we should have left him in his apartment if we couldn't move him somewhere safe."

I took out my phone. "There's only one safe way we're going to get Brian from here to the shop, ladies. I'm calling Joe to see if he can bring the SUV."

"Good idea," Olivia commended. "I'd hate to bring him back with a broken or missing arm."

"Although Dorothy would probably hate losing the man parts even more." Elsie giggled.

Dorothy's pale face turned a bright shade of scarlet.

Joe answered right away, and I kind of explained the situation to him. He said he was in the middle of a boring rehash of everything involving the case and would tell his captain that he had an emergency.

We waited on the sidewalk with Brian. He looked like a big ad for a young man who might be on drugs. Dorothy glared at the people who came too near.

About fifteen minutes later, Joe pulled up. "What's with him?"

"I can't explain. Thanks for coming so quickly." I smiled and kissed him. "He's going to the shop. We need to do some work on him."

He lifted one brow. "This is *club* work, right?"

Elsie giggled and Olivia laughed and fluttered.

"Club work?" Dorothy looked confused. "Oh. I get it. *Club* work. It's for our club. I see."

"Molly, there isn't a missing person report I should file, right?" Joe asked seriously. "The club has this in hand, right?"

"He'll be fine," I assured him. "I didn't want to take a chance on damaging him."

"You can't get the parts back, you know," Elsie confided.

"Okay. Let's get him into the back. I have some bungee cords to make sure he doesn't move around and hurt himself."

We wheeled Brian over to the SUV. Joe opened the back, and we were able to get Brian inside without using magic.

"We'll meet you at the shop." I handed Brian's car keys to Dorothy. "Are you okay to drive?"

She nodded. "I'm fine. I'm so sorry. I have to do something about this, Molly. I've never had a temper. I don't know why I keep lashing out with my magic."

Elsie and Olivia were quick to shush her with Joe standing right there. It struck me that I'd made a good bargain with the Bone Man to protect Joe, even if I wasn't quite sure yet how to fulfill my part of it. Accidents happened a little too frequently now.

"I guess we can't do the magic-bubble thing while I'm driving." Joe smiled as we pulled out of the parking lot. "I'd love to hear more about this."

"We may not need the bubble anymore," I told him. "I don't know for sure yet, though, so let's not take any chances."

"So does the *club* do this often? Was this some enemy you had to defeat?"

I smiled. Of course he'd think about it in terms of movies and video games. "No. Actually we were hoping he might join our club."

Joe grinned. "Probably not so much now. Does he know? I mean, does he realize that he's a statue?"

"I've never had the experience. It might be like a person

in a coma—some hear what's going on around them, some don't."

"I thought you had to be born into the *club*?"

"You have to be born a *potential* member of the club. It's difficult to explain in this context."

"Okay. Can the club fix this?" He glanced at me when we stopped at a red light.

"I hope so."

We reached Smuggler's Arcane quickly. I was a little worried about the potholes in the streets, but Joe took it slow. When we got Brian out of the SUV, he was fine. Not so much as a chip off his head.

Dorothy put her arms around him when she got there. "I'm so sorry, Brian. I wouldn't have done this if it wasn't necessary. I shouldn't have done it anyway. You couldn't help what you were doing. I'm sure it's the result of some kind of spell. At least you'll be here safe with us." She kissed his flat mouth.

Elsie giggled. "Watch that. We're right out here on the street. We don't want the shop to get a bad reputation."

We didn't have a hand truck. Our supplies came in smaller packages, or we moved them at night with magic. In this case, we couldn't wait until it was dark to hide our activities. Joe helped us get the "tree" up the stairs and into the shop. We made him tea and cookies for his efforts. Dorothy spent the whole time trying to find the right spot for Brian.

"I need to get back." Joe smiled at me, Elsie and Dorothy. "I miss seeing Olivia, even if she was a little crazy sometimes. I know she was a good friend."

Olivia fluttered close to him. "I can't believe you just said that, Joe Renard. I'm right here, you big lug. Take that."

I hadn't thought to tell Joe about Olivia. He couldn't see ghosts—why would the subject come up? I didn't think there was any point. He was becoming more involved with our witchcraft. I didn't like it, but it was hard to put the genie back in the bottle once it was out.

Olivia put her fingers together to pinch Joe's ear. He yelped, glancing around himself as he got up from his chair. "What was *that*?"

"She's not exactly gone," Elsie explained. "Olivia kind of hung around to help with Dorothy. She's her daughter, you know."

Two books moved from one of the big shelves on the wall to the counter where we kept the cash register. Olivia was in her glory. She danced across the ceiling like a beam of sunlight. "I did it! I really did it. I knew I could do it. I just had to keep practicing."

"You mean she's a ghost?" Joe's eyes scoured the room. "Really? Is that part of being in the club too?"

"What club?" Elsie asked. "Oh. You mean the coven. No. Witches don't particularly like ghosts. The council wants us to get rid of her. We refused."

"Elsie!" I couldn't believe she'd forgotten herself to such a degree around him.

"I'm sorry, Molly. I wasn't thinking." Elsie shook her graying curls. "I know better."

Dorothy held her breath, her dark eyes wide in her face. "Is it okay?" she asked finally. "Is the council coming for Joe?"

I could see my husband was completely confused. I put my arm around him. "Don't worry. It's nothing. I'll answer any questions you have later."

"Okay." He still looked uncertain. "You mean the bubble thing?"

"Oh, the enchanted bubble." Elsie clapped her hands. "Let's do it now. Then Joe will be protected."

Before I could protest, she'd created an enchanted bubble around the entire shop. Non–magic users wouldn't be able to see it, but it would stand out like a beacon to other witches. It couldn't stay up for long.

"Look, Molly!" Elsie held out her hands like a woman handing out prizes on a game show. "I can still do it."

"This is really weird," Joe said. "Anyone in the club can make one of these?"

"Pretty much," I told him, trying not to be angry with Elsie.

"I can't," Olivia complained. "At least not anymore. Not since I died. Who knows, now that my ghostly powers are coming in?"

Within the bubble, Joe could see Olivia. He jumped back and stared at her. "It's true! You're a ghost. I can't believe it."

"Oh, you can see me now, huh?" She put her hands on her hips. "Don't bad-mouth the dead, Joe. You never know when they might be watching and listening."

"I'm sorry, Olivia." Joe grinned at her. "But we've known each other a long time. You've always been the wild, crazy, sexy one."

"Sweet talker!" She patted her blond hair. "I suppose that's true. And I always had a better time than Elsie or Molly because of it."

"And Dorothy is your daughter?" he asked. "Was that by magic? I don't recall you ever being pregnant."

"Well, that's a long story. It all started when I met an evil witch named Drago. Of course, I didn't know he was evil. He was handsome, sexy and the best lover I'd ever had—"

Someone knocked on the outside of the bubble. I didn't even know that was possible. My world was getting crazier by the minute.

"Yoo-hoo. What are you people up to in there?" Cassandra pressed her face to the bubble.

"It must be the only time I've ever been happy to see her," Elsie muttered. "I didn't want to hear about Olivia's love life again."

"But what do we do?" Dorothy asked. "Joe is in here. She's going to know that something is going on."

"Hide!" Elsie said.

"It's too late for that." I grabbed Joe's hand. "Either the Bone Man is keeping him safe or we have a problem."

Elsie managed to disperse the bubble. Cassandra looked at us with a knowing gleam in her eyes.

"So what's going on?" she asked. "What's so secret that you can't do it out here in the open?"

She stared at each of us.

"We were just practicing," Elsie said. "You know, teaching Dorothy how to make an enchanted bubble."

Cassandra nodded slowly. "I suppose that's important, although many witches use that technique to hide their activities from the council. I know you ladies wouldn't do that, would you?"

I started to say something that would explain why Joe was there with us. I didn't have a clue what that would be, but I needed some defense against her judgment.

"At least you don't have anyone without magic in there with you." Cassandra studied her fingernails. "That's what most witches do with it. They think we can't hear them talking to a spouse or child about magic in the bubble. But we notice—especially if you make a bubble the size of a house."

"Leave now, Joe." I squeezed his hand. "I don't think she can see you."

Was it the Bone Man's magic? Had he completely taken Joe and Mike off the council's radar?

He nodded, his eyes still on Cassandra—I'd mentioned the herald's name a few times. He understood that part. He slipped out the door without her so much as blinking. I was so astonished and relieved that I had to sit down. I didn't know a witch who could do this, though many had tried.

Elsie watched him go. I hoped she wouldn't say anything. She looked at me and turned the key in the imaginary lock on her mouth before throwing it away.

"So, what brings you here, Cassandra?" I asked with wobbly confidence after Joe had left the shop.

"*You* had the big bubble, Molly. We check out these things."

I folded my arms across my chest and leveled my gaze at

her. If Joe was safe, I was prepared to take on the council. "You didn't come because of a magic bubble. I don't care what size it was."

Cassandra produced a small mirror, in which she studied her reflection for a moment. "You're right. I would've sent someone else. The truth is, Brian Fuller is missing. His grandfather and parents are extremely worried. I was able to track him to his apartment before his trail disappeared. Do any of you know what happened to him?"

CHAPTER 25

Looking for a good witch,
A true witch, a sweet witch.
Looking for a good witch,
Going to make him mine.

Elsie narrowed her gaze as she glanced toward Brian's stiff form in the window. "I haven't seen him for a while. Have you, Molly?"

Dorothy had covered him with one of the long robes that I'd put in the shop for the full moon festival. She'd also wound a scarf around his head. He appeared to be a paper doll in the window.

"No." I made myself look away from Brian. "Does his family check on him all the time? We were under the impression that they weren't very close."

Cassandra shrugged elegantly. "It's true. They aren't very close, but they keep tabs on him. When he vanished, they got concerned. Abdon Fuller's concern is *my* concern. So if any of you know what happened to him, now's the time to speak. Dorothy?"

Dorothy jumped when the herald addressed her. She looked blank for a moment but finally rallied her thoughts and forced her eyes away from Brian. "This is what I was trying to tell you earlier. Something has happened to Brian. He wasn't him-self. You acted like it was nothing."

"You mean until you did that cute little banishment spell on me." Cassandra giggled, but her black eyes held daggers. "Which, by the way, don't *ever* try again. I'm willing to allow for the fact that you're a newbie witch—for now. But don't ever turn your magic on me again, little girl. I thought Elsie and Molly were doing a better job training you."

Dorothy stepped forward with her mouth open. Olivia inserted herself between her and Cassandra.

"This is just a terrible pickle, isn't it?" Olivia laughed. "We've been looking for Brian too. Can't find him anywhere. Looks like he disappeared."

Cassandra turned her head. "I don't speak with ghosts."

But it didn't matter. Olivia's timely interruption had given Dorothy a chance to step back. She wrapped her arms across her chest and pursed her lips.

"What Olivia said is true," I told her. "We think someone may have taken him."

"Oh, you mean like the witch who's killing other witches, as Dorothy *tried* to explain to Cassandra?" Elsie asked.

"I'll check into it." Cassandra said the words through her teeth. "Be sure to let me know if you hear from him."

She disappeared in a puff of deep purple smoke that exactly matched the slinky dress she'd been wearing. As usual, it smelled like roses.

"I want to know what that costs," Elsie said. "I'd like to disappear one time before I die."

Our conversation spilled out into the room again when we were alone.

"She didn't even *see* Joe," Elsie said. "How is that pos-sible?"

"If he's being protected by a sea god, I guess anything is possible." Dorothy looked at me.

"I know. But she didn't know he was here. That must be what the Bone Man meant when he said he could protect Joe and Mike from the council." I was still stunned too.

"Does Mike know that you're a witch too?" Olivia asked. "Molly, that was very careless of you. You didn't know the Bone Man was going to take care of the situation. You could have lost Joe *and* Mike."

"Mike doesn't know. I only told Joe to save his life. I had to make it clear why he can't go after witches for murder." I bit my tongue, getting tired of defending my actions to my friends.

"What about the murders Joe is investigating?" Dorothy asked.

"Right now, let's not worry about what's going on with Joe." I wanted to put an end to that conversation. "It seems the Bone Man is holding up his end of the bargain. We need to figure out what's going on. Dorothy, you and Olivia stay here and work on reversing the spell you put on Brian."

"Maybe he'll be better off as life-sized cardboard for now, since we think this killer witch is hunting him," Olivia said. "At least he's safe here."

"But don't think everyone will ignore Brian standing there dressed like a male model. I really expected Cassandra to see through it. Abdon certainly would. Let's try to reverse the spell and get Brian back to normal before that happens."

"What are you and Elsie going to do?" Olivia asked.

"I'm going to see what I can find out about who's doing this to Brian. Then maybe I can find the Bone Man's wife before he changes his mind about our deal."

"And how are we going to do that?" Elsie asked. "Another fairy tale?"

"I hope not. I'm going to see Muriel the mermaid."

"Not *her*." Elsie sighed. "Can I stay here and Olivia or Dorothy can go with you?"

"No. We'll be back for lunch, I hope."

I knew Muriel was a long shot, but sometimes she came through for us. She lived in a salt marsh near No-Name Island, on the coast. She could be temperamental.

The first stop before seeing her was always the bakery, for cream puffs. She would never talk to anyone who didn't bring cream puffs. We bought a dozen of them and then headed toward No-Name Island.

Elsie ate one of the cream puffs we'd bought for Muriel and then saw a message on her phone. "Molly! Larry is back. I haven't seen him in days. Maybe you could drop me off."

That gave me an idea. "We need someone with a boat to take us to No-Name Island anyway. Why not Larry?"

She giggled as she wiped the cream off her face. "Why not indeed?"

Larry Tyler was a good friend, and a werewolf. He came to Smuggler's Arcane for magic supplies on a regular basis—except for the days each month that he took his boat out and changed into his wolf form. He'd been a vegetarian— and a confirmed pacifist—for many years. Even the sight of blood or the mention of death could make him woozy.

We drove slowly to the marina where his boat was tied up. He'd changed the name of the green-and-white boat to *Elsie* last year, when they'd started dating. Now we were harboring a ghost, Elsie was dating a werewolf and my husband knew about magic. All things strictly forbidden by the council. I didn't know what had happened to us after years of leading such uneventful lives.

"Hey, you two!" Larry greeted us after we'd parked the car and walked to his boat. "I wasn't expecting to see you until I had a chance to clean up, Elsie. But you're a sight for sore eyes."

Elsie and Larry hugged, and he kissed her. It was crazy, but I loved it. Elsie had been alone for too long.

Larry was the most ordinary person to be hiding such an extraordinary secret. He was short, a little lumpy and middle-aged. He wore his brown hair long, tied back in a ponytail. I didn't think I'd ever seen him when he wasn't wearing some kind of beach shirt. He had plain features and blue eyes. No one would ever suspect his other self as a werewolf.

"Larry, we were wondering if you could run us out to No-Name Island to see Muriel." Elsie's face was pink and her eyes were misty after their embrace.

"Not the mermaid?" He took off his fishing hat and re-adjusted it on his head.

"That's *exactly* what I said. Great minds think alike!" Elsie quoted. "But Molly wasn't moved by my protest."

"Why do you want to see Muriel?" he asked. "She's a big pain in the butt."

"I'm not disagreeing with either of you," I said. "But she might be able to help us find out who's murdering witches. We think the killer might be coming after Brian. He's safe for now, but I don't know how long we can keep him that way."

Larry whistled through his teeth. "Witches killing witches? Sounds bad. Sure, I'll help."

He'd done favors for us before he was dating Elsie, but I didn't want him to think we were trying to take advantage of their relationship. "There's money for fuel, a cream puff and lunch in it for you."

He grinned. "How could I pass that up? You all come aboard. I would've taken you anywhere just to spend time with my Elsie."

Larry held her hand so gently as she stepped aboard the boat. I held the railing and jumped down to the deck. Larry's boat wasn't very big, but it had a small cabin for sleeping, which made it ideal for him during the full moon. He made his living taking fishermen out to special places that he knew. He did very well with the werewolves who came to visit Wilmington.

"Let me get some fuel and we'll head out," he said. "Don't go below, whatever you do. It's the worst mess when I get back."

While he was gone, Elsie looked around at the area under the canopy, where he piloted the boat. She took a peek belowdecks but hastily retreated. "He wasn't kidding."

"What did you expect?" I sat in the sun on a chaise lounge. "How neat and clean would a werewolf be, especially during the full moon?"

"I'd like to find out," she said. "I have that full basement under the house. It would be a perfect place for him to change."

"I think he likes changing on the boat at sea. He knows he can't hurt anyone."

She sighed. "I suppose that's true."

"But maybe you could go with him and he could drop you off on an island or something during his change. I'm sure there are ways the two of you could work it out."

She sat next to me, her green eyes more alive than I'd seen them in years. "Do you really think so, Molly? I mean, everyone would give us such a hard time. The werewolves hate the witches as much as the witches hate them. And we're not young."

"Yes, but so what? You don't have to romance all the werewolves—you just want Larry. Who cares what other people think? As far as your ages, what difference does it make?"

Elsie hugged me. "You know, all those years with Bill, when I knew he was cheating, I kept hearing my mother tell me, 'Once you married, you married for life.' But I know that was wrong. I should have left him and started new while I was still young. Finding Larry has been like being young again."

"Then don't worry about anything but being with him."

"I'm not exactly ready to tie the knot yet—he hasn't asked me. I would, though, if it came up. Just letting you know."

"Thanks. I love you, Elsie."

"I love you too, Molly."

We heard Larry whistling as he came back from buying fuel. "It's paid for. I just have to pull over to the tank and pump it. We'll head out after that. Where's that cream puff? Just thinking about Muriel makes me crave sweets."

Elsie handed him a pastry out of the white baker's box. "Thanks for doing this, Larry."

"Anytime for you, sweet cheeks."

It only took a few minutes to get the boat ready to go out. Larry cleaned a little belowdecks—enough so we could go down if it started raining. But the sun was shining and it looked like a good day to visit Muriel. She liked the sunny days best.

"You know, someone got a video of her and stuck it on YouTube," Larry said once we were underway. "It caused a sensation until a few million people saw it and said it was a fake. Can you imagine? I guess mermaids don't have rules against being seen in public."

Werewolves strictly enforced their rules about changing in public. It didn't happen often, but it usually ended with the werewolf being killed by other werewolves. They were worse than the witches about protecting their secrets. At least the council didn't kill witches when people found out about magic.

"I'm sure Muriel enjoyed that," Elsie remarked. "She likes seeing her own face. I hope she got to see it on the Internet."

Larry chuckled. "Maybe, but there's not much cell phone service or broadband in the salt marshes."

The trip to No-Name Island was beautiful. The ocean was calm and blue, reflecting the sky above it. Elsie and Larry pointed out cranes, egrets and other birds as we passed them. We even got to see a dolphin and a school of sunfish swim by. Larry was careful to mark that location for his charter business.

We finally reached the swamp area around the island. There were some trees and coarse bushes, but mostly there were only plants that grew in the salt marsh. The seclusion of the spot, accessible only by water, made it a perfect home for Muriel.

There were tales of how she'd come to be here. A few people said that she'd been kicked out of the merfolk kingdom. Some said she was lamenting a lost human love.

Either way, she never ventured out into the Atlantic. She hid in the tall grasses of the island and watched humans. She'd learned to emulate them fairly well.

"You have to call her." Larry pointed out as Elsie and I looked over the side of the boat. "She won't just come on her own."

"It's always best to hold open the box of cream puffs," Elsie told him. "She's got a nose for them."

We waited patiently in the salt marsh as more birds and other small animals flew by and scampered across what little sand and rock they could find. The boat rocked gently in the water. In the distance, I saw two canoers making their way around the estuary.

"She may not come with other people around," Elsie whispered. "I swear this area gets more crowded every year. It seems an odd way to protect the marshes, by inviting groups of people to visit them."

Larry laughed. I shushed them both when I heard the sound of a mermaid's tail hitting the water.

An instant later, Muriel appeared at the side of the boat where Elsie held the cream puffs. She wasn't a pretty mermaid—not in the classic-myth sense of beautiful, long-haired, half-naked sea creatures.

She was older. Her white hair was green with bracken. It looked like steel wool on her head. Her eyes were narrow slits, and it was hard to tell what color they were.

Her breasts were bare, just like in the stories, but the scales from her waist down were the same color as her hair. There were no bright colors or sequinlike shiny flakes to her.

"Hello, Molly. I haven't seen you in ages. Elsie—nice to see you too, girlfriend. What are you doing with the wolf? I'll bet the council doesn't know about that. Am I right?"

"For not having Internet or TV," Elsie observed, "you talk just like someone from a late-night talk show."

Muriel laughed. Her teeth were small but sharp. She probably needed them for her main diet, which was crabs and raw fish. No wonder she liked cream puffs so much.

"I listen. I learn," Muriel said. "Just like now. I can guess what brings you out this way. It's the sea witch who's been killing your kind up and down the coast, right? Muriel *knows*."

CHAPTER 26

Listen—they cannot be heard.
Look—they cannot be seen.
Fear them, my child,
The ogres of the mind.

Elsie handed Muriel a cream puff. "What can you tell us about her?"

Muriel ate one of the puffs in a single bite, her strange eyes rolling back in her head with pleasure. "I know she's old—maybe older than me. I know she's looking for a man. That's why she only kills the male of your species—not that I have anything against two girls finding love together. But this is different."

"How is it different?" Careful not to let her fingers get too close to Muriel's sharp teeth, Elsie handed her another cream puff.

"She has to have him, you see. The others die until she finds the right one." She licked her lips with her peculiar green tongue. "It happens every hundred years or so. She eventually finds the right one and goes away."

"Goes where?" I asked as Elsie took out another cream puff.

"Who knows? Who cares? Just keep your loved ones away from the sea until she's done."

"What does she look like?" Elsie gave her another puff. "How would we know her?"

Muriel laughed, showing all her wicked white teeth. They looked like sharpened pearls in her mouth. "You won't. She's powerful, that one. She never looks the same way twice, and the way she looks isn't the way she is."

She gobbled another cream puff. Elsie and I tried to figure out what we could ask her that would help. That was always the trick with Muriel.

Larry filled in the silence. "Why does she kill the men?"

"It's the only way she can tell who's right." Muriel took the last cream puff. "A girl has to shop around. The sea witch is no different."

"What is she looking for?" I asked.

"What we're all looking for. *The perfect mate*."

I knew there were other questions we should have asked. As usual, Muriel had appeared, eaten and disappeared beneath the water before I could understand what she was saying. When the cream puffs were gone, so was she.

"Looks like you could've used a few dozen more cream puffs," Larry observed.

"I know." I sat in the chaise lounge again. "What does she mean by 'sea witch'?" Larry asked as he started the engine again. "Don't you each have an element that's special to you? Would that be the same as a water witch?"

"I don't know." Elsie shrugged her shoulders. "I've never heard anyone use that term before. Have you, Molly?"

"No. I've never heard there was a difference between water witches. That would be like having dirt and sand witches."

Elsie started laughing. "Sandwiches! I could go for one of those about now. Maybe with some fresh tuna on it."

"Too fishy for my tastes," Larry said. "Maybe some hummus. That sounds good."

"Oh, sorry. I forgot you don't eat fish." Elsie smiled at him. I thought she'd never looked happier.

While Elsie and Larry flirted and laughed on the way back to Wilmington, I thought about what Muriel had said. The sea witch—whatever that meant—was looking for a mate and, apparently, the mating process was killing the unworthy candidates. She sounded a lot like a spider's mating process.

When she found the right man . . . what? She mated with him? Was that to produce offspring? Was that what the whole process was about?

I could see why Brian would be on her radar. He was young, handsome, a powerful witch and a good catch.

But to find him, she had to have a human form, as Muriel had hinted. She had to stay close to the water. I understood that part. Being near the water made me feel better and stronger. It probably helped her disguise herself too.

But why use a disguise? Did she look like Muriel and would find it hard to trap a witch mate that way?

Her having magic from the sea went along with Joe's autopsy reports. I'd read once that water magic could cause a form of death that mimicked drowning, even when there was no water close at hand. I'd never gone further than the preliminary information. So there were some answers for our time and cream puffs, but almost as many new questions.

The one thing I felt safe about was that the witch was looking for young men with magic. She probably wouldn't come after Joe unless she felt threatened by him. If her magic was as strong as it sounded, she could elude the police forever.

We got back to the docks and waited for Larry to dock his boat so he could leave it. Driving the two of them made me feel like I had Mike in the backseat with a girlfriend. Elsie and Larry laughed, flirted and whispered. I saw a few kisses exchanged in the rearview mirror.

We stopped to get hoagies for lunch. When we got back to Smuggler's Arcane, there were several cars in the parking lot. I knew having customers would have made it more difficult for Olivia and Dorothy to come up with a way to return

Brian to his normal form. Elsie and I hurried inside to give them a hand.

But it seemed something else was happening. A witch who'd lost her son to the sea witch was there to mourn him with her friends and family. Many times, our shop was the only public place witches felt safe gathering.

There were hundreds of lighted candles around the shop. The smell of burning sage hung in the air. I hadn't realized that Belinda, a witch we knew well from Southport, was the one who'd lost her son.

I'd been so busy thinking about the Bone Man and Joe, Brian and the sea witch, I hadn't stopped to think that the two witches who'd been killed locally had families grieving for them.

"Molly." Belinda hugged me tearfully. "I was hoping you'd get back in time. What's wrong with everyone? Sam is gone now and no one can explain why. The council doesn't have any answers. I know Joe is with the police. Has he told you anything?"

I glanced at Brian's figure in the window. Dorothy shrugged when she saw me and kept pouring tea for our guests. There hadn't been time to figure out how to undo the spell.

Everyone glanced at Larry strangely, but he went to read at the back of the shop. He really was the most unobtrusive werewolf ever.

Olivia was happily mingling with a few of the witches. We'd known them forever and they seemed to accept her. Strangers were more likely to give Olivia a hard time.

"Come with me so we can talk," I said to Belinda.

We found a quiet nook in one corner. I told her what I knew about the killer from both a mundane and a magical sense.

"I understand about sea witches," she said. "I've lived on the ocean all my life. My father and grandfather were fishermen. Neither one of them had magic. They both married witches. I've heard stories about sea witches. My grandfather said they were the spirits of dead witches who had drowned and were trapped in the water. They could never come on land again for long, and missing the land made them crazy. Both men insisted that a sea witch could attack a large boat in the water and kill everyone aboard. They said they'd seen it happen."

"I'm sorry this happened to Sam." I held her hands in mine. "Was he dating someone who might be the sea witch? Muriel said she's using a disguise. He might not have realized who he was with."

Belinda wiped her eyes. "No. Sam was dating a nice young witch from Charleston. They were talking about getting married. She's from a good family too. Her parents were giving them some static about her being too good for Sam, but it was starting to look like the parents were going to give in."

"So you don't think it could've been her?"

"No. She wasn't even here. Sam had been dating her over a year, way before these killings started."

"Was there a witness to his death?"

"Yes." She sniffed and rubbed a tissue across her red nose. "There was a witness who said she saw the whole thing. She said it was a man who strangled Sam. But from what you're saying, it would've been the sea witch in disguise as a man. She's got strong magic. She can look however she chooses."

"We know from the practice of glamour that any of us can look different with very little magic expenditure. It's going to make it hard to catch the killer if she can look different every time she kills."

We talked about Sam. It seemed that he had experienced the same personality changes that Brian had exhibited recently. He'd also left home one night, and hadn't come back for three days.

"He was like another person," Belinda said. "I tried to talk to him, reason with him. Sam was always the calm, easygoing kind. You know. Suddenly he had temper tantrums and he couldn't sleep or eat. I knew something was wrong. I thought he'd snap out of it. Guys go through things sometimes."

It was beginning to sound more and more like it was a good thing that we'd brought Brian back with us. Maybe if he was gone for a short time, the witch would look for someone else. But we still had to turn him back into a human.

Belinda and I had some tea and burned some herbs in memory of her son. I couldn't imagine anything more devastating than losing a child. Thinking about her loss, I hugged Mike closely in my heart.

I noticed a change in the flow of muted conversation between the witches in the shop and looked up to see that we had a new arrival. The rune on my hand itched and burned as I got to my feet. Dorothy was making all kinds of pointing and head motions.

Abdon Fuller was there with his son, Schadt, and his daughter-in-law, Yuriza.

CHAPTER 27

Imagine the morning,
Imagine the day,
Imagine your troubles
Melting away.

I studied the three of them. The rune seemed to be saying that one of them was the Bone Man's wife. Was it Yuriza? Or was it one of the other witches in the shop? I hadn't noticed the feeling until she'd come in, but in all fairness, a few more witches had also come in since I'd started talking with Belinda.

"Where is my son?" Schadt's voice boomed over the sound of the memorial service. "What have you done with him?"

Dorothy was trembling so badly that I wasn't sure if she was going to continue standing. I immediately went to her side, and Elsie joined us.

"There's a memorial here now," I told Brian's family. "Your tone is out of line. Please come back later and we can discuss your son."

Abdon stepped in front of Schadt. His twisted mouth snarled as he looked at me. "We'll stay right here until you tell us what you've done with Brian."

By now Elsie was shaking almost as much as Dorothy. I put my hand on my amulet and stood my ground. "You can stay if you stop bellowing, light a candle and commiserate with our dead witch's mother. Considering that the Grand Council did *nothing* to keep this from happening, it's the least you can do."

Abdon opened his mouth to retaliate. Schadt and Yuriza began to look a little uncomfortable. I felt my friends come in closer until the thirty or so witches had formed a knot in the middle of the shop. I knew they felt the same and were ready to stand up to these three outsiders.

Schadt muttered something to his father.

Abdon stood down. "We'll leave for now—but you'd better have some answers for us when we return."

The family was gone from the shop as quickly as they'd arrived. There was a general sigh of relief from the witches around me. No one wanted a confrontation with the powerful Fuller family.

But that's where Dorothy, Elsie and I were headed if we couldn't change Brian back to himself.

The memorial lasted another hour. I was nervous and worried about someone discovering Brian, but I hated to ruin the celebration of Sam's life. There was also the problem with the rune on my hand. Even though the Fullers were gone, my palm was still itching and burning. Did that mean the Bone Man's wife was there with us? Or was it still reacting to the Fullers' presence?

"You look like you just ate a sour pickle," Elsie observed. "What's wrong besides the obvious?"

"The rune has been bothering me. I've talked to almost everyone here and it hasn't started bleeding, but I get the feeling the Bone Man's wife is either here or she's been here."

"Runes aren't an exact science," Elsie said. "You might have to shake hands with all the witches to make it bleed. I'm not sure you really want to do that."

"It's the only way Joe is going to remain invisible to Cassandra's radar. I can shake hands and handle some bleeding. I'll stand at the door as everyone is leaving."

As the group began to break up, I stood there like a party host wishing bright blessings to everyone as they left and touching them physically in some way. The rune continued as it had earlier without any significant change.

What had happened? Was the rune telling me that Yuriza was the Bone Man's wife? She was the only witch I'd seen who had left early. Everything had changed when the Fuller family had shown up.

I hoped that wasn't true. I didn't want to confront Yuriza about having another husband or trying to get her to visit the Bone Man. But what else could it mean?

After all our friends had departed, the three of us sank down on chairs around the table.

"Any bleeding, Molly?" Elsie asked with a yawn.

"No." I studied the rune on my hand, which was slowly going back to normal. "If the Bone Man wants his wife back, he's going to have to tell me who she is. This is stupid. I felt a presence—or at least my hand did. But I touched every witch as they were leaving. Nothing else happened."

"Not every witch." Dorothy pointed out. "You didn't touch Brian's mother—or the witches who were here when the Fullers arrived."

"Which witches?" Elsie asked.

"I saw them," Olivia said. "They were at the full moon celebration too."

"Since I'd rather confront anyone but Brian's mother, who were they, Olivia?"

"I don't know all of them. I mean, I'm only dead a few months, and there are new witches in the area already."

"Which ones *did* you know?" I asked.

"Well, there was Nora. I think she's from around here. And Adrian. She's from Kure Beach. And that new one with the long white hair who's here on behalf of the council. I saw her. And a couple of other new ones I didn't know."

"You mean Portia de Winter," Dorothy said. "She was here for a while. I think she left right before Brian's family got here."

"Yeah. Brian's family was a party buzzkill." Elsie started collecting dirty teacups.

"We know Nora," I summed up. "And Adrian. I don't know how we'll get the names of the other unknowns."

"Belinda had a memorial book." Dorothy snapped her fingers. "We could ask to take a look at it."

"Good idea." I got up to help Elsie collect the napkins and dirty dishes. "It shouldn't be too hard to figure out where Portia is staying."

"We have to antagonize the council from as many different directions as possible, don't we?" Elsie asked. "Portia is here on their behalf, you know."

"I don't want to antagonize anyone. I just want the Bone Man's wife to go back to him."

"Let's talk to Belinda," Dorothy said.

"I think we're getting ahead of ourselves," Elsie said. "There's the matter of a certain heavy cardboard cutout that has to be taken care of."

"I can't believe I forgot about him." Dorothy went to his side. "We have to change him back. There wasn't time when Belinda and everyone else got here."

"We should be okay as long as we locate the spell and change him," I said. "Find the spell, Dorothy. We'll clean up."

As Dorothy went through the transformation book, Elsie and I picked up after our guests. Olivia was trying hard to move objects with her ghostly powers, but it wasn't working well yet. Napkins and plastic forks were good to practice on—they weren't breakable. I smiled as she kept trying to lift objects.

"This is stupid," she declared. "I can't do witchcraft and I can't do things people without magic can do. There has to be some way to make this work."

"Practice makes perfect," Elsie sang out. "Keep trying."

"I found the spell!" Dorothy said. "Let's change Brian back."

"Has anyone considered how we're going to protect him if the killer witch is really stalking him?" Elsie asked.

"Which I believe is true after my conversation with Belinda." I told them about the changes Sam underwent before his death. "I don't know how we can protect him."

"I'll say," Olivia added. "First of all, we changed him into a poster person. He's gonna be angry about that. Maybe his grandfather will take him somewhere that he'll be safe."

"What about tagging him?" I suggested. "If we use a tracer spell, we should be able to keep an eye on him. We can spell the old binoculars to look for him if the tracer is activated."

"Good idea," Dorothy said. "How do we do that?"

"And what are our parameters?" Olivia asked. "Do we trace him when he uses magic? Do we use the tracer to tell us when he's having sex with the sea witch?"

"*Olivia!*" Elsie called out. "We are not voyeurs."

"I'm just asking." Olivia defended her words. "We'll need to be very specific to make a tracer work."

"We'll set that up later." I smiled at Dorothy's bewildered face. "Right now, we have the spell. Let's get Brian back to himself."

Larry was snoring in the back of the shop. He was probably exhausted from his change. It took a lot out of a man to become a werewolf and then change back—at least that's what he always told us.

"Don't mind him," Elsie said. "He won't even know."

Dorothy recited the spell from the book. After hearing it, we recited it with her. Elsie took out her sword. Dorothy held her emerald cull. I closed my eyes and held my amulet.

Nothing happened.

"I don't understand it," Elsie said. "I felt the vibe. Why didn't he change back?"

"You need to move him to the center of the room and join

hands around him," Olivia said. "Concentrate, girls. Brian doesn't want to be a poster boy forever."

We did as she suggested. It was tough pulling the heavy cutout into the center of Smuggler's Arcane.

"If you think this is hard," Elsie said, "dragging him into the cave will be even harder. Let's make this work up here, shall we?"

We joined hands around Brian and recited the spell again. This time there was movement in the cardboard, a slight rippling effect.

"Look!" Olivia yelled. "It's working."

We stared at her, only slightly irritated at the interruption.

"Oh. Sorry. I'll just go back to trying to lift one of these napkins."

"Again, ladies." I closed my eyes.

We kept reciting the spell to turn Brian back into a man until he stood between us with only his skin an odd color of gray. He was stark naked, but he was there.

Not sure why he'd lost his clothes—but at least he was safe.

"What's going on?" His teeth were chattering from the transformation. "I smell paper. What am I doing here at the shop? We were at my apartment, right?"

"Brian." Dorothy smiled. "We brought you here for safe-keeping. You'll be fine as soon as the shock wears off. Right, Molly?"

"That's right." I grabbed the robe that he'd been wearing as a poster and draped it around his shoulders. "Elsie, make Brian some tea, please."

"Wait a minute." Brian put his arms into the sleeves and pulled the robe closed around him. "Dorothy did something to me. You're not telling me everything."

"The important part is that we saved you from the evil sea witch who wants to kill you," Dorothy said. "We brought you here, and now we'll have some tea."

"Is orange spice good with everyone?" Elsie asked.

I shook my head.

Elsie puttered behind the counter looking for tea. "What about chamomile? That sounds soothing, doesn't it?"

"You turned me into a *poster*," Brian accused Dorothy. "And it wasn't for my own good either. You were angry because I'm seeing the most wonderful woman in the world. You can't compete with that. I'm sorry. We're over. I have to be with her."

"*Over?*" Dorothy wrinkled her nose. "I didn't know we ever got started. I don't care who you see. If she kills you, don't come haunting me."

The conversation was going downhill quickly.

"Brian, I know what Dorothy did was wrong," I told him. "But it really was for your own good. This is what's been happening to the other young male witches who have been murdered. You aren't strong enough by yourself to fend her off. She's very powerful."

He stared at me with glazed eyes. "I'm leaving. I don't want any tea. Just stay out of my life."

Dorothy grabbed the sleeve of the robe he wore. Another impassioned plea for understanding was on her lips. But Brian was gone—leaving only the robe behind.

"He can do that too?" Dorothy asked.

Elsie giggled. "I hope he's heading back for his apartment. Anywhere else could be embarrassing."

CHAPTER 28

Through the night to the witches' feast,
Through the night and up the street,
Baskets are passed with a Merry Meet!
Through the night on silent feet.

"I guess that's over." Dorothy sat down hard on a wood chair.

"What do we do now?" Olivia asked. "We can't just let him go to his doom."

"I invoked a tracer spell on him as I handed him the robe. We should be able to keep tabs on him."

"That was brilliant, Molly," Olivia said. "I was wondering why in the world you'd want to cover up that gorgeous form. I was beginning to think you were getting old for sure."

I ignored that remark. "Elsie, do you remember where we put those binoculars?"

"Not really. But I can look."

"What are the parameters of the spell?" Dorothy asked. "I know someone said there had to be parameters."

I nodded. "It's true. And they have to be very close to the individual person. In this case, we'll be able to track him if he goes within one hundred feet of the water. I think the sea witch takes her victims to the water. We'll know if that happens."

"But we should be able to keep track of him with this anyway." Elsie took out an old telescope. "I couldn't find the binoculars, but this should work, right?"

She moved it away from her face where she'd looked through it. It left a black ring around her eye. The rest of us burst out laughing. "What?" she asked without realizing what was wrong.

Dorothy gently took the telescope from her and used a tissue to clean the eyepiece. "Here's one for you too, Elsie."

"I don't know." Olivia considered Elsie's face. "I think the raccoon look is good on her."

Elsie cleaned her eye while Dorothy looked through the telescope. "What am I looking for?"

"All you have to do is say Brian's name when you put it up to your eye," she told Dorothy. Dorothy said Brian's name and looked into the telescope. "There he is. He went back to his place. He's leaving in his car."

"I hope he's not going to meet that awful sea witch," Olivia said.

"If he does, we'll know," I said.

"How are we going to rescue him if that happens?" Dorothy asked.

"I think our best bet is to find the sea witch before it happens," I told her. "I'm not sure yet how we're going to do it, but it would be better than waiting for her to kill him."

"Maybe Joe has some ideas," Olivia suggested.

"I'd rather not involve him in this. If the sea witch has enough power to kill Brian, she could definitely kill Joe." I mentally apologized to the Bone Man. Finding his wife was going to have to be put on the back burner for now. I wanted to keep Joe safe, but the danger to Brian was more imminent. "We'll have to look up what we can find on the habits of sea witches while we keep an eye on Brian."

"What about Belinda?" Dorothy asked. "Remember when my mother was killed and we could see some of what happened to her? Maybe we could see what happened to Sam."

Elsie groaned. "Do we really *want* to see that?"

"We might not have any choice." I agreed with Dorothy. "It could give us some clue to what the sea witch looks like."

"Good idea, Dorothy." Olivia applauded her daughter, her hands making no sound.

"We could get a look at the memorial book too," I said. "It's possible that the killer has been among us and we didn't know it because of her disguises. They say a killer always goes back to the scene."

"That sounds ambitious to me," Elsie said. "I might need a nap."

We spent a few hours in Smuggler's Arcane looking through dozens of books. We had a huge collection of magic treatises on various kinds of witches from around the world.

"Every one of these says the same basic thing," Dorothy finally said. "But all the sea witches in the world can't be the same."

"I'm sure they aren't." I stared thoughtfully at the book I'd just perused. "We're all different, but we have similar characteristics."

"It seems to me that the only thing sea witches have in common is that they kill when they mate," Elsie added.

"We need more personal information about this witch," Olivia said. "I think we're wasting our time here, girls. We need to get our boots on the ground if we hope to save Brian!"

We woke Larry and took him back to his boat before we headed to Southport. Joe had texted to let me know that the few leads he and Suzanne had been chasing had led to nothing.

"How's that working out with Joe and Suzanne, Molly?" Olivia asked from the backseat, where she sat with Dorothy.

"It's fine. There's nothing but the job between them now. I can feel it when I talk to Joe."

"I hope you're right," Elsie said. "There's nothing worse than having some strange woman in bed with you and your husband."

Olivia laughed. "I don't know. I never had a husband, but a strange woman isn't all that bad."

"What are we going to say to Belinda when we get there?" I asked. "I hate to get her hopes up that we can find Sam's killer. I'm sure she and her coven have similar ideas."

"I think she'll be glad for anyone to try anything," Olivia said. "It's better than people forgetting about Tyler."

"We won't be stepping on anyone's toes going out there like this, will we?" Dorothy questioned.

"I don't think so," I replied. "We'll see how Belinda reacts and go by that. I don't want to have hard feelings with her coven."

"But it's more important to keep Brian alive, right?" Dorothy continued. "Even if he never forgives me for turning him into a cardboard cutout, I'd like him to stay alive."

"I think we all agree on that," Elsie said. "Brian's almost a member of our little group. We can't let some traveling hussy take him out."

We got to Southport a short while later. I was surprised to see Joe and Suzanne at Belinda's house. His SUV was parked on the road. He and Suzanne were across the street on the beach. There was an area marked by crime-scene tape and guarded by a uniformed police officer. I assumed that was where Sam had been killed.

"Please try to be cautious what you say around Joe and Suzanne," I said. "I know it seems that Joe is impervious to the council seeing or hearing him, but we still have to be careful with Suzanne."

"Molly." Joe greeted me with a quick kiss on the cheek. "What are you doing out here?"

"Sam and his mother are part of our *club*," I explained with a lift of my eyebrows for emphasis. "We had a memorial for him at Smuggler's Arcane today. Belinda is such a good friend. We brought her a casserole."

Dorothy actually held out a casserole dish. "That's what we do in our club. When someone dies, we feed everyone."

Suzanne laughed. "I think that's what everyone in the south does. What kind of casserole is it?" She lifted the lid as I caught my breath, thinking it was only an empty dish. "*Mmm*. I love chicken and rice. It smells great."

Dorothy quickly closed the lid. "Thanks. It's a family recipe."

"So what brings *you* out here?" I asked Joe with a quick wink at Dorothy for her inventiveness.

"Still trying to figure out what happened. We decided to visit each crime scene again and hope that we missed something we can use."

"Is there any good news?" I asked him.

"I'm afraid not. We took our witness to the scenes and she drew a blank. We'll keep looking until we have a break in the case. You know how it is."

I did know how it was. Joe had been a homicide detective since I'd met him. He was methodical, and he never gave up. It was a difficult job that was sometimes very stressful. Some homicides cleared up quickly. Others were never solved, but he kept files on those and worked them on his own time.

"I guess we'd better go in," I said. "Good luck. I'll be glad when this is over."

"So will I." Suzanne smiled. "My goldfish misses me back in Savannah. Nice to see you again, Molly."

Joe and Suzanne went back to the SUV. I saw their witness in the backseat. As they drove by us, I was holding my amulet. The face on the witness wavered, somewhat like Olivia's ghostly visage.

I realized that the witness was using a glamour to disguise herself.

CHAPTER 29

*Look and see, look and see,
You will never know it's me.*

"Who was it under the glamour?" Elsie asked.

"I don't know. The face wasn't clear. But I think the witness may be using this opportunity to hide with Joe's help. She could even be the killer."

"There's nothing like hiding in plain sight!" Olivia suggested.

"How do you use a glamour?" Dorothy asked. "Is it like some magic makeup or something?"

"No." Elsie turned away for a moment. When she turned back, she looked like a different person.

"Lana Turner!" Olivia said.

Dorothy took a step back. "She looks like Elsie below the head. Just the face is different."

Elsie's face blurred for an instant, and then she looked normal again. "Wow. That was hard. I wouldn't want to try a full glamour."

"So a witch can change her appearance?" Dorothy smiled and nodded. "Cool. Is that a spell or what?"

"It's a spell, but a small one," I answered. "It's much easier to manipulate your appearance than to change Brian into a cardboard cutout. Even if you're doing a full body, all it takes is a little concentration and thinking about what you want to look like."

I walked away from her. When I turned back, her brown eyes were wide in her face.

"You look just like my mother."

"Now, that's not funny, Molly," Olivia complained. "At least Elsie did someone we don't really know."

"It takes a lot more to do a person's mannerisms and speech. You have to know your subject very well and concentrate to get it right." As I spoke, I'd taken on Olivia's voice and walk. I tossed my hair and wrung my hands as she frequently did.

"I'd say you've got that down," Elsie said. "Do me now, Molly."

I released the glamour I'd created and became myself again. "I think that's enough about glamour for now. We'll work on it later. Let's go inside and see Belinda."

Belinda and her sisters made up their coven. Elizabeth and Althea were there with her. The dining room table was heaped high with food, flowers and magic items to express sorrow at Sam's death.

"I'm happy to see you again so soon," Belinda said. "What made you decide to come all this way after we were just at the Arcane?"

"I know you've probably done some spells to discover who killed Sam," I started. "We think Brian Fuller may be next. We came out to take a look—with your permission. We don't want to cause any hard feelings, but sometimes extra eyes can be good."

Belinda and her sisters discussed it briefly. "We're fine with that, Molly, and welcome. Anything you can do to help catch Sam's killer is wonderful."

I took her hand. "I can't make any promises. But just as

the police look at the clues more than once, in this case, I think we should too."

"You'll have to do it." Belinda started crying. "I can't stand to see the shadows of Sam dying. I hope you understand."

"I do. We can go over there without you. Elizabeth and Althea are welcome to join us."

But Belinda's sisters decided to stay with her. They felt the same about seeing their nephew's death again.

Dorothy left the casserole on the table, and we walked back outside.

"You should've brought that with you," Elsie complained. "I'm starting to get a little peckish after that lunch. The rice smelled wonderful. What made you think of it?"

Dorothy smiled. "I was thinking about other funerals I've been to. My adopted mother told me you never go calling on people who have lost someone without food. I saw the recipe on the Food Channel last night. It stuck with me."

"Yes. She watches the Food Channel all the time," Olivia verified.

"I think that's just as good as you watching *Antiques Roadshow* all the time," Elsie said.

"It was very clever anyway," I congratulated Dorothy, "and some good magic. I like that you didn't have to be stressed emotionally to do it."

"Thanks, Molly." She smiled.

We took our time walking across the narrow, sand-washed street to the beach access. There weren't many houses at this end of Carolina Beach. Most of them were weathered and worn as though they'd been here for many decades. Some had a few new boards here and there from repairs to hurricane damage, but most had stood here facing the worst weather and survived.

I'd noticed that Belinda's kitchen window faced the ocean almost at the exact spot where the police were guarding

Sam's crime scene. I couldn't imagine anything worse for a mother than to have her child taken away.

The sea witch was clever and resourceful. If she was trying to mate, as Muriel had suggested, her path of destruction could keep growing. I thought again about Joe's witness. It could be her. She would know what was going on all the time by staying with him, and her account of Sam's death would protect her from the police—and other witches.

I hoped we'd be able to see the shadows of what had happened to Sam when we got to the murder site. We'd seen Olivia's death—it had been horrifying. I couldn't believe I wanted to see someone kill Sam. But if it would lead us to the killer, I knew it would be worth it.

"Are you sure about this, Molly? Elsie asked. "The last time, with Olivia, was dreadful."

"Elsie's right," Dorothy agreed. "I hoped we wouldn't have to do this again."

"I'm glad I wasn't there," Olivia chimed in. "I can't stand the sight of blood."

Dorothy shrugged and we kept walking.

An officer at the beach stopped us before we could enter the crime scene. The yellow tape, which was stapled to four poles, flapped mournfully in the ocean breeze. There were no swimmers, only a few surfers trying their luck with lackluster waves.

"You can't go past the tape," the officer explained. "There's been a murder. We might need to collect more evidence."

It made me feel a little better that I didn't know him as I muttered a confusion spell. I was as surprised as anyone when it worked and he wandered off to sit in his police car.

"Well, *someone* is feeling her oats today," Elsie remarked. "You didn't even ask for help with that spell."

"It's the amulet," Olivia said. "Even I can feel its emanations."

"I think it's great that Molly can do a spell by herself." Dorothy smiled and patted my back. "Congrats!"

Why didn't I feel any better after that glowing support? Instead I felt like someone who needed to have her hand held while she crossed the street.

Olivia and Elsie both snickered at Dorothy's response.

I took the high road and didn't say a thing about Dorothy's tone, which she might have used with a toddler at the library. "Let's get this done quickly. I didn't create the spell to last for long."

We went inside the crime scene. There were shoe prints and crushed plants but no blood, as Joe had said of the previous deaths. The police were lucky the attack had taken place far enough from the surf that the crime scene hadn't been affected by high tide.

"Let's hold hands and use our tools to enhance what we can see," I said.

Olivia was hovering over us, buffeted but not really affected by the strong wind. She had a look of profound sorrow on her face. I wished I could reach across and hold her hand too. But even a witch couldn't reach through that barrier.

Because there was no blood, it made seeing Sam's death harder. Bonds of blood and friendship had made finding the shadows that had remained after Olivia's death easier for us. But finally, Sam's shadow form began to reveal itself. We waited patiently to see the killer.

These were shadows from the past. Nothing could be done to change them. The shadows only revealed themselves for a short time before the past was wiped clean, like the beach after a storm.

The image of the killer began to form. It was the shape of a man. He was holding Sam in a passionate embrace— body pressed to body. If I hadn't known that Sam was dying, I would have thought the look on Sam's face was one of ecstasy. The killer's arms were wrapped so tightly around him that it was difficult to tell where one of them began and the other ended. I couldn't see the killer's face.

The terrible tableau was fading. The shadows were beginning to diminish in the bright sunlight. I was about to turn away, disgusted that we couldn't see more of the killer, when the man holding Sam let him drop to the sand. For one brief instant, I saw the man's face.

So did Elsie. "That must be the man you saw with Joe. He was definitely using a glamour to conceal himself."

"I thought you said it was a woman." Dorothy was crying. "It looked to me like Sam was killed by a man."

"That's glamour," I explained. "But it was an incredibly strong glamour. Hurry, ladies. Let's get back to the car so I can call Joe. He needs to know that his witness is the killer."

CHAPTER 30

Light pass through me, light pass through me,
No one can see, no one can see.
I hide amongst you,
No one can see.

We knocked on Belinda's door again. She didn't have a land-line, just a cell phone she had to take outside to find a signal. We walked around in her yard looking for bars with our cell phones up in the air, but we couldn't find enough to call.

"What happened?" Belinda demanded. "What did you see?"

I put my hand on her arm, conscious of the time that had passed since Joe had left us. The killer could have decided to end his or her masquerade and kill Joe and Suzanne.

"There was nothing that you missed. I'm so sorry. The killer was the witness I saw with my husband. He doesn't know."

"Wait! *What?*" Belinda yelled as she followed us back to the car. She jumped in with no explanation to her sisters.

I didn't wait any longer, and the sand flew under my tires as I put my foot down hard on the gas.

"Go, Speed Racer!" Elsie chuckled. "I can feel the g-force pushing me back."

"Molly, explain what you mean," Belinda said. "I saw

the killer on the beach with Sam. I saw Joe's witness too. They didn't look alike to me at all."

"I only caught the real witch out of the corner of my eye as Joe was leaving," I explained. "She was using a strong glamour."

"Why couldn't I see it?" she asked.

"Probably because you're too emotionally involved," Olivia offered. "Would you mind scooting over just a little? You're practically sitting on me."

"Oh, sorry." Belinda moved closer to Dorothy. "I'm not used to sharing space with a ghost."

"That's all right. It happens." Olivia seemed pleased with her answer.

As we were leaving Carolina Beach, Dorothy remarked that she had a cell phone signal. "It's like there was a little bubble of no-cell phone use over the beach. Maybe a witch did that so people could enjoy their vacations."

I stopped her meandering. "Call Joe."

"Sure. Sorry." Dorothy punched in his number as I gave it to her. "There we are."

The phone was ringing—she had it on speakerphone. I kept hoping Joe would pick up, but there was no answer.

"Maybe he didn't want to talk and drive," Elsie said. "Many people don't, you know."

"I think he would have answered if he could." I might be able to protect him from the council with my deal with the Bone Man, but there was no one I could make a deal with to protect him from everything.

My hands tightened on the steering wheel, and I sped up. The roads were empty. I didn't see where speeding could cause any harm. I needed to reach Joe. That was enough motive for me.

"I think we have a tail, Molly," Olivia remarked. "It might be an unmarked cop car. He's coming in really close. And—now he's turning on his siren and lights."

"You'll have to stop and explain what's happening," Dorothy said.

I put my foot down harder on the gas pedal. "No, I won't. Let him follow me, if he wants. He can help if Joe needs us. Or we can tell him what happened."

"Or you could do one of those nifty confusion spells and we could get away," Elsie said cheerfully. "Dorothy says you're *very* good at them."

"Seriously, Molly." Belinda was holding tight to the armrest on her side of the backseat. "How fast are you going? If we're killed, we can't help Joe or Sam."

But I wasn't slowing down. Not until I'd reached Joe and knew he was all right. I didn't flinch when the officer behind me started flashing his headlights or when another police car joined in the chase.

"Now, this is an adventure," Elsie said. "I don't think we've ever done anything like this before."

"I don't think we should be doing it now either," Olivia fretted. "Molly, you know my only child is in this car. Please slow down."

"Look!" I pointed and put my foot on the brake. "There's Joe's SUV."

The black vehicle was parked off the road on the sandy shoulder. Three of the doors were open. I parked behind it, skidding to a stop, and got out to check on Joe.

"Hold it right there, ma'am." A young officer jumped out of the first police car and drew his gun. "You're under arrest for speeding, reckless driving and failure to yield."

I completely ignored him and didn't stop moving until I'd reached the SUV.

Joe was slumped behind the wheel. I checked him. He had a pulse, but he was unconscious. There were no bumps or bruises, but the smell of magic was everywhere.

Suzanne was unconscious in the passenger seat.

The witness was gone.

"I said *stop*." The officer ran up behind me and grabbed my arm. "What the hell is going on?"

"This is my husband, Detective Joe Renard. He called me and said he and his partner were in trouble. We were a few minutes behind him leaving Carolina Beach. Call for an ambulance."

"Okay. Okay." He called it in on his radio. "Was there someone else?"

"They were transporting a witness in a homicide investigation. Joe had some idea that the witness wasn't who she was pretending to be. I guess she attacked him and fled the vehicle. Maybe you should look for her and we'll stay here until help arrives."

The officer wasn't sure. "You broke the law, ma'am. I understand you had a good reason, but—"

"I was speeding. The man you should be looking for is a *murderer*. Weigh your options carefully, Officer."

"Yes ma'am." He started across the road, calling to the other officer who'd parked behind him.

I slumped against Joe. I hoped the spell was something that would wear off quickly. I didn't dare try to get rid of it without knowing what it was. At least he was still alive.

Dorothy examined Suzanne. "She's still breathing."

"I didn't even check her," I said regretfully.

Elsie put her hand on my shoulder. "It's okay. You were worried about Joe. Who cares about his ex-wife anyway?"

That didn't make me feel any better as I watched the EMS techs arrive and put Suzanne on a stretcher. She might have been dead. I hadn't even thought about her.

Two techs were with Joe. They were trying to figure out why he was unconscious. He didn't respond to any stimuli. "Maybe he was drugged," one of the techs guessed.

"Let's get him out of here," the other said. "He's stable. They can figure it out at the hospital."

Because Joe's SUV was part of a crime, a tow truck arrived

to haul it to the impound lot. I gave the keys for my car to Dorothy so I could ride in the ambulance with Joe.

"He's going to be fine," she assured me with tears in her eyes. "I'm sure of it."

I hugged her. "Maybe you should take Belinda home first. You can drop Elsie off and go home. I'll take a taxi to your house when I know Joe is okay."

"Sure. Don't worry about a thing. I'll take care of it."

The young officer who'd wanted to arrest me helped me into the back of the ambulance. "We're calling for backup so we have more people to cover the area. The person who hurt your husband couldn't have gotten far on foot."

"Thank you. And I'm sorry you had to chase me. My husband would completely understand if you give me a ticket."

He smiled. "I hope my wife would be willing to disregard some laws to help me if I was hurt. Good luck, ma'am."

CHAPTER 31

I shall not fear.
Though fear stalks me,
I shall not fear.

The hospital was quiet and sterile, like always. I sat next to Joe and held his hand. He was still unconscious—after a barrage of tests that told the doctors nothing was wrong with him, except that he was unconscious.

They were still checking his blood for drugs, though they couldn't find needle marks or signs of ingestion or inhalation. I knew they wouldn't find conventional answers. I could only guess at the spell used against him. I knew it would be better to let him wake up on his own, if possible. At least he was safe from anything else happening to him until then.

I sighed when I thought of how many times I'd been at the hospital with him down through the years. There had been knife and bullet wounds, concussions and scrapes. He'd been punched, kicked and assaulted too many other ways to remember each one.

"I should've married an accountant," I whispered as I touched his face. "You don't hear of people in that profession getting hurt all the time."

But he was good at what he did, and he loved it. I had already faced the possibility that he might decide not to retire. It wasn't mandatory. It was a random number that he had picked.

What would he do without cases to solve? For that matter, what would I do without magic?

"Is he okay?" Olivia hovered over us.

"I think so. He isn't awake yet, but the doctor says he's fine except for that." My lips trembled as I smiled. "I guess if you're here, Dorothy and Elsie must be in the waiting room."

"I'm the advance scout." She grinned. "I'm so sorry this happened to Joe, Molly. Should you try something to wake him up?"

"I'm afraid to try anything without knowing the spell. And if this really is a glamourized sea witch, I don't know if our magic is compatible."

She nodded. "Best to let nature take its course, then. I'll tell Dorothy and Elsie that the two of you are decent. Elsie seemed to think you might be in here tickling the ivories, if you know what I mean. I told her you and Joe are too old for that kind of thing."

"Thanks. I don't think we're quite that old yet."

"I came in with my eyes closed, just to be on the safe side. I'll get Dorothy and Elsie."

I felt something odd envelop the room when she was gone. It was cold and damp. I could see my breath in the mist that developed. Without hesitation, I threw up a protective spell around us. I hoped it wasn't the sea witch returning to finish the job. I went quickly over spells I could possibly use against her, and held my amulet tight.

"Don't worry, Molly. I am not here to harm your man."

The Bone Man was standing in front of the door. I could hear Elsie and Dorothy outside knocking. He wouldn't let them in. Even Olivia seemed unable to cross that barrier.

"Do you know who did this?" For once my voice was quivering with anger instead of fear.

"Have you found my wife?"

"No. But I might have a lead on her."

He smiled, his black eyes laughing at me. "Then you have nothing to trade."

"We're talking about Joe's life," I reminded him.

"Yes. I know. And I am protecting him, as I promised. Your end of the deal is lacking, Molly. I do not like coming to your world to remind you of this."

I didn't like him coming there either. He dwarfed the small hospital room. The contrast of him against the white walls and sparse furnishings made him seem even more like a nightmare. It was different when I could control when and where I saw him. Seeing him in a place like this was terrifying.

"I'm doing the best I can. I don't have your magic, where you can make someone invisible to the council."

"Don't you?" He laughed, the sound scratching my nerves. "Yet you made the trade, not I. Finish what you began, witch. Find my wife."

He was gone as quickly as he'd arrived.

The door opened and Dorothy almost fell into the room. "What happened?" she asked. "Why didn't you open the door?"

"The Bone Man was here." I dropped into the chair beside Joe again. "He wants his wife."

"Molly, we have to give up trying to find this killer witch and find the Bone Man's wife," Elsie said. "You have to think of Joe first."

"Well, she's kind of caught in the middle," Olivia said. "If she doesn't find the Bone Man's wife, Joe won't be safe from the council. If she doesn't find the sea witch, she could kill Joe or Brian."

"Really, I think it would be better for him to lose his memory than to be killed," Elsie said. "But that's just me."

"No. You're right," Dorothy agreed. "We didn't get the memorial book from Belinda so we can check out those names. One of them could be the witch who did this to Joe. Who's with me?"

"I'm always with you," Olivia said. "At least, as long as you have the staff."

"I'm not leaving until Joe wakes up," I answered. "We'll have to go back out to Carolina Beach tomorrow. Belinda isn't going to throw away the memorial guest list. We can look through it as soon as I know Joe is all right."

"We can go without you," Elsie volunteered. "It's not like we have anything else to do. That way we'll have the names for tomorrow."

I got up and hugged both living witches. "Thank you for your help. I'll let you know if anything changes here. Be careful out there. We don't know exactly what we're up against."

"We'll pop by and check on Isabelle too," Elsie said. "You take it easy on yourself, Molly. We'll see you tomorrow."

I was so blessed to have such good friends. Dorothy was a lot like Olivia—she had a good heart. That was about where the resemblance ended. But I enjoyed being with both of them, and I was glad that Olivia had managed to come back and knew her daughter.

Joe was still sleeping at dinnertime. I ate his hospital food, which they brought in on a tray. I never cared for lime Jell-O, but it was better than nothing. The roast beef was soggy and the creamed potatoes were like glue. It was hospital food. I hadn't expected anything more.

He was still asleep at midnight. It was beginning to bother me. Not that I was upset with him—I kept thinking I should do something. I went to check on Suzanne. She was still out too. Whatever the spell was, it was powerful. It could last for another hour, another day, another year. There was no way to know.

My earlier feelings were that Joe should wake naturally, but suppose he didn't? I would have made this stupid deal with the Bone Man for nothing. It wasn't just a matter of backing out. Even if he weren't protecting Joe, he'd still expect me to keep up my end.

I took Joe's hand. Anything I did could make his condition better, or worse. Or could have no effect at all. The magic was so strong. I'd never felt its like before.

Try the magic in the amulet.

It was a random thought running through my head, and yet maybe it was possible. Was the sea witch's magic similar to what was in the amulet? Was it possible it could overcome the spell placed on Joe?

I looked at his dear, handsome face in the dim light. The heart monitor beeped in time to his breathing. Did I dare take a chance on his life? He might never wake up.

Either way—using magic or not—sounded bad to me. A year ago, before I'd begun wearing the amulet, I wouldn't have even considered it. My aging magic had been too erratic. I couldn't have trusted it. Now, with the amulet, I felt the new strain of magic flowing through me. I felt strong again, young again. I believed I could help Joe and Suzanne.

But did I dare?

CHAPTER 32

I am not afraid,
I am not afraid.
Moon guide me,
Sun aid me.
I am not afraid.

Before I could make a less emotional decision, Joe's heart monitor began making an odd sound. The number of heartbeats had slowed, alerting the medical professionals to the fact that he was failing.

It seemed as though my hand was being forced into using my magic to help him. I couldn't stand there and let him die. I had to act.

Before the nurses and doctors could respond to the new emergency, I placed one hand on his chest and held the amulet in the other hand. I closed my eyes and recalled a rejuvenation spell. It was all I could think of with no spell book to guide me. I repeated the old words again and again as my hand grew warm against him. The amulet felt as though it were on fire.

"Get the crash cart," someone yelled from behind me. "I'm sorry, Mrs. Renard. You'll have to leave the room now."

A bevy of nurses buzzed in behind the lead doctor. I finished my spell with a cleansing breath and gave thanks for Joe's life.

"Someone get her out of here!" the doctor yelled again. "Get that crash cart. Wake up, people! One of Wilmington's finest is dying."

Joe's eyes fluttered open. He stared at me for a long moment, and then finally smiled. "Molly?"

A nurse reset the heart monitor. "I think the machine was just going crazy, Doctor."

Another nurse helped Joe sit up as she saw him struggling to move.

"What's going on?" Joe asked. "Where am I? Where's Suzanne?"

It hit me that I needed to pay Suzanne a visit before she started crashing too. I had ignored her at the accident scene. I wouldn't do it again.

The doctor and nurses hovered, taking Joe's vitals and asking him questions. I waved to him and then went to find Suzanne. My heart was still pounding. It had been terrifying taking his life in my hands.

Suzanne was still slumbering peacefully when I went into her room. There was no one there with her. Savannah was a long way off. Maybe there wasn't time for family to come here, or maybe she didn't have anyone. I wasn't sure.

I did exactly the same thing for Suzanne that I'd done for Joe. A moment later, her eyes opened and fixed on me. "Molly? Where are we? Where's Joe?"

"We're at the hospital. Joe's here too. What do you remember about the witness's escape?"

Her brows knit together. She looked confused. "I'm not sure. I heard him laughing in the backseat. A minute later, something stung me—at least, that's what it felt like. The pain was terrible. I guess I blacked out. Then I woke up and you're here."

"It's going to be fine now, Suzanne. You and Joe are okay, although you might be off the street for a few days. Take care. I'm going back to see Joe. Is there anyone I can call for you?"

She smiled sadly. "Nope. Joe is as close to family as I

get. I hope that doesn't bother you. I don't mean it in a bad way. Joe and I aren't like that anymore."

"I know. Rest now. You'll be fine."

I left Suzanne's room and put my back against the cool wall to take a deep breath. I was so grateful that I could help them—and that nothing bad had happened when I'd done it. I fingered my amulet with a smile. Maybe Olivia and Elsie thought that using this ancient magic was bad, but it had served me well.

Joe's room was right down the hall. I straightened up and went to see him.

Only his main doctor was left in the room. He was explaining what he believed had happened to Joe and Suzanne.

"It sounds ridiculous, but we found that both of you were affected by puffer fish poison."

"That doesn't sound so much ridiculous as impossible," Joe said.

I went to stand next to the bed, and I took his hand.

The doctor shrugged. "Maybe so, but that's what our tox screens showed in both of you."

"We were driving down the road when we were attacked," Joe told him, "not in the water."

"Well, whatever. It looks as though you're going to be fine. I'd like you to stay until at least tomorrow—maybe another night."

"Thanks, but no thanks. We're in the middle of a homicide investigation. It looks as though the one witness we had is involved in the two local deaths. He may even be the killer."

"It's two A.M." The doctor looked at his watch. "Get some sleep, and we'll see how it goes later today."

"Sure." Joe shook his hand. "Thanks, doctor."

When we were alone, I sat beside the bed again. "How do you feel?"

"Starving. I hope you have a big T-bone and a baked potato in your purse."

"I have a few Tic Tacs." I smiled at him. "I'm sorry. I ate

your yummy green Jell-O for dinner with your terrible potatoes and soggy roast beef."

"No wonder I'm hungry." He grinned. "I guess they'll have to bring two trays so I don't starve to death."

I kissed him and smoothed back the silver streaks in his black hair. "That was too close. What do you remember?"

"I felt something—like a bee sting—and nothing after that. Was that some kind of *club* thing?"

"Yes. I think your witness is actually your suspect. The *club* noticed that the man's face was shifting." I couldn't think of any other way to explain it without going into a lengthy explanation of glamour.

"Shifting?" He glanced around the room and whispered, "You mean like a hologram?"

"Something like that. Hiding in plain sight, I guess."

"And now he's gone."

"I have good club information that your suspect is really a woman. Her club is very strong. You were lucky she didn't kill you."

"But why use puffer fish poison? Where would she even get something like that?"

"She's one with the sea. She probably brought it with her. I can't explain everything to you right now, but she's very dangerous and powerful. Maybe you should take some vacation time. You and Suzanne have both earned it."

"Suzanne!" He sat up. "Is she okay?"

"Yes. Lie down. Get some rest. I'll see if I can find something for you to eat."

He pulled me back. "You're not doing anything with this woman's *club* from the sea, are you?"

"No. Don't worry. I'll be right back."

I went to the cafeteria and found some crackers, a candy bar and a Coke in a vending machine. I took it back to Joe, but he was asleep again. It was nice to see that it was a natural sleep.

Thinking that Suzanne might be hungry too, I took my

haul to her room. She was awake and hungry. The doctor had told her the same thing that he'd told Joe.

"I'm not sure I've ever heard of a killer using puffer fish poison as a weapon." She munched down the crackers between gulps of Coke. "Things keep getting weirder. I wonder if that's what the killer used on all the victims. I doubt the medical examiners would have thought to check for that poison. But how did he inject it? I searched him. He didn't have a needle on him."

"I don't know. I'm glad you and Joe are okay. I think maybe you should take some time—both of you."

"Seriously?" She frowned at me. "In the middle of a homicide investigation? I don't want to trail this killer up to Virginia Beach. We need to stop him now."

I knew she'd feel the same way as Joe. I doubted that I could convince either of them to take a break. I couldn't even use magic references with her. I'm sure she thought I was just overly concerned.

"It will be okay, Molly." She ripped open the candy bar. "We know to keep a better eye on this guy now. I'll take care of Joe."

With their recent history, I doubted it, but I smiled and kept it to myself.

"Joe is a wonderful person. He always has been," she said. "I'm glad he found someone like you."

"Thanks. I'm glad he did too."

"We just had too many issues when we were married. It was kid stuff, looking back on it. I didn't want to stay in Wilmington. He did. I was looking for adventure. Joe was never the adventurous kind. He liked being at home, watching football on Sunday. That wasn't for me, although you'd never know it now. Where did I go? Savannah. What an adventure!"

"You've been there awhile," I reminded her. "I guess that's what you were looking for."

She grinned, but there was something in her eyes that made me realize she was serious. "I think I've been looking for Joe ever since we split up. I just didn't realize it until we met again. I was stupid to leave him. I wish he had a brother."

I laughed at the last part—Joe was an only child. But knowing she meant what she said about wanting to be with him again made me aware again of their previous relationship.

After she'd finished eating, I told her that I should go so she could get some rest.

"Thanks for being here with me, Molly. I know this has been awkward for you. Me too. I appreciate you not holding it against me."

I was exhausted. I took a taxi home and fell into bed. Isabelle promised to keep watch while I slept. I barely heard what she said before I was asleep. I dreamed about the ocean and Manannan MacLir being chased by a hideous-looking woman who I assumed must have been the sea witch.

There was something to these dreams—to the interplay of the Bone Man's wife and the sea witch killing young men. I felt as though the dots were starting to connect for me.

It was nine A.M. when I awoke to an overcast day. I couldn't remember when I'd ever slept so late. As I became more aware, I realized that I wasn't alone. Elsie was sitting on the bed beside me. Dorothy was in the chair. Olivia was hovering over me.

"Thank goodness," Elsie said. "I thought you were going to sleep all day."

Dorothy moved over and sat on the bed too. "How's Joe? What time did you get back?"

I sat against on my pillow, realizing that I was still wearing the clothes I'd come home in last night. I really had been tired. "Joe and Suzanne are both fine. I got back around three. I need a shower, a few minutes alone and a strong cup of coffee."

"Green tea and breakfast would be better," Elsie said. "I'll make you some eggs. You have to keep up your strength."

"Have we considered that Suzanne could be the sea witch?" Olivia asked. "She's been everywhere the killings have taken place. She wants Joe. I think she could be evil."

"I don't think she's evil." I threw back the sheet and blanket. "I think she's lonely and looking back on the mistakes she's made in her life. Not too much different than any other woman her age."

"Did the doctors know what was wrong with them?" Dorothy asked.

"They were both injected with puffer fish poison, although Suzanne swears she checked their witness carefully before they left the safe house."

"But a magical, dead creature of the sea could have access to that kind of thing," Olivia said. "It's a wonder they both aren't dead."

"I suppose that's true." I got up and stretched. "I'll see you two in the kitchen."

When I had showered and dressed, I felt much better. I called the hospital. Joe was being released later that afternoon. Suzanne too, so I could pick them both up. I'd have to go to Dorothy's house to get my car. The world seemed a better place again.

Elsie had scrambled all the eggs in the refrigerator. She and Dorothy helped me eat them at the table in the garden. All around us life was coming back to the world. Birds nested in the trees and added their voices to the morning. Azaleas were splendidly in bloom along with daffodils and tulips. There was even some wisteria perfuming the garden for us.

"So we got the memorial guest book from Belinda last night." Dorothy produced the small book out of her bag. "Mom and I went through it last night and I created a spreadsheet from the names."

"She's very efficient." Olivia beamed at her daughter.

"Who'd have thought she'd be good at something like that? I never was. She must get it from her father's side."

"Is all that necessary?" Elsie righted her peach-colored hat. "We could just separate the names magically like this."

She muttered a spell and the printed spreadsheet Dorothy had created caught fire and burned in her hands. Dorothy jumped up with a yelp and dropped the paper to the ground.

"Sorry." Elsie sipped her tea and looked the other way.

"I guess we're back to looking through the book and writing the names of the witches we don't know on a piece of paper." Dorothy smiled, but she was obviously a little annoyed.

We pulled our chairs together and studied the book. Olivia looked over our shoulders.

"We know the sea witch isn't Phoebe or Kay," Elsie said. "We've known them for years. Oh look—Larry signed the guest book too. Doesn't he have lovely penmanship?"

She giggled, and we moved on.

"Not Adrian, or Nora," Olivia said. "They're old friends too. And Althea and Elizabeth are Belinda's sisters. We've known them forever."

"What about Marlie Eubanks? I don't recognize that name." Elsie pointed at it.

"Let's write that down." I grabbed a piece of paper from the desk in the living room. "I also don't know Zack Nelson or Emma Rhodes."

Olivia and Elsie agreed.

"What about Portia de Winter?" Dorothy questioned.

"She's only been in the area for a few months while she was setting up the full moon celebration," I told her.

"But she's with the council," Elsie reminded us.

"We should check on her for sure," Olivia said. "Since when do we trust the council?"

"Four people we don't really know from the list." I looked

at the names. "That's not too bad. We can find them and be on guard against the sea witch's glamour."

"We should be able to do that." Elsie looked away, and when she looked back, her face resembled Cary Grant's. "By George, I believe we can do it."

Dorothy laughed and even Olivia chuckled.

"I wish it was that obvious," I said. "Everyone be sure to bring your magic tool with you. I don't have to get Joe from the hospital until later today. We should have enough time to check out these witches."

"Fortune favors the bold," Elsie/Cary said as she picked up her plate, glass and silverware. "We shall come back victorious, or on our shields."

CHAPTER 33

Witch's cat, witch's cat,
Watching the night,
Run away, run away
Into the light.

We went to Dorothy's. She and Olivia wanted us to come inside and listen to Hemlock talk about his past.

"He only spends time in the library," Olivia said. "I think he might actually be reading the books."

We spent ten minutes listening to Hemlock recount tales of his life in ancient Greece. He seemed a little puzzled to be in the New World, as he called it.

"He thought this was Atlantis," Dorothy said with a laugh. "He was disappointed when I told him it wasn't. It's amazing all that information was inside my cat and I never knew it."

"People who don't talk to cats don't know what they're missing," Elsie said.

I reminded everyone gently that we were on a mission. It was lovely conversing with Hemlock, but there were things to be done.

We took my car back to my house, and Dorothy drove the Mercedes. Olivia insisted the car wasn't being driven enough, since Dorothy only wanted to drive the Beetle.

We were in the process of changing cars when Abdon Fuller joined us with Cassandra at his side.

"I'm looking for my grandson. Have you seen or talked to him?" he demanded with no preliminary.

"Good morning to you too, starshine," Elsie said. "The earth says hello."

He frowned at her and focused on Dorothy. "I know he was at that hovel you call a shop yesterday. I lost track of him after that."

He glanced at Cassandra with a murderous expression that said that *she* had lost track of him. She pushed her hair back behind one ear and feigned boredom, staring at her fingernails.

"He was at Smuggler's Arcane," Dorothy admitted. "But he left. I tried calling him several times during the night. There was no answer."

"You have strong magic," Elsie said. "Why don't you do a finding spell? Or a locator spell?"

"Don't you think I've tried that? It's as though he disappeared from the earth."

"He may be underwater and in danger," I told him. "The sea witch that Cassandra warned us about has killed two young men in the area. I'd hate Brian to be the third, but he's showing signs that he could be next."

"No sea witch would *dare* attack my grandson," Abdon roared. "He's probably hiding himself from the likes of you. I don't know why I bothered coming here. Come, Cassandra."

Abdon vanished. Cassandra stayed long enough to tell us to call her if we heard anything from Brian. Then she was gone too.

"And you can buy that ability to pop in and out, huh?" Elsie asked. "I wonder how much it costs. I have some money saved up. I'd like to be able to dramatically disappear at will."

"I'm afraid Brian is really in trouble," Dorothy said. "I

went to his apartment again last night. He hasn't been home. Could we try looking for him through the telescope before we go talk to those witches?"

We were at the shop ten minutes later. I fed Harper while Elsie and Dorothy took out the spelled telescope to search for Brian. Olivia tried to get Harper to play with her, but while he acknowledged her, he wasn't interested in playing.

"It's really odd not hearing his thoughts," Olivia said. "After years of having him in my head, it feels empty in there now."

"Any sign of him?" Elsie asked Dorothy who was holding the telescope to her eye.

"No. I don't see him anywhere." Dorothy turned to me. "Would we be able to see him if the sea witch took him underwater?"

"I don't think so. I think we'd need a different spell for that."

"And maybe a pair of magic goggles," Elsie said. "How else could you open your eyes underwater?"

"What should we do?" Dorothy was suddenly panic-stricken.

"I know this is only a theory." I put my hands on her shoulders. "But I think the sea witch is the Bone Man's wife. I think they're the same."

Elsie drew in a deep breath. "Why would you think that, Molly?"

"Dreams and intuition. The sea witch and the Bone Man's wife keep coming back together. A sea witch is a dead witch given to the ocean. Sometimes they return. The first dream I had was about the sea god getting there too late to save his love from the fire. I know it sounds crazy, but I'm sure that was the Bone Man and his wife. I think he couldn't let her go. He put her in the water even though he knew what she'd become."

"Why wouldn't he tell you about it?" Elsie asked.

"Because that's the way he is," Olivia answered. "We all know he's as slippery as an eel. He doesn't admit anything unless he has to. I wouldn't put it past him to set Molly on the track of a murdering witch just so he wouldn't have to go get her himself."

"That's harsh," Dorothy said. "I thought you had a good time with him on the island when he took your staff."

Olivia fussed with her blond hair as she would have when she was still alive. But now it never changed. "That was different. I understand the way he thinks—though I didn't know he was a sea god. I suppose that could explain a few . . . *different* things."

I didn't want to know what those things were. "Let's stay focused, ladies. If the sea witch is actually someone from the memorial book list, we'd better be careful how we approach this. She could have Brian stashed somewhere. She could try to kill us."

"How are we ever going to get her to go back to Oak Island?" Elsie asked. "Obviously it's not somewhere she wants to be."

"Or maybe she goes out and sows her wild oats every hundred years or so and then goes back," Olivia suggested.

"But if that's her normal routine, why ask me to find her and bring her back?"

"And how do we rescue Brian from her?" Dorothy asked.

There were no answers to the questions. We piled back into the Mercedes. Dorothy brought the spelled telescope with her. Elsie hid her sword under her green-and-peach-colored shawl.

I looked at my amulet in the mirror before we left the shop. I hoped it was powerful enough to help me through this.

Elsie had managed to spell a phone book so we could find the witches we needed to talk to. The closest one to us was Zack Nelson. He lived in downtown Wilmington, close to Thalian Hall, the old theater.

"Maybe I should pop over there while you all talk to Zack," Olivia said. "You know everyone claims Thalian Hall is haunted. I wouldn't mind spending some time with my people. I might learn a thing or two. It would be nice to understand my ghostly powers."

"I think you should stay with us, Olivia," I told her. "Remember the part about one of these witches possibly being a murderous sea witch? We might need your help."

"Well, of course, Molly. But I don't know what good I can be without knowing what I can do. Maybe I can visit Thalian Hall alone later."

"I'll be glad to take you over there, Mom. I'm surprised there aren't any ghosts in our house, as old as it is."

"Honey, I'm sure if there had been any ghosts, witches would have kicked them out years ago. As you've noticed, we aren't exactly ghost-friendly."

Zack lived in an older house that had been made into apartments. We found his name by the door on his mailbox in the downstairs entrance. When we pushed the call button, he answered and we explained that we were from Smuggler's Arcane and wanted to talk to him for a moment.

He was happy to see us, and he even brought out homemade chocolate chip cookies and milk, which completely endeared him to Elsie right away. Olivia was taken with his charming Southern-gentleman manners and good looks.

We sat in a small solarium, eating and drinking, while I tried to devise a plan so we'd know if he was the sea witch. Because the power of glamour could be so strong, I couldn't trust my eyes. I didn't think I'd have been able to see the glamour the killer had put on before attacking Joe and Suzanne if she hadn't been distracted.

"Would you mind if I used your restroom?" I asked.

Zack smiled handsomely. He'd been showing us dozens of the orchids that he grew. "Of course. It's the third door to the right, Molly. Be sure to try the lavender soap. I made it myself. The perfume is exceptional."

Dorothy seemed to be the only one cognizant of my dilemma. "I have to go too, Molly. I'll come with you."

Zack and Elsie both looked surprised, but no one said anything. Olivia sighed as she continued to study his beautiful face and muscular body.

"This looks odd," I whispered to Dorothy as we went to the bathroom together.

"Women always do it in restaurants." She shrugged. "What do you have in mind? What's the plan?"

"There isn't one. We should have thought of what we were going to do before we got here. I think Elsie and Olivia might be too taken by Zack to be much good."

"Maybe we could throw water on him," Dorothy suggested. "What's the standard practice for taking away a sea witch's glamour?"

"I don't think there is one. Sea witches are so rare—like witches who become ghosts. I'm not sure what to do."

We surveyed the bathroom, admiring its homey touches. The lavender soap perfumed the entire room. The hand towels matched the color of the soap, and pretty purple plants grew in the windowsill.

Dorothy nodded. "Leave it to me. I have a plan."

Before I could ask what that plan was, she was already on her way back to the solarium. I stayed in the pretty bathroom and filled the sink with water, bathing my face, using my fingers to smooth water on my eyelids. I invoked a water spell for clear sight and hoped that might help. I realized it might not be enough for a really sophisticated glamour, but it was the only appropriate spell that came to mind.

I smelled the lavender soap. It was very nice, but I only needed pure water. I went back and sat in the chair I'd vacated.

Zack looked the same as he had before I'd done the spell.

Either he was who he said he was or I couldn't crack his magic. I *was* able to see that his credit score was poor and he was having trouble with his wisdom teeth.

I shrugged when Dorothy raised her brows.

She nodded, assuming I couldn't see anything, and got to her feet. She closed her eyes and invoked a spell for strength before she punched Zack hard in the face.

He dropped back in his blue velvet chair, his hand pressed to his jaw. "Why did you do that, Dorothy?"

She narrowed her eyes, studying him closely. "Are *you* the sea witch?"

"What is she talking about?" he asked Elsie in pain and confusion.

"Unless I'm very much mistaken, I think she was trying to make you angry so you'd shake off your glamour. A good ploy, really."

"Except that anyone can tell that no glamour could make a face so perfect," Olivia simpered, probably trying to make amends. "You'll have to forgive her. She's new to being a witch."

"At *her* age? What has she been doing all her life?" Zack stared at Dorothy in horror. "Of course I'm not a sea witch. Your mother is right. *Anyone* could tell that."

Dorothy's actions put an end to the almost partylike atmosphere there had been only moments before. We left soon after. I didn't expect to be invited back at any time in the future.

"I think we can cross him off the list, don't you?" Elsie asked. "And by that I mean *any* list that young man ever makes with witch's names on it."

"What in the world were you doing?" Olivia asked Dorothy. "I can't believe that adopted mother of yours didn't teach you better manners."

"Back me up here, Molly," Dorothy implored. "It would've worked if Zack was the sea witch. I punched him so he'd be distracted and in pain, like it said in the books we looked through. If he'd been trying to hide who really is, his glamour would've slipped."

"I think, before we visit anyone else, we should come up with a better plan," I said in the kindest way possible. "I really don't think Zach is the sea witch. Who's next?"

CHAPTER 34

Water clear and water bright,
Clear my mind and make it right,
Cleanse my eyes and cleanse my soul,
Let the truth now be whole.

Emma Rhodes was next on the list. She lived in the newer part of Wilmington just off Military Cutoff Road. We passed the big branch of the New Hanover Public Library, and Dorothy squealed.

"I've always wanted to work at this branch," she said. "I just don't want to drive every day."

"We're going to have to write down the next addresses," Elsie informed us. "The spell on the phone book is fading."

"I can just look them up on my phone," Dorothy volunteered with a smile.

"I suppose you could do it that way." Elsie frowned and muttered something about gadgets.

"She lives in those apartments." I pointed when I saw the sign. "This time, let's be more prepared. If Zack had been the sea witch, I'm afraid we'd be dead by now."

Elsie giggled. "Or asleep like Joe and Suzanne."

"And Zack could kiss us to wake us up." Olivia sighed. "Just like a fairy tale."

"Except that Zack would be the one who'd have put the curse on us," Dorothy reminded her. "It's unlikely that he'd want to help us."

"I suppose that's true," Olivia agreed. "You're not very romantic, are you?"

I interrupted. "What can we do to make sure we're safe? All I could think of was a water spell for clarity. It worked, but what I saw wouldn't have saved us. Any ideas?"

"If we had our spell book, we wouldn't have this problem," Olivia chided.

"If you hadn't been murdered, we'd still have our spell book." Elsie grinned at me. "There you go, Molly. Don't let her bully you."

I smiled as Dorothy parked the car. "Ladies, this isn't a plan. Think of poor Brian. We have to find the sea witch to save him."

"What if you're wrong and we find the sea witch but she *isn't* the Bone Man's wife?" Elsie asked.

"Then we'll save Brian, and I'll have to figure out another way to keep Joe safe."

"You know it's not as easy as you make it sound," Olivia warned.

"What about if we work on that spell you used at Zack's, but we do it together, before we go inside?" Dorothy said.

"Great idea!" Elsie smiled. "And I have just the thing that we can spell to see what we're really looking at." She produced a small, handheld mirror from her bag.

"Excellent!" Dorothy said. "Come on. Fist bump!"

Awkwardly, Elsie and I bumped fists with Dorothy. Olivia did her own ghostly version of it. We got out of the car and stood under the shade of a large cedar tree. We all put our hands on the mirror. I repeated the spell for clarity, and we said it together a few times before trying to spell the mirror.

Closing our eyes, holding our tools of magic, we recited the spell until the mirror began to glow.

"I think that's got it," I said. "Let's try it out."

I held the mirror up to my face. It showed me with the Bone Man standing right behind me. I jumped and glanced back to see if he was really there.

"Why is it showing him, Molly?" Dorothy asked.

"The spell shows who we really are," I replied. "In this case, it's showing a large influence in my life. You try it."

Dorothy nodded and cautiously took the mirror from me. She was almost too nervous to hold it up to her face. "That's not too bad. Look. It's showing Hemlock and Mom's house. I guess that's who I am right now."

"It's your house too, honey," Olivia told her. "I'm not surprised at all that being a wealthy witch is influencing you. It's your birthright. Be proud of it."

"Let me try." Elsie wasn't afraid of what she'd see in the mirror. "There I am. I look amazing holding my sword. I've never seen it on fire before. What's up with that?"

We all looked at her image in the mirror. She looked strong and powerful, much more so than she looked in real life.

"Maybe you accidentally stuck it in the fire," Olivia said. "You *can* get a little careless at times."

"We know the spell works. We'll have to figure out a way to gaze at Emma in the mirror." I shivered, still a little nervous after seeing the Bone Man standing behind me. "We'll deal with that once we get inside."

Elsie insisted on carrying the mirror, since it was her idea. We found Emma's apartment easily enough. Dorothy knocked on the door, and we waited.

"Yes?"

I remembered seeing Emma at the memorial. She was very short, almost pixielike, with golden blond hair and blue eyes.

I smiled at her. "I'm sorry. I'm Molly Renard from Smuggler's Arcane. Someone at the memorial left behind a valuable antique watch. We're trying to find out who it belongs to."

Her blue eyes widened. "I don't think I left anything

there. That poor boy. I felt so bad about his death. It could've been any of us. Would you like to come in? I have gingerbread in the oven."

We gladly agreed and went into Emma's very modern apartment. She chatted the whole time about her job as a nurse and Sam's death. Elsie fidgeted, having a hard time sitting in one of the plastic scoop-type chairs. They were too low to the floor, and she was afraid she wouldn't be able to get up.

"I'll help you before we go," I whispered. "Let's just get this over with. Give me the mirror."

Emma brought us each a slice of gingerbread with dollops of fresh cream. It was heavenly, though I thought after eating it that we probably shouldn't have tasted it in case she *was* the sea witch. It was too late then.

I managed to get behind her with the mirror. Dorothy looked over my shoulder.

The only image we could see was Emma, dressed as a nurse, with a young child who looked as though she was recovering from cancer. Her small, bald head and thin face were pathetic.

"What are you all looking at back there?" Emma laughed and grabbed the back of her blue top. "Is my tag sticking out or something?"

"Yes." Dorothy pretended to push a tag down at Emma's neckline. "There you go."

To further distract, Elsie pointed to a picture on the mantel of a pretty young girl with curly blond hair. "Is that your daughter? She's very cute. How old is she?"

There was no way she could have known that the dying girl we saw with Emma in the spelled mirror was the same girl from the picture. She didn't look like the same person.

"Yes. Brandy was three in that picture. She died last year. There was no magic, no medicine that could save her. I almost gave up being a witch." Emma wiped tears from her eyes. "Then I realized that I couldn't abandon my beliefs because of her death. I was teaching her to be a witch too. She loved writing spells."

"I'm so sorry." Elsie managed to push herself out of the bright yellow chair and took Emma's hand. "I can't imagine what you went through."

"It hasn't been easy. I give everything to my job and then spend hours trying to contact her spirit." She held up her hand. "I know. I shouldn't be messing with that stuff, but I see you have a ghost. I'd give anything to have Brandy here with me."

Olivia dropped down from the ceiling. "Oh, my dearest woman, she is here with you right now."

Emma got to her feet. "Really? Where? Why doesn't she show herself? I can see you."

"It may be your sorrow," I said. "I don't know everything about ghosts, but my mother told me once that grief can keep us from contacting our dead loved ones. You'll have to let go of it to see her."

By this time, we were all crying, our arms wrapped around each other. Olivia was crying too, and she pressed as close as her ghostly flesh would allow her.

"Thank you," Emma said. "Thank you so much for coming today. The watch you found isn't mine, but what you've given me is invaluable."

"When you find her," Elsie warned, "beware the council. They've already threatened to take Olivia from us. They might do the same with Brandy."

Emma's face was fierce. "Let them try. Where is she now, Olivia?"

Olivia pointed to a corner where a blond doll sat on a painted chair. "She's right there. Come on and give your mama a hug, sugar. She wants to see you in the worst way."

Until that moment, I couldn't see Brandy either. Then, suddenly—there she was. She looked as she did in the picture on the mantel, with a big smile on her face.

"Mama?"

"I'm right here, baby." Emma sobbed as she saw her daughter's spirit for the first time. "We'll never be apart again. Someday I'll cross over and we'll really be together."

We left Emma and Brandy together. All of us were still crying, trying to keep our eye makeup from running.

"Definitely not the sea witch." Elsie blew her nose on her peach-colored handkerchief. "We're so lucky to have you, Olivia. That poor woman. At least they'll be together again."

"I couldn't see her," Dorothy remarked. "Do you have to be related to a ghost to see them?"

"No. Not usually," I replied. "I couldn't see her at first. She had some reason that she was hiding. I hope it was nothing to do with her mother."

"I know what you're thinking, Molly, and don't you dare." Olivia shook her finger at me. "Sometimes a ghost has a hard time getting used to where she is, and she can't appear right away. It has nothing to do with how much the mother loves the child. And it certainly doesn't mean she was being abused or something. I can't believe you even thought that."

I *had* been thinking that. It came from years of teaching school and trying to help children who were being abused at home. I didn't always think the worst, but I had in this case. "I'm sorry. I'm sure you're right. But how did you know?"

Olivia looked surprised by the question as we got back in the Mercedes. "I don't know. Maybe I'm learning things about being a ghost. It's taken long enough."

"Quick," Elsie encouraged her. "Try to pick up that tissue Molly just dropped on the floor."

"Sorry." I leaned forward to retrieve the tissue off the immaculate gray carpet. It was force of habit. I didn't reckon with Olivia doing the same.

Our heads collided—or would have if Olivia had been solid. Instead, her head went right through mine. Her arm went through mine too. It was an eerie experience.

"I did it!" Olivia was grinning as she held up the tissue. "I actually did it. I'm getting a handle on this whole ghost thing. It won't be long until I can look for a new lover."

We all laughed at that even though my head and arm were still tingling from our encounter.

"Leave it to you to think of that," Elsie mocked. "Of all the things in the world, that was the first one?"

"I think that might be the most important one," Olivia shot back, still holding the tissue. "Where are we off to next?"

CHAPTER 35

May my sword stay between myself and all danger.
May my magic protect from all who would harm me.
Blessed Be.

We stopped at Marlie Eubanks's house on the way to South-port. She also asked us in for tea and cookies. The spelled mirror saw her with a very young lover and an older man we assumed must be her husband. He didn't look very happy.

As we went back to the car, Elsie shook her faded red curls. "I'm glad this is almost over. I'm going to gain weight from looking for the evil sea witch."

"There's only Portia de Winter left on the list," I said. "What address do we have for her?"

Dorothy consulted the list. "She lives out here too. We're only a few minutes from her place."

I glanced at my watch—the antique I was using as a prop to talk to the witches we suspected. "That should be fine. I'll have to go right after to get Joe."

We were beginning to give up hope on the plan. The mirror seemed to be working, but none of the suspects had turned into dead witches when we'd looked at them in it.

"Are you sure you're doing it the right way?" Olivia asked.

"We appeared correctly in it. The other witches seemed the same. I don't know what else we can do."

Dorothy started the car. "We only have one more witch to try. Either it will be her or we'll have to come up with a new plan."

"What are the chances that someone working for the council is a sea witch?" Olivia asked. "I know we don't think much of the council, but surely they would check out those who work for them."

Elsie chuckled. "That might be true, but don't call me Shirley."

Dorothy laughed too, and I smiled.

"That was really lame, Elsie," Olivia berated her. "You have to find some new jokes."

We drove to an older house on the beach. The windows were boarded up. Half the roof was gone. It looked as though it had been the victim of a hurricane, but not a recent one.

"Are you sure this is the right place?" Dorothy asked. "We couldn't verify the address with my phone since she's only been here a short time."

"That's what the memorial guest book said." I looked at the house. "There must be some mistake."

"Or she's the sea witch and lives over there in the water and not in a house at all," Elsie added. "Did none of you think that could be the case?"

"I think she's right." Dorothy took a deep breath. "I have a bad feeling about this."

Portia de Winter came around the side of the old house. The ocean breezes blew at her silky silver hair and whipped at her long blue skirt. Her pale blue blouse was studded with silver stars.

"Hello, ladies!" She greeted us with a big smile on her classically pretty face. "Come around back. I'm staying in the guesthouse. I'm hoping to get this old monstrosity torn down and build something later. I'd love to stay here in the area. It's a charming place."

"Maybe not so much the sea witch after all," Elsie whispered.

We followed Portia behind the house, where an old swimming pool was empty, the concrete cracked and overgrown with weeds. The guesthouse was small but perfect for one person. She invited us in for lemon meringue pie that she'd made that morning.

Elsie groaned before she smiled and accepted a slice.

"I see you brought your ghost," Portia said. "You know the council doesn't look favorably on her being here."

"We know," I answered. "We don't care how the council feels about her. She's our friend and Dorothy's mother. The rule is wrong. Why feel like witches can't be ghosts?"

Portia shrugged as she cut the pie. "I think being a witch is all about the natural order of things. When you die, you move on. Don't you believe that, Molly?"

"I do. But when there is strong purpose, and not just a lingering shadow, I think there should be an exception. Olivia had no time to get to know her daughter. This is all the time she has with Dorothy."

I didn't mention Brandy, Emma's daughter, but I knew that witches who were firmly against ghosts clinging to life wouldn't care that Brandy was only a baby separated from her mother.

Portia passed out the pie on wonderful china plates that were painted with delicate seashells and other ocean life. "I'm sure you're right. The council is stubborn and slow to change."

The little room we sat in was pleasant in the watery sunlight. There was an old fireplace for heat and a tiny kitchen area. A bed was in one corner with a chest and lamp beside it.

It looked as though this was going to be another dead end. Dorothy was eagerly eating her pie. Elsie was only looking at hers and sighing.

I glanced at my plate, about to take a bite. But where the beautiful china had held luscious lemon pie, there was now only a piece of barnacled metal with seaweed on it.

"Don't eat it!" I dropped the plate on the tile floor. "It's not real. It may be poisoned!"

Elsie dropped her plate right away. It was too late for Dorothy.

"I don't feel very well, Molly," Dorothy said. "I don't know what's wrong with me."

She fell to the floor, not moving.

Portia smiled. "Don't worry. She'll be fine. What gave me away?"

I looked at my hand. The rune was seeping blood around the edges. That had also been masked by her glamour. "You're the sea witch, and the Bone Man's wife."

Her brows lifted. She appeared pleasantly amused. "I haven't heard that term. What does it mean?"

"You haven't been here long. That's what the witches in this area call your husband."

"Really? How does he feel about it? I'll bet he thinks it's funny. I think it's funny that he still thinks of himself as my husband."

I got to my feet, holding my amulet. Elsie pushed to her feet, clutching her sword.

"He's charged me to bring you back to him," I told her. "But I think you'll have to face the council for the witches you've killed."

She laughed. "I see. You must be his personal messenger. I noticed the amulet you wear, Molly. So much power for one *old* witch. What do you plan to do with it?"

"This isn't about me. It's about you."

"You won't do anything with it." Her voice cracked and thinned. "He won't *let* you. It's hard for me to believe you even have it. Where did you find it?"

"He gave it to an ancestor of mine, I think." I thought

telling her might crack her shell of amusement. I was right—
I was also sorry.

Portia's appearance began to shift and change like a kal-
eidoscope. Colors whirled and danced until there was nothing
left of her.

Nothing *human* anyway.

Elsie caught her breath, but stood her ground. I swallowed
hard, wishing I had a sword too. I went to the other side of
the table, where Dorothy lay prone on the floor, and picked
up Olivia's staff.

"It won't do you any good against that thing," Olivia
hissed a warning. "You need your magic, Molly. You can't
bludgeon it."

I knew she was right, but the feel of something sturdy to
defend myself made me feel better about facing the sea
witch. We'd wanted to see her true form. We didn't need a
spelled mirror now.

Portia's body turned into something green and wrinkled.
She resembled a large cucumber that was going bad. There
were prickly spines all over her. Her long, beautiful silver
hair shriveled and turned green. Her hands became like
lobster claws with spines on them. Her mouth was a hideous
gaping maw filled with sharp teeth.

All that remained the same were her very human blue
eyes. They were the same eyes I'd seen on the witch burned
at the stake in my dream. I immediately felt pity for her as
well as a kind of empathy. What had he done to her? She
would have been better off dead.

"Look out, Molly," Elsie warned. "She's coming after you."

CHAPTER 36

I am a witch,
I do not fear.
I hold my magic strong.
I do not fear.

"I'd like my amulet back, witch," the sea creature that had been Portia said as she leapt toward me. "He had no right to give it away. He knew I'd be back for it."

I was mindful of the spikes on her claws. I had a feeling that was what Joe and Suzanne remembered stinging them in the back. No doubt those spines contained poison.

"It's mine now. It's been in my family for hundreds of years." I held the staff between us.

"Magic, Molly," Olivia reminded me. "Do something with your magic. You can't hold her off with the staff. And you might break it."

I glanced up at her. "Seriously? This thing is trying to kill me. You can't even use the staff anymore."

"Yes, but who knows what will happen to me if the staff is destroyed."

I couldn't disagree with that.

"Just give me the amulet," Portia's new form demanded. "I

don't want to hurt you. You've been as deceived by MacLir as I was."

"You killed those boys," Elsie shouted. "Don't think we feel sorry for you."

"I didn't want to hurt them either," the sea witch said. "Every hundred years I must return to the land and mate with a witch. If I don't, I'll die. I've fought to stay alive. I won't give up now. I've found the right one, finally. I don't need any others. Give me the amulet. Leave me in peace. I swear you won't see me again."

I couldn't help it. I felt bad for her. She was right. This was what the Bone Man had made of her. None of it was her doing except for keeping herself alive.

But I had to harden myself against her. It was obvious she was talking about Brian being her last victim. While I felt pity for her, I couldn't let her kill him—if she hadn't done so already. Logic told me that we wouldn't have found her here if she'd finished her deadly ritual. She'd be back in the sea and far away by now.

"Olivia's right," Elsie shouted as I tried to keep the sea witch from taking my amulet. "We need magic to fight her."

"I'm working on it." I pushed the sea witch back with the staff. "I can't think of a spell. Can you?"

Her forehead furrowed. "I'm thinking of a protection spell. Remember that wonderful spell that makes a shield? Maybe that would work."

"Maybe—if I could remember it."

"It's something like *Protect me now from harm and fear. Lead me to shelter that is near.*" She panicked. "Oh dear. That's all I can remember."

"The enchanted bubble," Olivia called out. "You just did that, Molly. Use the enchanted bubble."

"That won't keep her out," I reminded Olivia. "I need something stronger."

The sea witch's mouth opened to laugh at me. "Poor Molly. You can't fight me with water magic. I *am* water magic."

Her spiny claws were getting closer. I couldn't hold her back much longer.

"Oh, the hell with it!" Elsie yelled out a spell and held her sword high. It burst into flames just like the image we'd seen in the spelled mirror. "Begone, I command thee!"

The sea witch made a horrible shrill noise and reached for her.

Elsie swung her blade without an instant of hesitation. She chopped off one of the sea witch's claws. The creature cried out in pain and anger. The smell was terrible. I hit her with Olivia's staff, using one hand while clutching the amulet with the other.

The sea witch ran out the door. Elsie and I stood paralyzed for a moment. It only took that long before the glamour affecting the guesthouse was gone too.

The guesthouse was in no better shape than the main house. The roof had collapsed and the windows were broken. There was no furniture. Everything around us that had made the guesthouse hospitable was gone.

"She's gone." I realized that wasn't a good thing. Though I was afraid for my life, I ran through the debris to find her. There was no sign of her outside in the yard or in the street. She might have looked like a cucumber, but she moved like a jellyfish.

Dorothy was sitting up and holding her head when I returned. "What happened? Where's Portia? Did I miss something?"

Elsie pushed back her hat and carefully sat on what had once been an old sofa. "That's a long story."

"It can't be that long." Dorothy glanced at her watch. "We've only been here for twenty minutes."

"We should talk while we search for Brian. I have a feeling he's in here somewhere. It's unlikely she'd let him out of her sight if he's the right witch for her." I set down Olivia's staff.

"That was a close one, girls," Olivia commented. "Wait. I see Brian over there. I can't believe that sea witch's glamour was so good that we didn't even notice him. Where do you think she learned to do that?"

"What?" Dorothy frowned. "The sea witch? She was here?"

We pushed aside old chairs and fallen pieces of the ceiling and walls to reach the tattered bed where Brian lay. Olivia kept a running commentary to explain what had happened after Dorothy had passed out.

"I guess I was lucky I didn't end up like Joe and Suzanne," Dorothy said. "What about Brian?"

Elsie put her hand on Brian's forehead. "He's dead. She must have finished the spell before we got here. She was just playing with us."

Dorothy sat beside him and took his hand, heedless of the spider-infested, moth-eaten draperies around her. "He *can't* be gone. There must be a spell or something to bring him back."

"We don't bring back the dead, Dorothy," Elsie said. "It's just not done."

"I've read about it in some of the books at the shop." Dorothy cried as she argued.

I covered her hand with mine. "We don't do that kind of magic. The price is too high. When it's someone's time to die, we have to respect it."

"What's the price?" Dorothy yelled. "I'll pay it. I don't care. He can't be dead. How can it be his time to die when the sea witch killed him?"

"You don't understand," Elsie said. "The price is another life. Another soul that isn't ready to go. You can't pay that price. You'd hate yourself."

"We have to save him." She fell on top of him. "I can't lose him this way."

Despite the shock and sadness of Brian's death, Elsie and

I realized we couldn't let Dorothy continue grieving in this way until her emotional magic was triggered and she did something she'd regret.

Together we recited a sleeping spell that we'd used to help when both our children had colic as babies. It would ease her sorrow until she had a chance to live with her loss for a while.

"It's for the best," Elsie said when Dorothy was asleep beside Brian on the bed.

"I know." I wiped the tears from my eyes. "I don't know what to do now."

Elsie leaned on her sword with the point jammed into the wood floor. "The sea witch is gone. You can't take her back to the Bone Man. We can't take her to the council for justice. Brian is dead. We screwed up."

"There has to be something we can do." Olivia ghost-stroked Dorothy's dark hair. "My poor baby."

"We can't leave him," I said. "We have to get him—and Dorothy—out of here."

"We should take him back to the shop," Olivia replied. "We have to call Cassandra and his parents. Oh, girls, this is the worst thing that's *ever* happened to us."

Elsie pointed at the sea witch's claw that she'd lopped off. "I know we can't do anything about it right now, but later maybe we can use this to lure her back and kill her." She stabbed it with the sword and wrapped it in her scarf. "I never liked that scarf anyway."

CHAPTER 37

All deeds great and all deeds small,
All deeds must balance through it all.

Elsie and I managed to get Dorothy and Brian to the car. It was part magic and part physical strength. We were both exhausted by the time we were done.

We took them to Smuggler's Arcane. Dorothy was awake and a little calmer when we got there. She checked on Brian again. He was slumped in the backseat beside her. "He's cold. I guess you were right. He's dead. What do we do now, Molly?"

"I'm so sorry." I got out of the car and hugged her as we cried. "We should call his family and let them know."

"I can't believe this is happening." She put her hand to her forehead. "He was supposed to be all right now. We were supposed to win. We're the good guys."

It wasn't easy to get Brian into the shop. It didn't seem right to ask Dorothy to use her magic to transport him inside—besides, it was still daylight and there were shoppers at the other stores in the Cotton Exchange. We couldn't risk it.

We wrapped him in an old blanket and were barely able

to lift him between us. Going up the stairs with him was grueling—one stair at a time with a moment to catch our breaths between. I was glad no one called the police when his hand slid out of the blanket and flopped out on one side.

We put him on the old wood floor and covered him with a dark blue cloth that had been embroidered with moon-blessed silver threads. There was nothing else to do but call Cassandra.

When she appeared, her gown was like blue smoke around her thin body, her black hair surrounding her beautiful face. She lifted the moon cloth. "What have you *done*?"

"We tried to save him from the sea witch," Elsie told her. "It was more than *you* or any of his family tried to do."

"Abdon is going to be furious. Brian's parents are going to want revenge," Cassandra warned.

"Let them," I told her, though I didn't feel as brave as my words. It was more than just me. It was Joe and Mike, Elsie and Aleese, Dorothy and even Olivia. They could take everything from us. "You know where to find us."

"What about the council catching the sea witch and making sure she doesn't ever kill again?" Olivia whimpered.

"We'll deal with this first," Cassandra said.

"Which is what got us all into this mess in the first place!" Elsie raged.

"I'll take him to his family, and then consult the council. Stand away." She moved her hand and his covered body began to rise from the floor. "The Fuller family will remember this loss for years to come, ladies. I'm sure the council will try to mitigate that rage, but you might have to stand trial for it."

Cassandra disappeared with Brian. Sobbing and covering her face, Dorothy collapsed at the table.

Joe texted me. I had to wipe tears from my eyes to see what he said. He and Suzanne were being discharged from the hospital. "I have to go."

"We'll be all right here, Molly," Olivia assured me. "Go on."

Half an hour later I was at the hospital as Joe and Suzanne were being released. I watched as they got out of their wheelchairs at the pickup ramp.

"There you are." Joe kissed me as he got in the front seat. "I was beginning to worry about you." He studied my puffy, red eyes and tear-stained face. "Everything okay with the club?"

"It's hard to say right now." As soon as Suzanne was in the backseat, I hurried out of the parking lot. It was hard to keep my voice from trembling and not let my feelings show. "I'm sure the two of you are off the rest of the day. Where can I take you, Suzanne?"

She gave me the address of a hotel on Market Street, where she was staying. I managed to make it through several traffic lights as they turned red by swerving around any slower moving traffic.

"Are you in a hurry to get back to the club?" Joe frowned. "I think I might be about to give you a ticket for careless driving. What's wrong?"

"I'm in a hurry." I tried, but I couldn't smile at him. "It's not like I actually ran a red light, *Officer*. I have to get back."

"Leave her alone, Joe," Suzanne said. "She's a woman on a mission. Thanks for taking me to the hotel, Molly. Is there anything I can do to help?"

"No. I'm afraid not." I pulled into the hotel parking lot and dropped her at the front door with a squeal of brakes. "Feel better, Suzanne. I'll see you later. Call if you need anything."

"Thanks." She laughed. "I will. But I'll be sure to wait until after your mission is accomplished."

As soon as she was out of the car, Joe turned to me. "Don't leave until you explain."

"There's not time now." I put my foot on the gas. "The club has an emergency. Something—terrible—has happened. Brian is dead. I wish I could explain more right now, but I have to drop you off and get back. I don't want to leave everyone for long."

"Brian is dead? What happened? Is everyone else okay?" He stared at me. "Tell me what happened. What's going on?"

"Really, Joe. I *can't* tell you. Not now. You know what I mean. Please don't make this any harder than it is. I'll tell you everything later."

"Are *you* in danger, Molly?"

"No. For now, the danger is past. We have to figure out what to do next." I drove in the same haphazard manner from the hotel to our house. "I have to go. Do you need anything? There's plenty of food in the refrigerator. The doctor said you should rest. I'll see you later."

Joe's dark eyes were filled with questions and fear. "I don't like this. I wish you wouldn't be involved in club activities that could be dangerous."

I kissed him and smiled, though I knew there were tears in my eyes. "Don't worry. We're going to make it right."

CHAPTER 38

Death is but a doorway to another path.

Brian's funeral was a solemn affair. None of us had expected to be invited. We were surprised when Cassandra came to tell us that the Fuller family wanted us to attend. We were reticent at first—maybe they wanted to exact revenge while we were there. But I knew they wouldn't attempt it in public, and Dorothy needed this closure. We all did.

We dressed in our finest, knowing how many upper-crust witches and members of the council would be present. None of us had ever attended an event of this kind. We were more the celebrations-in-the-park-and-backyard-type witches.

I still wondered, when the large black limousine came for me, why the family had invited us. They'd been very clear about their feelings toward us. Even though I wanted to attend, I had my doubts as to what sort of reception we'd receive.

"I think your ride is here." Joe was looking out the kitchen window. "This Brian who died was well-to-do, huh? He didn't really seem that way when I met him."

"He was a very nice young man." I pulled on elbow-length

black gloves and made sure my silk scarf was perfect across my head and around my neck. "I still can't believe he's gone. I feel so responsible. I wish I could've done more."

Joe hugged me, mindful of my makeup and black crepe gown. "You know I always feel the same way. What do you say to me?"

I smiled. "You did your best. Sometimes bad things happen."

"That's right." He glanced out the window again. "Don't blame yourself. You didn't kill him. I'll see you later."

We'd talked about the *club* aspect of Brian's death. Joe was still following up on the other two murders. He had refused to give up on finding the sea witch—she had a human identity he thought he could track. He wasn't happy about not being able to log Brian's death in the case, but he understood that some things were impossible for him.

Elsie and Dorothy were already in the car. The driver got out and opened the back door for me. The windows were so dark that there were small lights illuminating the interior of the limo.

Dorothy's eyes were red and puffy. She'd brought a box of tissues with her. Her simple black dress was made elegant with one of Olivia's beaded scarves and her diamond earrings.

"I've been trying to convince her that we could do that spell that makes the magic handkerchiefs," Elsie said. "No witch worth her magic goes to a funeral carrying tissues. It looks bad. I could give her my handkerchief, but that sounds nasty."

Elsie was dressed in a long dark purple silk gown that was covered by her full-length purple cloak. Her red-gray curls were up on her head and held back by a rhinestone tiara. She wore too much blush and her very red lipstick was smeared as she'd attempted to find her lips, but she looked like a queen.

"I'll be fine." Dorothy blew her nose. "I wish Mom could have come too. It's just stupid how witches feel about ghosts. It's prejudiced. If this was the real world, it would be illegal."

I put my hand on hers. "I know. I wish she were here too. But Elsie's right about the tissues. We can make a nice handkerchief for you from one of them."

The three of us held one of the tissues. Elsie was proud that she could remember the spell, since it was one she used every day. She spoke the words and the tissue began to change. When it was finished, the tissue was a lacy, red handkerchief.

"Red?" Dorothy asked.

Elsie brows knit together. "I'm sorry. I thought it would be white. Maybe we should try it again."

"I think we should leave it the way it is," I said. "We got lucky. Let's not push it. At least it's not an octopus or something."

We were only in the limo for about ten minutes when it slowed to a smooth stop and someone opened the back door. "Ladies." A young man in a black livery and white gloves inclined his head as we stepped out.

"Where are we?" Dorothy asked in a scared voice. "I don't think I've ever been here. I didn't know Wilmington had a castle."

"We're not in Wilmington anymore, Dorothy." Elsie chuckled. "It makes me wish I had a small dog in a basket. Very *Wizard of Oz*, right?"

"Really?" Dorothy frowned. "Like I didn't get that my whole life."

"Sorry." Elsie put her hand on her tiara and looked up at the castle. "Wow. I guess this is where the Fullers live? Where do you think we are, Molly?"

"I have no idea. Let's not stand here and gawk. We should go inside. Dorothy—no temper tantrums. Elsie—no magic or snarky remarks."

"What about you?" Elsie said. "What are *your* restrictions?"

"I'll try to think of some." I started up the steps toward the castle door.

The place was immense. I could see at least five floors with several turrets on top. All of the turrets flew black flags. Hundreds of windows on the front face were made of colorful stained glass that sparkled in the light. The stonework was ancient, white and gray, with the letter *F* worked into the pattern.

Music poured out through the open doors. Hundreds of witches were ascending the steps with us. Servants wearing the same black livery as the man who'd opened our car door were standing at the top of the stairs.

"Very posh," Elsie whispered. "Glad I wore my tiara instead of my plaid beret as I first had a mind to do."

"*Shh,*" I said. "Let's be very careful what we say here. The place is probably crawling with council members and their people."

"I think I see a lemur in that bush over there," Dorothy added. "We might be in Madagascar."

"Welcome." Abdon Fuller was standing immediately inside the door welcoming visitors as they entered. Schadt and Yuriza were beside him. All three looked elegant and stately. Yuriza was the only one who was red-eyed and haggard. It was easy to see that she was deeply mourning the loss of her son.

Abdon faltered when he saw us, but he quickly took hold of whatever he might have said to us and welcomed us as he had the witches before us. "Welcome, sisters."

Elsie impulsively grabbed his hand. "We are *so* sorry for the loss of your grandson, sir. He was a wonderful boy who didn't deserve to end that way."

"Thank you." He cleared his throat, but his authoritative voice was still gruff.

Yuriza and Schadt said the same words. I caught Yuriza's eyes on me when she nodded her head. I wanted to say something, but was too aware of our cultural differences. Elsie was always the spontaneous one.

Dorothy started crying again. She reached for the red handkerchief and accidentally dropped a small glass vial from her sequined evening bag. The glass shattered on the stone floor, drawing everyone's attention. If they had stared a little longer, they would have seen Olivia's ghostly form fly out of the vial.

I hurried Dorothy into an alcove. "What were you *thinking*? You brought Olivia with you?"

"You don't have to make it sound like I'm the plague or something," Olivia whispered. "I knew Brian before any of you. I should be here."

"Mom and I were experimenting with a spell last night. It seemed to work," Dorothy said.

"Until you broke the vial," I reminded her. "Now here she is. We know how everyone is going to react."

"I can do another quick confinement spell," Dorothy offered. "I don't have anything to put her in, since the vial broke, but—"

"I have a plastic sandwich bag with peanuts in it," Elsie offered. "You know how these affairs can be. I was worried I might get hungry."

Cassandra was coming our way. There wasn't time for a spell—and it would be worse than embarrassing if it didn't work.

"Hide behind the drape," I told Olivia. "Stay out of sight for now."

"But Molly—"

"Please, Olivia. We'll figure out some way for you to pay your respects to Brian before we leave. But not now."

Olivia was sulky about it, but she managed to conceal herself behind the massive burgundy drape. I hoped no one around us would notice. If I'd known this was going to be an issue, I wouldn't have come.

"Molly. Elsie. Dorothy." Cassandra had inclined her regal head after each name. "I'm so glad you could be here. It wasn't easy to convince Abdon and the rest of Brian's family that you belonged here for his memorial, but I believed it was the right thing, since you fought so hard to keep him alive. And I *am* the herald. That makes me the liaison between the council and other witches."

"Thank you," I said. "I wish no one had to be here today. I hate that Brian is gone."

"So do I." She sighed. "We had such hopes for the boy."

"I want to see him," Dorothy said. "Where is he?"

"It would be better manners to mingle with the other witches before you view him," Cassandra counseled, as though she also determined protocol for the council.

"We can do that," Elsie said. "We'll be fine, Cassandra, if you want to mingle with some other witches too."

"First let me introduce you to the rest of the Grand Council of Witches. I don't think you've ever met them."

She was right on that score. We weren't the kind of witches who went to soirees or consulted on long-term plans for the witches of the world. We were housewives, mothers, schoolteachers and other ordinary people who happened to be blessed with magic. If anything, we were careful to avoid attracting the council's attention.

But what could we say?

Cassandra led the way through the crowd. I looked up at the high ceiling, where several large crystal chandeliers hung, illuminating the event. There were velvet couches of various sizes and colors scattered throughout the ballroom and long tables filled with any kind of food one could imagine.

"I guess I really didn't have to bring the peanuts," Elsie muttered. "Do you think a plastic bag with a zip top can hold a ghost?"

I shook my head. We were walking between richly garbed witches with elaborate headdresses. Most were dressed in black or shades of dark purple and blue. It was more like I'd imagined a royal ball to be than a memorial, although large banners with Brian's face on them floated throughout the room.

"I think I'm underdressed," Dorothy muttered, taking my hand. Hers was freezing.

I squeezed her fingers. "Most of them only wish they had your youth and beauty. You can't dress up and create *that*."

She smiled tearfully and looked at the banners. "I'm not sure I can see Brian. I mean, I want to see him, but I'm not sure if I can handle it."

"You don't have to decide yet. But if you don't want to see him, we won't go over there."

"Thanks, Molly."

There was a raised dais at the far end of the room. It had been so far from the door that I hadn't even seen it as we came in. There were eleven men and women seated in thronelike chairs that were embellished with coats of arms and gold inlays.

I knew this was the Grand Council of Witches—minus Abdon Fuller. These were the people who made our lives miserable from time to time. They were feared, sometimes hated and respected by the ordinary witches.

Cassandra was her most charming self as she introduced the members of the council to us. "This is Molly Addison Renard. Elsie Clarrett Langston. And one of our newest witches, Dorothy Dunst Lane."

All the men and women on the council nodded their heads stiffly.

"Ladies, allow me to present your council members: Owen Graybeard. Sarif Patel. Joshua Bartleson. Larissa Lonescue. Zuleyma Castanada. Rhianna Black. Makaleigh Veazy. Arleigh Burke. Bairne Caelius. Hedyle. And Erinna Coptus."

Elsie tried to curtsey and almost fell over. I grabbed her arm, and she managed to right herself. I inclined my head in respect without going overboard. Dorothy did a cute little-girl curtsey without Elsie's drama.

I wasn't sure what we should do next. Were they going to speak with us, or was that it?

Cassandra smiled. "I'm so glad I could introduce you to the council," she said. "This is a solemn time, but I hope you enjoy yourselves."

I assumed that was it and started backing away, bringing Elsie and Dorothy with me. Cassandra had already moved on. The members of the Grand Council sat like statues overseeing the memorial.

"I'm not sure what I expected the council to look like," Elsie finally said. "But it wasn't those witches. Do you think they've ever had a new member of the council?"

"Not in our lifetimes," I said. "I think it's time to make a decision, Dorothy. Do you want to see Brian or not?"

CHAPTER 39

Do you love me?
Tell me now.
I see your eyes in the mirror.
If you love me, tell me now.

The three of us sat on one of the velvet sofas. Servants in black liveries offered us food and drinks. None of us had anything. Even Elsie chose to eat her peanuts instead, saying that she might need the empty bag to take Olivia home.

Dorothy stared at the people around us with a blank expression in her eyes. I wondered if she was thinking about whether or not she wanted to see Brian or if she'd been overwhelmed by meeting the council.

A few witches examined us in disdain, but no one else spoke. I didn't recognize any local witches or even any witches we'd met on our travels, which had taken us around the world. It was as if this was a different level of witches, one that didn't make friends with ordinary people like us.

"I want to see him," Dorothy suddenly blurted out. She reached for a glass of wine as a servant walked by, and downed it in one swallow. "I can't leave until I see him. I can't believe it's real until I'm sure he's dead."

Having examined Brian before Cassandra had come for him, I believed we all knew that Brian was gone. I understood what she meant by wanting to see him one last time. Somehow the brain refused to accept that a horrible truth was possible. Sometimes it helped seeing the person again. Sometimes it didn't. But I was willing to do whatever she needed. Despite what Olivia thought about her relationship with Brian, I knew her heart had never been involved with him. Dorothy's was.

"All right." I took her hand. "Olivia is going to have to wait behind the drape until we're ready to go. I'm sorry. I don't like the council, but I don't want to be the witch who was kicked out because she brought a ghost with her."

"I understand. I'm sorry." She sniffed. "How are we going to find him?"

"I think Brian might be over there, where the large group of witches is standing. They're filing past something and it's not the dessert table."

Dorothy and I looked where Elsie was pointing. There were many witches slowly moving past something that was against a stone wall.

"Let's go see." I held Dorothy's hand as we got to our feet.

"If Mom couldn't be here, I'm glad that you and Elsie are," she whispered.

Olivia was peeking out from behind the drape. She hissed at us a few times and tried to flag us down. I ignored her and kept walking. I didn't want Brian's memorial to end in a brawl with a ghost-versus-witch theme. Nor did I want to rub it in the council's faces that we were harboring a ghost. That could be the deciding factor to them for making her disappear forever, as Cassandra had hinted many times.

"Ladies." Richard Brannigan approached us with a plate of food in one hand and a champagne glass in the other. "It's good to see you. No hard feelings over what went down the last time we met, I hope."

"None at all," I told him with a pleasant smile. The dwarf witch lawyer had been Olivia's attorney for her will. He had also tried to take my amulet—at the council's request, of course.

"I'm glad to hear it. I did what was necessary with the werewolf and such." His beady eyes behind his wire-rimmed spectacles coveted my amulet. "I see you've managed to hold on to it, Molly. Good for you."

"Thank you. Excuse us. We're going to see Brian." We walked around him as he called out a farewell. I was glad we weren't saddled with talking to him as we had been with Cassandra. I wasn't particularly fond of him.

We found the end of the long line and stood together, not speaking. The line moved slowly, as the witches paid their last respects in muted voices to Brian as they passed him.

When we finally reached the point where we could see his coffin, Dorothy gasped and her hold tightened on my hand. "What in the world? Are *all* witches buried that way?"

"Oh no!" Elsie's green eyes were riveted to the sight before us. "There's no way I want people looking at me in a glass coffin when I die."

The glass coffin was incredibly ornate, with gold fittings and a blue velvet interior surrounding Brian's handsome face. He was dressed like a prince, in a gold-and-white costume that looked as though it had come from a Renaissance faire. Heavy gold chains lay around his neck and on his chest. His hands were adorned with gold and jewels on every finger.

"Why did they dress him like that?" Dorothy mumbled, crying.

"Maybe that's the way they saw him," I replied.

"The young Fuller prince." Elsie completed my thought.

The coffin was set on a small platform so that no one had to bend over to look closely at Brian. The light from the crystal chandeliers danced in the glass. Brass incense burners wafted the heavy scent of sage and bay laurel around us.

"How can anyone be at peace that way?" Elsie whispered. "He looks uncomfortable."

"Let's go," I urged. Nothing more could be gained by standing and staring at him.

"No." Dorothy shook her head, her dark hair swinging from side to side. "*No*. This isn't right. I just know it isn't."

Afraid she was about to make a scene, I squeezed her hand. "You have to let him go. I know it's painful, but you have to go on without him."

Witches behind us were making subtle and not-so-subtle sounds reminding us that there was a long line behind us. Elsie took Dorothy's other hand to console her.

"No!" Dorothy yelled and shook free of both of us. "This isn't happening. It's not right. I won't let him die."

Elsie and I had no time to react as Dorothy smashed open the glass coffin with one of the brass incense burners. A woman behind us screamed and fell to the floor in a faint. Someone else yelled for security. Most of the people in the line scattered into the large hall.

I tried to reach Dorothy, but there were too many shards of glass preventing me from easily getting her away from the coffin. I coaxed. I pleaded with her. She had become like a possessed mad woman, clearing away the glass from Brian's body until her hands were bloody.

"What in the world is going on here?" Abdon came down on us with his full fury. His mouth was twisted, his eyes blazing with anger when he saw Dorothy on top of what was left of the coffin.

"Maybe we should leave now, Molly," Elsie suggested. "There's no point in all of us being persecuted, thrown in a dungeon, boiled in a cauldron. Let's *leave*."

Brian's parents rushed to the scene. Yuriza gasped and grabbed her husband's arm. Schadt balled up his fists and reached for his wand.

Dorothy had finally cleared away most of the glass from Brian. She looked into his young, handsome face and brushed his hair from his forehead with a light hand. "You can't be dead. I won't let you be dead. I love you. I know you love me too."

Elsie took my hand. "Molly, I think I've seen this movie. Only the girl was in the coffin instead of the boy. I can't remember the name right now."

"*Snow White*," I whispered.

Dorothy planted her lips on Brian's, her arms going around him to almost lift him out of the coffin. It happened so quickly that no one had time to react. Two security people stood beside me but didn't move.

"Brian." Dorothy sobbed against him. "You have to wake up."

There was no flash of light. No clap of thunder.

But suddenly, Brian was alive again. He sat up in the coffin and put his arms around Dorothy before he kissed her.

"What's going on?" He looked away from her to the astonished faces that surrounded them.

"Son!" Schadt yelled, advancing on the coffin.

"He's not dead." Yuriza followed him.

"That's ridiculous!" Abdon roared. "Of course he's dead. I checked him myself."

"I don't think he was dead at all." Elsie spoke up. "I think it was just the sea witch's spell. Or I guess the old 'true love's kiss' works too."

I put my arm around Elsie, tears flowing freely down my cheeks. "She did it. She saved Brian."

Dorothy still sat on Brian in the demolished coffin.

"True love's kiss, huh?" Brian kissed her through her tears. "Thank you. I love you too."

"Someone get them out of there before the girl bleeds to death on my grandson," Abdon shouted. "And get all these mourners out of here too. I need some peace and quiet—and a large whiskey."

CHAPTER 40

Rejoice,
The dark times are gone.
Rejoice at your life.

We waited. We weren't going anywhere without Dorothy. A healer was called in, and she took care of the cuts on Dorothy's hands and arms. Brian carefully climbed out of the coffin after Dorothy was lifted out by two security people.

"Hi, Molly. Elsie—you look great." Brian, back to his usual self, grinned at us. "What are you doing here?"

"You were dead," I reminded him. "We came to pay our respects."

"That was nice. But I'm glad I'm not really dead. What happened? I remember opening the door to my apartment and someone was standing there. That's it."

"It was the sea witch," I explained. "She wanted to mate with you."

"Was she hot?" he asked with a teasing expression on his face.

"When we last saw her, she looked like a big cucumber with spikes all over her and a green Brillo pad on her head," Elsie said. "Not really your kind of date."

"I think I'll pass on that." He looked around. "Where did they take Dorothy?"

"Let's go somewhere more private," Abdon said. "The others don't need to hear all this."

But for my money, this was too good an opportunity to miss. "Excuse me, I think you're wrong."

"What?" Abdon's scar on his cheek stood out purple against his skin. "You are a *guest* in my house."

Frightened, but determined to say what needed to be said, I cleared my throat. "And you are on the Grand Council of Witches, which is supposed to protect all witches. We told you long before this about the danger facing Brian. The sea witch has taken the lives of twelve other young witches. Where was the council when that happened?"

"We sent the herald to inform you."

"I believe you should have done more, and now all the council needs to hear what we have to say. Deny me if you like, but in the end, the council will pay the price for it."

Abdon opened his mouth to rebut my words, but Makaleigh Veazy held out her hand. "I would be interested in what she has to say."

I was grateful, and I managed to take a breath at her intervention. She reminded me of Whoopi Goldberg. Her dark hair was like a halo around her beatific countenance.

"The council shouldn't indulge one witch," Joshua Bartleson said in a lofty tone. "I am certain it is against our principles."

"Maybe it shouldn't be," Makaleigh said. "We've gone too long without getting our hands dirty. Why are we here if not to help our fellow witches?"

She seemed to be the only council member interested in listening to me or helping defeat the sea witch. The rest left with Abdon and Brian's father. Yuriza stayed, casting a defiant look at her husband.

Brian showed us to a small room with a big fireplace that was carved from crystal. There was uncomfortable furniture set on valuable Persian carpets. Crystal sconces lit the room. "You hash this out. I'm going to check on Dorothy."

Makaleigh sat back like a queen in a large chair. "Tell me of this sea witch, Molly Addison. I knew your great-great-grandmother. I recognize her amulet around your throat."

Elsie and I took turns explaining everything that had happened. I didn't include the Bone Man in this description, because I didn't want the council to know about the deal I'd made with him to protect Joe.

When we were finished, Yuriza nodded. "I am not part of the council, but you have my undying gratitude for saving my son. I don't know why Schadt and my father-in-law deem this to be of no merit. I promise to speak with them on your behalf."

"What can I do for you, Molly?" Makaleigh asked.

"We need help capturing the sea witch. I believe it's the only way Brian and other young witches will be safe from her, the only way you can make sure justice is done."

"Why capture what you could kill?"

"I'm not convinced we could kill her." I kept the real answer to myself. "Can you help with that?"

"I grew up along the Nile many centuries ago. There were many such water creatures at that time. Let me consult the archives, and I will tell you if I find anything that might be useful to you."

"Archives?" Elsie perked up. "I'd love to take a look at the archives."

"It is forbidden for anyone not on the council," Makaleigh said. "Perhaps someday you will sit beside us."

"Thank you." Elsie inclined her head with respect, but whispered to me, "Yeah. Right."

"Is there any other grievance I might return to the council for you?"

I thought I might as well air one of the biggest grievances witches in the real world had with the council. "Would you consider lifting the ban against non-magic spouses and their children knowing about witches?" It was a long shot, but if I didn't have to worry about Joe, I wouldn't have to figure out how to get the sea witch to the Bone Man's island.

Makaleigh's arresting face grew stern. "This can never be allowed, Molly. There is too much at risk. I lived through a time of torture and death for all witches. I never want to see that time return. Witches should marry witches. They should have children who are witches."

"How would that happen every time?" Elsie asked.

"There are ways to tell if the child in the womb has magic. If not, the couple should try again."

Elsie and I couldn't have been more horrified by her decree if she'd told us to go out and murder every person who wasn't a witch. The arrogance and self-righteousness of her statement took my breath away.

"I will talk with you again, Molly. As I will you, Elsie. You can be sure that I will keep you in my special sights from now on. Thank you for enlightening me." Makaleigh swept from the room with Yuriza at her side.

Elsie and I put our arms around each other. "What have we done now?" she whispered. "I don't want that monster's special sights on me."

"It won't take long for her to forget she ever met us," I murmured. "I didn't think anyone could be worse than Abdon."

Dorothy and Brian joined us in the smaller room. Dorothy still had blood all over her.

"But the red looks very nice with that black dress," Elsie complimented. "I'm glad you're all right."

"What made you *do* such a thing?" I hugged Dorothy. "If Brian had really been dead, your emotional magic might have brought him back anyway. There would have been a price to pay."

"I know," Dorothy said. "Elsie told me we can't resurrect

dead people. But in my heart, I knew he wasn't really dead. I could still feel him there."

Brian kissed her cheek. "Lucky for me, or I'd have been buried looking like Prince Charming." He glanced down at the jeans and T-shirt he'd changed into. "For future reference, before you put the torch on the wood, this is how I want to go out."

"I like your spirit!" Elsie grinned.

"And I know I've been hedging about joining your coven." Brian took Dorothy's hand. "But it's what I want to do. I like all of you—and love some of you. I want to help you."

"And you might find that we can help you too." I was thrilled that he'd finally made a commitment. I didn't care if it was because of Dorothy. There were no rules against lovers or spouses being part of the same coven. "Welcome, Brian. And I think we should go."

"I won't argue with that," he said. "The council is up in arms—which keeps my grandfather off my back for now. Let's go."

"What about Mom?" Dorothy asked.

"Is Olivia *here*?" Brian questioned.

"She's hiding by the door," Elsie said. "Maybe we could stop and make a plate of food before we leave too. I'm starving."

"We'd better get Olivia out of here before we do anything else," Brian said. "I don't want to think what could happen if someone from the council sees her."

"I'm glad I had peanuts," Elsie complained.

There were still dozens of people milling around the big ballroom. Many more had left, but it looked as though most of the council was still there. Abdon was arguing with Makaleigh near the dais.

Olivia peeked out from behind the heavy drape. "Are we ready to go yet? This is really boring and not at all what I had in mind. Brian! You're not dead. That's so wonderful.

Dorothy—what happened to you, honey? You've got blood all over your pretty dress and my diamond earrings."

"Not really yours anymore," Elsie remarked.

"We don't have time for this," I told them. "Let's get you out of here, Olivia."

"Can we just walk out the door with her?" Dorothy asked.

"I don't think so." Brian nodded toward Abdon, who was coming our way.

"Quick." Elsie emptied a hand-cream bottle into a nearby planter. "Get in here, Olivia. They won't know you're here."

"Really?" Olivia whined. "I don't like the smell of that rose hand cream you use, Elsie."

"It's that or nothing," Dorothy told her. "Just do it, Mom."

Olivia turned into a gray mist that squeezed into the tiny hand-cream bottle. Elsie put the top on it and dropped it in her bag.

"Where are you going, Brian?" Abdon only had eyes for his grandson.

"I'm going home with Dorothy. I'll talk to you later."

"After all you've put this family through, young man, you're staying right *here*. The sea witch hasn't been captured yet. She won't give up until you're dead. We can protect you here."

"I can help Molly, Elsie and Dorothy find a way to defeat her."

"That's not your concern."

"Yes, it is. I'm going. Wish me luck." Brian grinned at him and put his arm around Dorothy as he started out the front door.

"We won't help you, you know," Abdon called out after him. "If you're one of them, you're on your own."

Brian turned. "I've been on my own most of my life. I finally have a family. We'll take care of the problem. Don't worry. *You're* safe."

I grabbed Elsie's hand and we walked quickly out behind Dorothy and Brian. I didn't want to hang around to take the brunt of Abdon's anger at his grandson. Once outside, the limousine we'd come in was waiting. We all jumped into the back and left the castle.

"That was close." Elsie wiped her forehead with her handkerchief. "I managed to pick up a few sweet rolls and some grapes as we walked past the food table. Anyone want some?"

Dorothy was frowning as she sat beside Brian. "You should've stayed there. We all know the sea witch isn't going to be happy until you're dead. We don't know how to protect you. I'm scared."

He hugged her and kissed her lingeringly on the lips. "Don't worry. We're gonna take care of this cucumber chick. All of us together—who can fight us?"

But his words were hollow. We all knew it. Dorothy was right. Unless Makaleigh came up with a plan to fight the sea witch, we didn't know what to do. I wished I could go to the Bone Man and ask him, but I knew he wanted her alive. If he did have the answer, he'd want to trade for it. I had nothing else I was willing to give. We'd have to face the sea witch on our own.

CHAPTER 41

A witch's hat,
A cauldron blessed,
A sacred spell,
A night to test.

"We need to use me as bait," Brian said when we got back to Smuggler's Arcane.

The limo driver had dropped off all of us. We had no cars, but I had already called Joe.

"That's crazy," Dorothy said. "She'd take you for sure. There must be a better plan."

"Her magic is really strong," I cautioned. "She probably already knows that Brian is back. She won't wait long before she tries to take him again."

"We'll have to keep him here with us," Elsie said. "At least until we figure out what to do. We may not have the strongest magic in the world, but we might win through sheer numbers."

"What about the Bone Man?" Brian asked. "Would he be willing to help?"

"He and I are in a complicated situation right now," I explained. "I don't think we can count on him. I'm still work-ing on my part of the bargain to find and deliver his wife."

Elsie nodded. "Who, as we all know now, is the sea witch. I need some tea."

While the kettle heated, we sat around the table in the shop and tried to figure out what to do with the sea witch. Elsie had taken out our individual cups—the goldfish cup for me, the flamingo for her, the star for Olivia and the tree for Dorothy.

"I hope you like your cup, Brian." Elsie clapped her hands. "Call it a premonition that you'd be here with us eventually."

Brian smiled when he saw it. "Thanks, Elsie. Do I have to drink tea to use it? I'm more a coffee man."

"I'm sure we can conjure up a coffeepot." Elsie waved her hand, and a can opener appeared on the counter. "*There* that is. I've been looking everywhere for it."

"Allow me." Brian took out his wand and concentrated. A small black coffeemaker was on the counter. "I've wanted to get a new one for the apartment anyway. Maybe now that there will be two of us, I'll have a reason to invest in one."

Dorothy smiled and kissed him. Elsie also smiled and released Olivia from the hand cream bottle.

"It's not gonna happen!" Olivia sniffed and then frowned. "I'm covered in that stuff now. I wish I could take a shower."

"Maybe he could move in with *us*," Dorothy suggested. "We have lots of room in that big old house."

"Think what you're saying," Olivia demanded. "No man has *ever* lived in that house. It just hasn't been done."

"But he has nowhere safe to go," Dorothy argued. "The house is completely spelled, right? The only place he might be safer is here, and he can't stay here while all of us go home."

Elsie poured tea for everyone—spiced chai—except for Brian, who ended up with green tea made in his coffeemaker. "Sorry, no coffee. Olivia, you might as well give in. Dorothy is right. He needs to be somewhere safe."

Olivia put her hands on her ghostly hips. "Well, why don't you take him home with *you*, Elsie, and keep him safe?"

"That won't work. Aleese would think he's my new boy-friend. And what would Larry think?"

Olivia stared at me.

"I have enough problems with the Bone Man visiting me and Joe's ex-wife popping in for pizza. You're going to have to do this, Olivia. It's not forever. We'll catch the sea witch and then the three of you can argue about it."

"It's just not fair," Olivia complained. "Only the female members of my family have lived in that house. I'm not too sure a man won't be struck down by the protective runes."

Elsie snorted. "You better get that changed before you have a grandson."

"Grandson?" Olivia's tone was startled. "Dorothy isn't ready to have children. She's not even married."

"Not like that stopped *you*," Elsie reminded her.

"Oh, I really wish I could drink that tea," Olivia whimpered. "And how am I supposed to get rid of this awful rose smell?"

"Olivia." Brian grimaced when he tasted his tea. "It's not like you and I don't know each other."

"Oh my lord!" Olivia screeched. "Did you really just *say* that? I wish I could turn you into a beetle!"

Elsie giggled and then the rest of us laughed at Olivia's indignation.

"It's settled, then," Dorothy said. "Until we can get rid of the sea witch, Brian is staying with us."

The two kissed, and Olivia blinked out of the room.

"This is going to be so much fun to watch." Elsie rubbed her hands together. "So, what's the plan to catch the sea witch?"

There was no plan, of course. I thought we should wait a few days to hear from Makaleigh. She would know better than we did what to do. In the meantime, we started training again.

It was better, knowing that Brian wanted to be with us. He was more open and less filled with angst. We practiced spells—beginning with another protective spell to keep the sea witch out of the cave and the shop. We got a chair for Brian and made room for him in our lives and our coven. He spent hours with us and then went home with Dorothy and Olivia.

There wasn't too much complaining from Olivia. She was sidetracked trying to train herself to be more solid. She kept practicing picking up paper and books around the shop. It was good to know she had a purpose again. Ghosts could be very powerful—sometimes more so than witches. Olivia probably wouldn't be one of those ghosts, not for a long time anyway.

A week had passed. Joe had gone back to work after I'd explained everything that had happened and how it had happened. We'd used the enchanted bubble—I was still afraid of the Bone Man deciding not to keep his end of the bargain. I was constantly on edge, worrying that he could show up at any time. He stayed away, though, and everything seemed almost normal.

Until the day we met at the shop and Brian had begun having dreams about the sea witch. "This is how it started last time." He was already more pale, hollow-eyed and restless. "I dreamed about her all the time"

"What are you dreaming about her?" Dorothy asked.

"She's calling me. We're not finished yet. She knows that I'm alive and she still wants me to finish the spell to keep her alive."

"You mean mate with her," Elsie said.

"Yes." He glanced at Dorothy. "I'm sorry. It's not what I want to do."

"I think anyone could tell that much by the way you screamed out last night," Olivia observed.

"I heard you too," Dorothy admitted. "I didn't want to say anything, but I can hear you all the way down the hall."

Elsie giggled. "I guess that answers *that* question."

"What can we do? I don't think we can wait much longer," Dorothy said. "We've got to stop her."

I didn't like going it alone. We had no experience dealing

with a witch as powerful as this one. But we couldn't let her have Brian again.

"What's your plan, Molly?" Olivia asked. "I know you have one."

"I sure hope it's better than the one we had to get Brian away from the sea witch. We're lucky to still be alive," Elsie reminded us

"All we have to do is figure out how to catch a sea witch," I said. "I'll bet Muriel knows the answer to that."

Brian insisted that he was going along despite the rest of us disagreeing. "We're safer together. Protection spells on the shop or the house aren't as strong as our combined real-time magic."

We finally agreed, and Elsie called Larry to make sure he was at his boat. Lucky for us it wasn't his time of the month.

Larry was cleaning his boat when we got to the docks. He was happy to take us to see Muriel again if it involved another boat ride with Elsie.

"What about the cream puffs?" Olivia asked. "Will she talk without cream puffs?"

I glanced at my watch. "We'll have to think of something else."

Larry scratched his head. "I have some jelly donuts. Will that help?"

We decided to take a chance on it. Larry was a little nervous about taking Brian with us, since the sea witch was after him again. "It's possible she could attack the boat to get him back," he reasoned. "She's bound to be more powerful on the water, just like you, Molly."

But we'd already made that decision, and Elsie convinced Larry that it was safe.

My magic wasn't a match for the sea witch—I wasn't convinced all of us together could stand up to her. Knowing more about the amulet made me feel somewhat safer. I agreed with Brian that leaving him anywhere was risky. I worried that she could compel him to come to her. We might need to fight him *and* her.

Larry's boat went slowly into the salt marshes near No-Name Island. He and Elsie had kissed and talked the whole way. Olivia and I tried to help Dorothy keep a positive outlook on our venture. Brian had a better chance of survival with our plan—whatever it was—than he would without it.

Brian stared off at the water where it met the horizon. Several times, when Dorothy had spoken to him, he hadn't heard her. I was afraid the sea witch was already eroding his will. Soon there wouldn't be any way to stop him from going to her. I was angry that I'd waited too long. I'd believed Maka-leigh really meant to help. I had obviously been mistaken.

We found Muriel basking in the sun. She saw us coming and hid in the weeds.

"We need your help again," I called to her. "Will you speak with us?"

I held out the jelly donuts that Larry had volunteered. Muriel peeked around a coarse bush and sniffed. "Those aren't cream puffs."

"They aren't," I agreed. "But they're really good. Look. Larry will eat one."

He munched it down quickly and smacked his lips. "*Yum.* Try one. You might like it better than cream puffs."

Muriel ventured from her hiding place and daintily picked up a donut with her ringed fingers. She chewed a bit and smiled. "These *are* good. What do you call them?"

"Jelly donuts." I took another for her. "We found the sea witch."

"Lucky you! She's a pistol, isn't she?"

"You could say that. We have something she wants. I don't want to kill her. How can we trap her?"

Her tiny feral eyes locked on my face. "I'm going to need something more than jelly donuts to give you information that will hurt her. If she isn't dead, she could come for me."

Elsie offered her hat. Muriel turned it down. Dorothy offered her bag. Muriel didn't want that either. I rummaged around in my bag for something she might take.

She sniffed. "What's that? I smell magic."

It was the spelled mirror. "Is this what you want?" I asked.

"Yes. Let me see it."

I handed her the mirror. I only caught a glimpse of what she saw in it. The image was that of a beautiful, young *human* girl. I could see something in her face that resembled Muriel. Had the mermaid once been human? There were old stories that hinted at that possible transformation.

"I'll take it." She clutched it to her bare bosom. "I know exactly how to capture the sea witch. I don't know how to kill her, unless she can't mate. Then she'll die. Once you get her, you'd better do something with her quickly or she'll escape and kill you. No sea creature likes a net."

Elsie and I exchanged glances. "What kind of net?" I asked.

"You'll have to gather seaweed and weave it with witch's hair into a net. Then it must be blessed with your tears. The hearts of the makers must be emotionally involved with capturing the sea witch for the magic to work. That's all I know. Thanks for the donuts. Can I have the rest?"

I gave her the remaining jelly donuts, and we left the salt marsh.

"Sounds like a major project," Olivia said. "Do we have time to weave a net? Maybe we could buy one and put seaweed on it. The sea witch probably won't know the difference."

"That was always your problem," Elsie scolded her. "You can't take shortcuts with magic. Sometimes you have to do what the spell demands."

"Well, it doesn't matter to me," Olivia snapped back. "I can't contribute, so it will be up to you all to save Brian. I was just trying to help."

We gazed at Brian—the breeze in his hair, his eyes far

away. Dorothy called him back from wherever he'd gone, but the light had gone from his eyes and his face was haunted.

"Whatever we're going to do, we'd best do it quickly, like the mermaid said," Elsie advised. "We can't hold him if he wants to go. He's strong. We may not have much time."

Elsie and Larry said a long lover's good-bye when we got back to the docks. He'd wanted to come with us, but I knew his presence would be a distraction to Elsie and an irritation to any other witches we might ask to help us. Werewolves and witches didn't get along.

"Maybe we can do it by ourselves," Elsie suggested with a besotted smile. "We might not need any other witches. Larry could help us."

"I have no idea how to weave a net or anything else for that matter," Dorothy said, holding Brian's hand as she was getting off the boat. "I hope we have instructions."

"I can repair nets," Larry said. "I could probably weave one."

"You're wonderful, and I love you for it." Elsie patted his cheek. "But Molly is right—we need more witches. I don't have enough hair to donate for a net. What about Belinda and her sisters? They have emotions involved with catching the sea witch—and hair."

"Exactly what I was thinking," I said. "I hope her phone number is in the memorial guest book."

We went to Smuggler's Arcane. It was an eerie trip, as we could feel Brian slipping away from us. He was almost unresponsive when we got back. I wondered what he heard, what he felt. Like Ulysses tying himself to the mast of his ship so he could hear the mermaid's song, I was curious. Dorothy wasn't able to rouse him, but she did coax him into the shop.

I saw a familiar shape across the street as I closed the shop door. It was Portia de Winter in her glamourized form. She already knew we had him. I spelled the door three times when we were inside. I knew the moment of truth was close at hand. She would strike that night.

We found Belinda's phone number, and Elsie called her to ask for her help.

"Should we put him in the cave?" Dorothy asked as she watched Brian staring at the door. "He might try to break away."

"No. Let's not take a chance on our spells holding up that close to the water. The sea witch might be able to go in and out with no problem given the close proximity to the river." I glanced at the trapdoor. "In fact, let's barricade the trap-door from the cave with magic and those boxes of children's books you brought."

We tied Brian to a chair, spelling the ropes that held him. I could tell Dorothy felt bad taking this measure, but we all knew it was for his own good.

"Belinda says she and her sisters are on the way," Elsie finally said. "They'll bring the seaweed. All we have to do is stand watch over Brian until they get here."

"Is that all?" I asked when Brian was secure in the chair. He was no longer himself, completely dominated by the sea witch. "Stay close to him, Dorothy. Use every ounce of love you have for him. She might own him right now, but you still have the advantage. Don't let him get to her or we'll probably never see him again, and all this will have been for nothing."

She bit her lip. "Do you think he knows what's going on?"

"I don't know. Keep whispering a protection spell. Don't falter. Keep him safe."

While we waited for Belinda to arrive, Elsie and I took out the old net that Larry had given us as a guide to create a new one. We thought we could weave new rope and sea-weed through this net.

"It doesn't look like much," Olivia said. "I don't think it will hold her."

"It's not finished yet," I told her. "It will be stronger when we're done."

We laid the net on the hardwood floor. I cut large swaths of Dorothy's and my hair to put in a basket. We blessed them with our magic and our hopes for trapping the sea witch. Elsie contributed a faded red curl, but her hair was thin and fine. I didn't expect her to give as much as we had.

After that we used sage smudge sticks to purify the shop for the spell. Elsie handled the candle lighting, one of her favorite pastimes, since she could still do it without matches. We were as ready as we could be when Belinda, Elizabeth and Althea arrived.

Night was starting to fall when the three sisters walked in the door. I peered into the shadows outside but couldn't make out the sea witch. I could feel her there waiting for the right moment. We couldn't allow that to happen.

The sisters were wearing long, hooded cloaks in matching deep purple. They'd twined seaweed into their hair, and extended their blessings as they'd come into the shop.

"Blessed Be." Belinda bowed her head.

"Let's kill this chick," Elizabeth added.

"We're ready for you," I told them. "Please close and lock the door, Olivia. Pull the blinds too, and turn off the lights."

CHAPTER 42

Help me face my fear
On this dark night.
Stars, guide me,
Moon, shield me.

Olivia had played around with pulling the shades on the front windows and had finally been able to accomplish it. She was like a child with the thrill of doing something new.

"Is the dead woman staying?" Althea asked. "I've always heard it's bad luck to attempt a spell with a ghost present."

"We've done many spells with our sister present," I told her. "But if she bothers you, she'll wait in another room. We don't want to be handicapped by prejudices. What we're doing is too important."

"*Another room?*" Olivia whined. "The only other room is the supply closet. You're not banishing me in there, are you?"

"Never mind," Althea said. "Just tell her to be quiet."

We took our places at the borders of the old net and blessed it again. We each took turns giving small parts of our elements to the enchantment. We were very fortunate to have witches with earth, air, fire and water magic represented. It would make for a more powerful spell.

The three sisters added their hair to ours in the basket. They presented us with a big plastic bucket full of seaweed. It seemed that we were ready to start.

As we began weaving the seaweed and hair through the strands of the old net, Belinda began to cry. She mourned her son as she worked. We all centered on Sam's loss and shared our tears in the spell. I could feel the power growing.

It took about an hour to weave the thin rope, hair and seaweed into the old net. It was already damp from our tears. We were ready to start.

"Open the front door, Olivia." I hoped she was up to the task.

The front door swung open. The evening breeze held the scent of the Cape Fear River—and something else—*magic*. It was powerful, frightening—a storm coming toward us that I hoped we could survive.

The sea witch—for she was no longer Portia de Winter or anything human—swept up the stairs bringing cold, wet air with her. The candles in the shop immediately went out. The icy tendrils of her power threaded through me.

The six of us continued chanting the protection spell we'd agreed on. Slivers of doubt entered my mind as to whether or not it would be strong enough to hold her. I clutched my amulet and forced myself to concentrate. It was difficult to ignore the strong water energy she'd brought with her. It was as though we were standing in the middle of a hurricane and trying not to notice it.

"You think to trap me with your weak, foolish magic?" The sea witch laughed, her voice grating up and down my spine. "Your magic is nothing compared to mine. You can't hold me. Give me the boy and all of you will live."

We kept chanting and holding hands as she came into the shop. Dorothy's hand was tightly clutching mine. I knew it was probably harder for her than for any of the rest of us. Not that Elsie and I had ever battled, or hoped to trap, a sea witch.

But this was only one of a few dozen spells that Dorothy had ever participated in. I hoped she could hold steady until the spell was done.

"*You!*" The sea witch singled me out, grasping me by the throat and lifting me from my place at the net. "You think to use my amulet against me? You have no idea how to wield that power. Give it to me now."

I gripped the edge of the net with desperate fingers. She shook me like a rag doll, but I refused to let go. Except for a brief glance from Dorothy when the sea witch grabbed me, she continued chanting.

I continued chanting the protection spell, though one of the sea witch's strong claws was painfully wedged in my skin. It was a good distraction from her real motive for being there. She hadn't gone after Brian yet or called him to her because she was so intent on taking the amulet.

She put her bony claw under the chain and tried to pull off the amulet. The chain didn't break, and I continued chanting, even though my feet dangled above the wood floor.

"What magic is this?" she demanded. "The secret is no doubt your death, woman. I can help you with that."

I could feel the magic of our spell building. Olivia slammed the shop door closed as the net began to glow. Our energy began to make the net stick to her. She tried to writhe away from it, but the harder she tried to escape, the more she stuck. She was pulled to the wood floor, the net encompassing her. Her hold on me was finally free.

I hit the wood hard too but managed to get to my feet. "Now, sisters. We must do it *now*."

Together we lifted the enchanted net and covered the sea witch in it. She flailed madly and tried to remove it, but our spell held strong and wouldn't be thrown off. She screamed, and her uncanny eyes burned into ours. She was trapped by our magic and the pain of loss. Witchcraft is emotion, and there was plenty there to force her to submit that night.

Finally, she lay there, limp and powerless. "Is she dead?" Belinda whispered.

"I don't think so," Elsie responded. "But no magic."

"Are you okay?" Dorothy asked me.

"I'm fine." I moved my neck experimentally. "Just a little sore and bruised. Check on Brian."

"What now, Molly?" Elsie asked, moving away from the sea witch.

"She can't do anything else now. It's over."

"How can you be sure?" Elizabeth demanded. "I think we should throw her in a fire."

"I have to take what's left of her to the Bone Man, and then to the council." I didn't go into an explanation. "She won't bother anyone again."

Sam's mother and aunts weren't happy with that resolution. They'd wanted to see her explode or perish in some other theatrical event. The victory seemed as though it should have been more remarkable. "We should at least kill her." Althea's pretty face was harsh in the dim light.

"That won't bring Sam back," Belinda said. "I don't want that stain on my life. So done to another, done to me. Let her take the guilt."

We acknowledged each other and gave blessings before the sisters left Smuggler's Arcane. Althea and Elizabeth were unsatisfied, but Belinda was happy with the outcome.

I still reserved judgment. What would happen when I took the sea witch to the Bone Man? Was I wrong not to give her to Cassandra and the council first?

"I don't know about anyone else, but I could do with a glass of elderberry wine," Elsie said. "I think there's still enough from last summer."

"That doesn't do me any good," Olivia protested. "But I *was* able to close the door. Did you all see that?"

"I saw it." Brian's voice joined ours as Elsie switched on the lights. "I'd like some of that wine too. Thanks for saving my life *again*."

"You're okay!" Dorothy squealed and kissed him at least a dozen times.

"I don't know if I can handle my daughter being in love," Olivia drawled. "Maybe that's why parents change poopy diapers when their kids are small—to prepare them for the *real* nasty parts."

I sank into my chair with a sigh. "So mote it be!"

I wrestled with my conscience through what was left of that night. Elsie, Dorothy, Brian and I spent the night at Smuggler's Arcane to be certain the sea witch didn't escape.

I talked with Joe, explained what had happened and why he and Suzanne would never be able to close this case, even though it was over.

Everyone had their opinions on what should be done first—taking the sea witch to the council or to the Bone Man. But I knew that, if the council took the sea witch, I wouldn't get her back to give her to the Bone Man. He wouldn't continue protecting Joe, and his reprisal for not fulfilling my part of the agreement might be terrible.

She had to go to Oak Island first and then be handed over to the council. I couldn't force the Bone Man to give her up to justice for the young witches she'd killed, but nothing I did would bring them back, and I had to look to my own.

I didn't want to visit the Bone Man alone again. I was scared and wanted someone to hold my hand, I suppose. And I wasn't sure I could get the sea witch to the island by myself. Though she hadn't moved or spoken since we'd trapped her in the net, her eyes still followed our movements.

Everyone went along, as though it was a picnic or some

other fun outing and not delivering a prisoner to whatever
fate awaited her.

Even Olivia went, although she planned to wait by the
lighthouse until we'd talked to the Bone Man. It meant a lot
to me that she was willing to go that far after her personal
experience with him right after her death.

I made sure that all of us were on the ferry at the same
time—no more sudden swells that sent the ferry off without
warning. I even made us hold hands and invoked a spell for
clarity. I didn't let on to them that I was scared to go out
there again. I'd always been nervous about visits to Oak
Island, but after the last time, I was extra cautious.

The sea witch stood looking out over the gray ocean,
which slapped against the boat. We'd put one of the hooded
robes on her, and no one asked any questions. I could still
feel the strong pull of her magic on my amulet. I wouldn't
allow myself to look into her eyes. I wasn't afraid of her
now, but I didn't want to know what was hidden there.

"She survived at the cost of other lives," Elsie whispered,
her hand on my shoulder. "Don't pity her, Molly. This is
magic beyond us. There's nothing we can do for her."

"What a lovely day for a boat ride." Dorothy had kissed
Brian a few dozen times.

"If you don't mind being on the water." Elsie kept her
hands on the boat rail. "I'm not partial to it myself. But that's
not surprising, since I'm a fire witch."

"It's okay," Brian said. "I can take it or leave it. I'll bet
Molly enjoys it."

"Yes I do. Although going to see the Bone Man is always
a little frightening."

Elsie had regaled Brian and Dorothy with tales of our meet-
ings with the Bone Man through the years. Neither of them
seemed impressed by what she'd told them. I reminded myself
that the Bone Man had to be experienced to understand. I

didn't know a single witch who'd asked him for help who wasn't terrified of him.

"Why come to him at all if he's so scary?" Brian grinned. "You could go online or ask through the grapevine for what you need."

"I don't know about online," Elsie said. "But the grapevine eventually ends up at the council's ears. No one wants that."

Brian's eyes searched the horizon. "My family expects me to take my grandfather's seat on the council one day. I don't think I want to do that."

"Why not?" Dorothy asked. "Think of all the good you could do."

"There are too many other voices and opinions to change anything meaningful. You heard what Elsie and Molly said about Makaleigh's opinion of non-witch babies. I can't imagine being part of that."

Elsie patted his shoulder. "There will be new voices and new opinions on the Grand Council, Brian. Change will come. The beliefs of witches who have lived through evil times in the past will fade."

"You might be right," he partially agreed. "But I also know you're a big optimist, Elsie. Life isn't always as pretty as you see it."

She blushed. "Why, thank you. I'd rather see the pretty life than the ugly one. It's all a matter of perspective."

The ferry finally bumped against the dock on Oak Island. It had been a rough crossing, the sea unusually gray and choppy. Spray from the water hitting the rocks beside the walkway splashed us as we got off the boat with the sea witch between us.

"Looks like rain," Elsie said. "I knew something was coming—my bunion hurt all night."

"Does every witch have a part of their body that foretells something?" Dorothy asked with a smile. "Mom was telling me about her elbow that used to hurt when the stock market was about to take a dive."

Olivia, who'd been unusually quiet on the trip, joined in the conversation. "That's right. My mother had migraines when she was going to find a new lover."

I saw her glance around the island and bite her lip. I realized she was as afraid as I was. Both of us had had unusual experiences with the Bone Man that we didn't want to repeat.

Was it my imagination or were Olivia's features stronger and better defined? Maybe it was everything she was doing to become physically stronger. I'd heard stories of ghosts that were so well formed that they couldn't be differentiated from the living people around them. If that was the case, I'd be glad when she was substantial enough that I could hug her again.

"My mother had a green thumb—literally. An earth witch, she loved her garden. Her thumbs would turn a pale green right before one of her prize flowers bloomed." I smiled at the memory. "My physical malady is an earache if a hurricane is coming close to Wilmington."

"That's right." Elsie clapped her hands. "I remember that one back in the nineteen seventies. Molly knew three days before the weatherman that the tropical storm was going to become a hurricane."

"What about you, Brian?" Dorothy asked.

"I don't know. I can tell when someone is cheating at poker. Does that count?"

We laughed at that. Dorothy didn't have a physical manifestation of her magic yet either. But they were both very young, just getting started in their lives.

Elsie and I took the lead, the sea witch subdued and silent between us as we started walking across the island toward the lighthouse. The wind whipped foam on the water as people visiting the lighthouse struggled to keep their souvenir hats that said SHRIMP FEVER on their heads.

I smiled at Olivia as she stood in the shade of the old lighthouse. "We'll be back before you know it."

"Just be careful out there, Molly. You know that the Bone Man is more than he appears to be—although goodness knows that's frightening enough. Don't let him talk you into anything you don't want to do."

"I won't. Don't worry. I have plenty of backup."

She nodded, and I could tell she wished she could go back there with us too. But she was too vulnerable. Maybe some other time, if her ghostly abilities kept growing. It was ironic that she'd spent her whole life trying to be a better witch only to find herself learning to be something else.

"When you're ready," I said to Brian and Dorothy, who were kissing again near the woods.

"We're ready," Brian replied. "The Bone Man doesn't scare me."

Elsie shushed him. "Be careful what you say."

Her words were blown away by a sharp crack of lightning over the sea. Rain gushed from the dark, swirling clouds above us.

"We have to follow the path through the woods to the old cemetery!" I shouted at them to be heard above the weather.

Elsie was right beside me. Dorothy and Brian were behind us. Following the well-worn path, we trudged through the wet sand between the trees. The storm came down hard on the island. It was hard to see anything that wasn't right in front of me. I kept my eyes open for the first of the old settler's tombstones.

I reached the center of the cemetery. This was where the Bone Man usually made his appearance. I tried to still the rapid beating of my heart by taking deep, slow breaths. I looked back for Elsie, but she wasn't there. Neither was Brian or Dorothy. I forced myself to stop clutching the sea witch's arm.

The rain suddenly stopped and the wind grew quiet. It was as though I were standing in the eye of a hurricane. The sky above me was blue and birds were singing in the trees.

I called for Elsie, Dorothy and Brian. That inner sense that usually told me they were close by was gone. I felt alone and disoriented. I started to retrace my steps through the woods.

"Molly." The Bone Man suddenly appeared—as he always did—from behind a tombstone. "You brought her to me."

"I did, but we have to talk." My voice trembled and I fought to get hold of myself. "Let me find my friends . . ."

He grinned, black teeth showing in his red mouth. "No need. They've returned to the lighthouse. You weren't clever to bring them with you. We don't need them."

"I brought her to you, but she must answer to the Grand Council of Witches for the deaths of the witches." My voice shook despite my best intentions.

"The witches' council means nothing to me. You've done well, Molly. You saved your friend, and honored our agreement."

"One of those young witches was the son of a friend of mine. Magic won't bring him back. His family requires justice."

"Human life is fragile and short," he mused. "Even a witch's life."

I didn't like how this was going, even though I had expected it. I knew there was nothing I could do, as Elsie had said. "Easy to say that when you're a sea god, eh, Manannan MacLir?"

When I said his name, an immediate transformation took place. His frightening shape as the Bone Man was only glamour too.

In his place stood an average-sized man with very pale skin and long black hair. He was amazing to look at, like no one I had ever seen. His eyes were constantly changing color from blue to green to gray. He exuded magic that was stronger even than what I'd felt from the sea witch. My amulet grew warm and animated as he changed.

"You know my name." He smiled and took my hand. "You are indeed worthy of that amulet, Molly."

The sea witch changed at the same time. She was the beautiful, red-haired woman who'd been in my dreams, the one who'd been burned at the stake as a witch hundreds of years before. The magic net slewed off her to the ground. She stood tall and proud at his side, her hand on his arm.

"I thank you for returning me to my home, Molly," she said with a graceful nod of her head. "I was lost and could not find my way back. Only here am I safe. Only here can others be safe from me."

My heart thudded in my chest and my breath came faster. I was caught in a net of magic just as the sea witch had been, the passionate emotions between these two people swirling around me. What was I going to do? How could I force the Bone Man to give her up to the council?

Easy answer—I couldn't. I wasn't even sure it was the right thing to do.

"That's right." He looked at his mate again with love in his eyes. "I could not give her back human life, you see. All I could offer was shelter here with my magic. We were separated. I couldn't find her."

"I swear I meant no harm to you or your kind," she assured me. "The magic is too strong for me to contain unless I am here."

"Why didn't you use your magic to go get her?" I asked in the throes of conscience.

The sea god put his arm around her. "I am punished here forever for my deed after her death, as she is punished with me for our love."

I thought about the deaths of the colonists that I'd seen in my dream. I looked at the two lovers, who were doomed for what they'd done to be together. I knew I wouldn't tell the council what had happened.

I felt sorry for him and the sea witch. It was better to have

Joe for a human lifetime than to live so long going into and out of the spell MacLir had cast.

"And now you know my secret." He took both my hands in his. "If you agree to keep my name to yourself, I vow to always protect you and your family, as I vowed to protect your family when I gave the amulet to your ancestor."

I had no intention of telling anyone that I'd had a conversation with an Irish sea god. Who would believe me? It was an easy deal to make. "From this day forward, I won't tell anyone your real name."

"Then the deal is made."

I knew it was time to go. I smiled at the handsome couple, wondering how I would ever explain this to Belinda and her sisters, or to the council.

"One last word of warning," he said. "Never give that amulet to anyone not in your family. It could be dangerous in the wrong hands."

I started to speak, but he was gone. I took a deep breath and made my way back through the trees. As he'd said, everyone was waiting for me at the lighthouse. There were too many questions to answer. The storm had stopped as soon as I'd vanished. Dorothy, Elsie and Brian had looked for me. They swore I hadn't been in the old cemetery.

"Did you give the sea witch to the Bone Man?" Elsie asked. "Should we call the council now?"

"She's with him," I told her. "I'm not volunteering any information to the council. I'll explain later. Let's catch the ferry before it leaves without us."

EPILOGUE

We discussed plans for training Brian and Dorothy on the way back to Wilmington. Though Brian refused to admit that he needed some help in that department too, he grudgingly agreed to let us show him a few things.

"I think this is a new golden age for us, Molly," Elsie said as we reached Smuggler's Arcane. "I can feel all that young magic coming together with ours. Gives me goose bumps all over."

Olivia laughed. "Are you sure you're not thinking about Larry?"

I started to open the door to the shop—it was already open despite magic and mundane locks.

"Let me go in first," Brian volunteered. "It's probably someone from my family. I hope having me around isn't going to be too much of a problem."

Cautiously, we made our way into the shop, noticing that

there was a stranger sitting at our table. He got to his feet. He was tall, lean, handsome and dressed like a pirate. "You must be Dorothy," he said, walking right up to her with a broad smile. "Yes. I'd know you anywhere."

Olivia's jaw dropped. "Drago? Is that really you?"

WELL-CRAFTED MYSTERIES
FROM **BERKLEY PRIME CRIME**

- **Earlene Fowler** Don't miss these Agatha Award–winning quilting mysteries featuring Benni Harper.

- **Monica Ferris** These *USA Today* bestselling Needlecraft Mysteries include free knitting patterns.

- **Laura Childs** Her Scrapbooking Mysteries offer tips to satisfy the most die-hard crafters.

- **Maggie Sefton** These popular Knitting Mysteries come with knitting patterns and recipes.

- **Lucy Lawrence** These brilliant Decoupage Mysteries involve cutouts, glue, and varnish.

- **Elizabeth Lynn Casey** The Southern Sewing Circle Mysteries are filled with friends, southern charm—and murder.